'Celeste Kelly's eye-opening transc
university doctoral candidate to un
dimensions is compelling reading. 1   _...es
the worlds of quantum physics and me _...ysics for Celeste's
transformation as she establishes the Research for Quantum
Metaphysics program to inspire people to design their own
destiny. A must for those searching for their greater purpose in
life and open minded enough to make it happen.'
—**Barry Eaton, broadcaster & host of** <u>RadioOutThere.com,</u>
and author of the internationally released trilogy *Afterlife, No*
Goodbyes **and** *Past Lives Unveiled.*

'How did author Peter Smith make a story about one
woman's quest to understand the true nature of the universe such
a page-turner? It helps that he's one of the world's leading experts
on quantum consciousness, so it's meticulously researched. But
more than that, he's used fiction to explain complex facts in a
form that is absorbing, fascinating, and eminently readable. I
found *The Transcendence of Celeste Kelly* a hard book to put down.
If you're interested in how the Universe really works, then so will
you.'
—**Bill Bennett, award-winning filmmaker (***PGS – Your*
Personal Guidance System **and** *Facing Fear – the Film.*)

The Transcendence of Celeste Kelly is a fascinating journey
which focuses on the nature of reality. It's a fictional story about
a scientist faced with experiences which challenge her notion
of reality, taking her on a multidimensional journey exploring
metaphysical principles, psi abilities, and non-ordinary states
of consciousness. Celeste comes to realise that there is much
that modern day physics has yet to explain when exposed to the
multidimensional nature of human consciousness. It is a journey

that many of us will explore when we challenge the 'conditioning box' of 3D reality and beliefs and the scientific model of reality. A wonderful and insightful journey for those who are seeking to understand human consciousness and the nature of reality. A great read, highly recommended.'
—**Mary Rodwell, founder and principal of ACERN (Australian Close Encounter Resource Network), author of** *Awakening* **and** *The New Human.*

'*The Transcendence of Celeste Kelly* is a delightful adventure into mysteries of quantum consciousness. Interweaving leading-edge science with powerful mystical concepts, the book offers an insightful, mind-expanding forum for exploring our multidimensional existence—a pathway to know and experience the deep, hidden truths of reality.'
—**Kim Chestney, author of** *Radical Intuition* **and** *The Illumination Code,* **founder of IntuitionLab.**

'Poignant sentences drop like nectar throughout this book, luring your consciousness into its own expansion. By the last page you will find yourself changed in some way, from the inside out. An alchemy of consciousness in its own right, this story profoundly and subtly rewrites the future by paving the paths within you that bring more of your own future self into the here and now. Whole worlds, past life experiences and future versions of yourself will follow you through the pages of this book, transcending that which no longer resonates. Somewhere near the end, you will find the newest version of yourself emerging— just as its key character Celeste does, through her openness to find the 'more' we were never told about.'
—**Carmel Cathie, creator of** <u>www.beingandbecoming.life</u> **and consciousness art at** <u>www.carmelboone.art.</u>

'Celeste carries with her the promise of tomorrow, of a better world and limitless possibilities. The narration of her story is the story of the new methods of accessing our higher states of consciousness as discovered/created by Peter Smith, trailblazing pioneer into the expanded states of awareness and our own magnificence, whom I have had the privilege to study under. If you are, like me, an incurable romantic and an optimist, this book is a must read. It will make you laugh, cry and leave you at the end with a glowing smile and hope for the future. I intend to read it again and recommend it to my consultants thoroughly, for it breaches complicated subjects in a simple, novelised manner that gives us all the right information about who we really are and what we can become in the shape of characters who are personable and all too human. I loved the book, I could not put it down and that hasn't happened to me in quite a long while! Thank you Peter for bringing the story of you and these incredibly powerful methods as quantum and universal consciousness into the lives of people who might have never heard of them otherwise. May *The Transcendence of Celeste Kelly* transcend space and time and create the wave of consciousness needed in the world today!'

-**Dr Milly Diericx, author of** *The Konscio Method* **and** *Befriending the Wolf*

'There are writers looking to propel humanity forward, even ahead of scientists and their struggles with the quantum challenges to linear thinking. As with Verne, Wells and Clarke, Peter Smith can offer humanity a perspective allowing advancement at a pace which science is yet to match. In the footsteps of Pauli and Jung, Smith melds the human wish for a better life with a universe patiently waiting for humanity to attain sufficient awareness to step across the threshold from science to science consciousness.

Simply combining science with consciousness into metascience, humanity springs forward as it has been building toward for millennia. Here, Peter Smith offers a roadmap, as unfolded by Celeste, we can all use to navigate a way to a better world for all. Allow yourself to take this journey of yet another human pioneer. Allow yourself to see the approach of the new human existence. Feel the optimism Peter Smith offers. Read this story, feel into it, and know that there is so much more out there than ever thought possible.'

—Dr. C. Eldridge PhD, Author of *How life works: The Fireside Companion past life series.*

'A compelling, unputdownable tale of a doctoral student in quantum physics who makes a scientific breakthrough regarding the nature of our universe and our evolving understanding of consciousness. A must-read!'

—Ann J Clark, Ph.D., former Director of Research for the Michael Newton Institute, co-author of *Wisdom of Souls*, and author of *Great Loss.*

THE TRANSCENDENCE OF CELESTE KELLY

PETER SMITH

AIA PUBLISHING

The Transcendence of Celeste Kelly
Peter Smith
Copyright © 2023
Published by AIA Publishing, Australia
ABN: 32736122056

ISBN: 978-1-922329-47-9

DEDICATION

*This book is dedicated to those who seek new horizons.
It is for the people who see past the illusion of the physical
universe and have found the knowledge within that we
are more than we have ever been told, magnificent in ways
we are yet to understand and have potential beyond our
wildest dreams.
If we stop and listen, we will hear our souls calling us to
this truth … and our lives will be forever changed.*

Chapter 1

Celeste woke, as she always did, as though she'd arrived back from elsewhere.

Sometimes she felt separate from her body and had a hard time squeezing back in, but then she'd always had a vivid imagination. It took a few seconds to remember where she was, then the environment of the family home came into her awareness.

This morning, she felt the exhaustion of the last two years more present than usual. Twenty-three months had passed since she'd lost her father in the accident. He'd been her rock, her inspiration and her safe place in the world. As so often happened in these first moments of the day, the story flashed past, and she felt the pain in her heart. She recalled the police coming to the door and asking if this was the home of Dr Benjamin Kelly. The chill and shock still remained in her energy field from that devastating moment when the police officer told them of the accident and her mother collapsed to the floor beside her. Though that was just the beginning …

The vehicle had been retrieved from a deep gully in a part of the mountains that her father never visited. The toxicology report showed cocaine in his system. Neither of them could understand why a seventy-four-year-old retired professor of engineering would turn to drugs. It was too much for her mother, already highly strung and prone to panic attacks. She'd literally curled up in a ball, manifested cancer as a way out and was gone within six months. As an only child, Celeste had then truly been alone. She'd moved home to look after her mother and see her through her grief and had ended up being her carer. Her tiny flat down in the city had fetched a mediocre price as the market bottomed out, and she'd only just cleared the mortgage and expenses. But home she came so that the two of them could grieve together, though her mother had been inconsolable. Lifelong friends had drifted away, and Celeste realised it was her father's personality that had drawn other couples into the friendship orbit of their social circles.

She shook her head to be rid of the story, though a part of her recognised the deep sadness seeping through in the first moments of the day—before she could use any one of several distraction techniques. A powerful intellect and a strong personality had made her an expert in that realm, and after all, life goes on, doesn't it? You can always find a worse story than your own.

There was a deep and profound irony in the fact that she'd inherited the family home by losing her family. Without siblings or parents, and given she'd never had a family of her own—yet, anyway—it was no longer a family home. She was flying solo in life, housed by her inheritance.

She'd always loved this home. As the place in which she'd grown up, it held many fond memories. While the city had borrowed her for a while to build her career, the mountains had remained within her, ready to call her home.

Celeste loved the Blue Mountains. They had something that couldn't be found elsewhere. Only one road passes through, dotted with towns and engulfed by endless bush on either side, a small trail of very recent civilisation, tolerated by nature, that winds through an expanse of bush the size of a small country. The presence of the First People of the land has remained indistinguishable from the bush itself for a hundred thousand years. Celeste could almost hear the echoes of the ancestors still reverberating through the valleys and rivers, bringing something that can't quite be explained. Just a feeling, ever present. A consciousness holding something that will forever permeate the landscape, transcending time and space.

The town of Glenbrook is the first town at the start of the mountains. When you head east towards the heart of Sydney some sixty kilometres away, you descend into the smog, noise and frenetic energy of Australia's busiest city. As you travel down the Lapstone Hill, you can see the cloud into which you descend. However, when you come back out again on the return journey, it's bliss. Celeste's father had always said that Glenbrook was where you could get your first breath of fresh air. It was a beautiful place to make their home.

The house and the acre of land on which it rested, situated about a kilometre away from the main village, were purchased by her parents around the time she was born. They bought at the right time and restored the old sandstone home to its former glory. With four large bedrooms, two open fires, an old-style kitchen and plenty of living space that they had no trouble filling, it was a wonderful place to grow up. Outside, deciduous trees surrounded the house. They brought shade in summer and in winter let the sun into the wide wrap-around veranda where she and her father sat and played chess. A running tally of games won went into the hundreds, remaining neck and neck. It was his gentle and loving way to build determination and intention in a young girl who had incredible potential yet to be tapped.

Her mother's art studio and her father's old shed completed the structures. Each had their own mini kingdoms among the expanse of gardens and trees that made up the acre. Her creativity and his tinkering nurtured each of them individually and brought peace in their final years. Celeste was yet to dismantle these monuments to each of her parents. They sat in the garden, patiently awaiting her attention, waiting for a day when the pain would lessen.

Musings over, Celeste pulled the covers back and stepped out of bed. The old floorboards felt cold under her feet, though that served to bring her even further back into her body. She'd set up in the guest bedroom when she came back. The bedroom of her childhood remained exactly as it'd been for over twenty years, which was both cute and a little creepy at the same time. Going back in there would feel like regressing somehow, like all she'd done in between was pointless. She couldn't have that!

The master bedroom was where she'd held her mother's hand as she gradually slipped away. A kind palliative-care nurse had been her companion those last days and offered both unfathomable support and an incredible example of what compassion looked like. The nurse gently took charge after her mother's soul had left her body. Celeste had been amazed at how someone could bring so much into your life for just a few days and then disappear, never to be seen again.

The master bedroom was also a time capsule that she'd yet to bring into the present, with its contents and furnishings, not unlike how her old bedroom had been kept. Perhaps she was more like her parents than she'd thought, after all.

She walked out into the main area past the 'Celeste-ial Wall' as her mother called it, where her parents had lovingly hung all her

4

qualifications and awards. It was her father who had steered her towards quantum physics originally. The quantum philosophies had opened new pathways of thought and possibility for him. Engineering hadn't quite brought the inspiration he sought, even though he'd earned an excellent reputation in his field as a consultant and teacher.

His work had taken him around the world, and he'd consulted on some of the biggest projects of his day, though from age seventy-two onwards he'd slowed down. He spent a great deal of time tinkering in the shed and was content to just chat with old friends about their latest theories or ideas.

In Celeste's late teens, she and her father discussed all manner of theories exploding out of the realm of quantum mechanics, as he loved to call it. This somehow brought a trail- blazing engineer closer to the 'science of possibility'. Another of his favourite terms.

The end result of that shared interest hung on this wall. Celeste had been drawn to the University of New South Wales (UNSW) with its reputation for quantum physics, the wide and varied research opportunities, and their unique approaches to embracing a field of work still coming to terms with its own radical possibilities. She'd graduated top of her cohort in her Bachelor of Science (physics major) degree before extending into postgrad studies focusing on astrophysics and theoretical physics. Things really took off when she undertook a project at the *Max Planck Institute for Extraterrestrial Physics* in Garching, near Munich, Germany. She spent time looking into black holes but didn't find any extra-terrestrials (disappointing given the name of the institution), though her broken high school German became more conversational in the six months she spent there. A vacation research scholarship to CERN (*Conseil Européen pour la Recherche Nucléaire*) in Switzerland, the Mecca for all quantum physicists, topped up her CV like nothing else could. When she emailed a photo of herself standing in front of the Hadron Collider, it made the front page of the UNSW Alumni Magazine and went viral on a new social media platform called Facebook, still in its early days.

It had taken her till three years ago to decide the subject of her doctoral thesis. She'd been in and out of research projects in UNSW for almost twenty years and had become the darling of the School of Physics. She'd also been used as a circuit breaker in difficult projects and had the vision to bring in something that broke deadlocks in emerging theories. Celeste knew that scientific types could disappear into the data when they might gain better insight from an elevated view. Her father had told her about this a number of times over the years.

'You are a rare commodity, Lesty, an idealist disguised as a scientist. You will be able to bring new thinking to old situations. Use it to your advantage. Remember, it's quantum physics … stay open! Never close a door or you lose the limitlessness of what the quantum field is about. It's the greatest travesty of science to want certainty, when the landscape we exist in is an ocean of limitless uncertainty.'

'Stay Open' had become her T-shirt ever since, maybe even a tattoo across her heart. It was possibly engraved on her soul, so deep was its reach into her being from the words her father had offered. It's a shame that her PhD review panel hadn't purchased that T-shirt, and if they had, Celeste was sure it was probably misspelled. Today was the meeting with the full panel she'd been dreading, though there was plenty of time to gather her thoughts and build trepidation on the journey into the city.

Having passed the Celeste-ial Wall and her role in life as a quantum physicist, she entered the bathroom and threw off her robe. She stood naked in front of the mirror, moving more into her personal identity, the vulnerable part of her that she disliked, as there was nowhere to hide.

Celeste took in her reflection, observing the dark wavy hair of her mother and the light-brown eyes that came from her father. She'd recently turned forty, and soft crow's feet were emerging from the corners of the eyes that looked back at her from the mirror.

She stood around 165 cm tall, with long and slender legs, and her once-firm bikini body still held strong echoes of a younger self. Though attractive, she would never dress in a way to turn heads in her direction. That aspect of society was shallow and superficial. The tests of character were the ones most needed to be passed in life. In tough times, you stand strong, even though others may head for the hills. The last two years had shown her that she had more resilience than she realised. She still carried some heavy energy, mainly the hole in her heart that was a constant companion, reminding her of tragic loss. Time would heal her wounds, but in the meantime, sometimes at night she rolled over in bed and felt their jagged edges pressing into her side.

'Stop moping and get in the shower,' she said to herself and ran the hot water so the mirror would fog up quickly and shroud the reflection of her vulnerable self.

Thirty minutes later, she left the house and walked to the carport, where the blue Wrangler Jeep waited. The accident had badly damaged the other car, and by the time it'd gone through the investigation, she and her mother had never wanted to see it again, so she'd sold it for scrap. The Wrangler gave her a sense of durable resilience and navigated the practicalities of getting down a driveway prone to flooding when the big rains came. It had been her father's all-time favourite car, and he'd spent hours making modifications, so much so that she hadn't been able

7

to part with it. Today, it only needed to get her to the railway station, which was barely a challenge for Jeeps, her father's term of affection for the vehicle.

An hour's train ride and twenty minutes on the bus was better than a couple of hours in Jeeps at this time of day, and she needed reflection time to think and prepare for what lay ahead. It would be an interesting conversation. Her personal brand at UNSW had diminished recently. You could say her star had started to fade, given her lack of sparkle over the past two years. Project staff coming out of graduation were much cheaper to contract than she was, and she'd had run-ins with a few key project leaders in recent years. Some of this had been due to her suppressed grief emerging as anger on occasion, though in the words of one close colleague, 'Celeste, you can't call the professor in charge of the research project a "neanderthal knucklehead" and expect to have your contract renewed.' That sort of made sense, but even if she'd been accurate, it could've been said better. Over the years, she'd become a little less tolerant of career academics with fragile egos. Her doctorate had already been creating waves well before the tragedy of her father's death. Celeste had put her PhD on hold for a year, allowing her time to deal with everything.

The proposed scope of her thesis wasn't just ambitious, it had been described by some as 'impossible' and subsequently career suicide, though she no longer cared about that.

In the past two years, Celeste had realised that some things were more important than career status, and acceptance by peers as one of their approved members of the collective mindset was really about minimisation of unique creativity and a dumbing down of talent.

She gave one professor a verbal barrage over the concept of the peer-review process. 'So you mean to say that if I do something that hasn't been done before and it breaks new ground, it has to go to colleagues in our field for peer review, to people who may not know what I'm talking about?' When she was given the affirmative and told that it was a tried and tested system that had been in place for decades, she shook her head. Her parting remark was, 'If I wanted to design a process to hold humanity back, this would be it. No wonder science is dying ...' She wasn't asked to join any more research work for that professor.

Celeste looked out the window as the train descended through the Lapstone Gorge. She always paused her reflections to take in this scene of sandstone formations that were older than life itself. The morning sun heralded possibilities yet to be known, and the sheer beauty of the landscape inspired her. There was only peace, and for a moment, she was part of the gorge, feeling the sunlight and knowing true freedom. The train came around a bend, and she was back in her thoughts.

She knew word for word the introduction of her thesis, which would form the abstract as it matured, though it had raised the eyebrows of all who'd read it

> *'The many worlds' interpretation (Everett et al.*
> *1957 etc.) and superstring theory (M-theory*
> *– Witten 1995) both opened the possibility of*
> *other dimensions mathematically. If we expand*
> *Heisenberg's uncertainty principle beyond third-*
> *dimensional reality, we can then prove the existence*
> *of these other dimensions.'*

No one had yet tried to bring two of the major theories of quantum physics into a single theory. She was combining three. At times her head hurt, though in her heart she could feel the incredible possibilities of what she was suggesting. As for her review board, it was more than likely they felt she'd finally cracked and was off in la-la land or alternatively had stopped taking her medication. The second alternative was a no-go, anyway. She was no fan of the pharmaceutical industry, given her mother's experience with prescription drugs over the years.

After alighting at Sydney's Central Station, Celeste walked through to Eddy Avenue to wait for the 891 bus, which would take her to UNSW. Twenty-five minutes later, she was walking through the main gate on her way to the lecture room that had been set aside for her meeting.

CHAPTER 2

Celeste took her seat in the lecture room, a small wave of trepidation washing over her. A long table had been set up with three seats on one side and one on the other. It was clear which seat was hers, so she took it, reached for the water jug and poured herself a glass. The seating dynamic seemed to be a cross between a job interview and a firing squad. Often professors fired questions like bullets, and it was her role to be bulletproof by knowing her subject and putting their minds at rest, showing that she knew what she was doing. Given the subject of her doctorate, her professors grilled her regularly. Two out of the three overseeing her thesis didn't believe she could do it.

She heard voices in the corridor, and the three of them entered the room.

Dr Bartholomew Kindred was first through the door and smiled warmly. Dr Bart, as she called him, had been her first lecturer all those years ago and her mentor since postgrad days. He'd recommended her for the scholarship to CERN in Switzerland. A thoughtful and kind man in his early sixties, he had terrible taste in sports coats, shirts and ties, which always did their best to go in different directions. His clothing was a personal testament to chaos theory. Though underneath that level of disorder was a good heart and a brilliant mind.

The universe works in balance at times, so Professor Mildred Shrewberry walked through the door next. The name said it all, really. A career academic who had never soared to great heights; in fact, she'd hardly left the ground. Professor Shrewberry walked the planet as a rotund person with an unfortunate personality and had never been a fan of Celeste. Her nickname on campus was 'QB', which was less than complementary given it stood for 'quantum bitch', as many an intimidated freshman would attest to. If Dr Bart was echoing chaos theory in his clothing, then she was more than likely constructed from dark matter, emanating from a collapsed star with the usual absence of light. Some said she would benefit from a certain type of rocket, delicately placed to ease her frustration.

The final member of the panel was Dr William Nicholson. He had a solid grounding in astrophysics, had written some well-received papers over the years and was heading for retirement. He was solid, but a bit of a non-presence, and on this panel to fill in time till he was sent out to pasture, though he did make an occasional contribution. He was well known for observing the universe and people in a certain way, particularly women, as his gaze often dropped to their chests. Beyond that, he had a penchant for cats and often took strays into his cottage, just outside the campus grounds. He had a network of cat boxes in his backyard, where the feline community came and went. All of this had earned him the inevitable nickname of 'Schrodinger'.

Dr Bart, QB and Schrodinger offered their greetings, shook Celeste's hand and took their seats.

12

QB started the conversation. 'It's been three months since we last met. I assume you've settled back into the work since your time off?'

Such compassion, Celeste thought. 'Yes, Professor, I'm back in the flow.'

QB continued, 'I still have to admit to not being entirely enrolled in your subject matter, so perhaps you could recap the high-level concepts you're exploring once more, just to bring it together. Assume I'm a lay person with only a rudimentary knowledge of quantum phenomena.'

Finally, some self-awareness. Celeste looked at each of their faces, reading the energy before she spoke. Schrodinger's eyes dropped about twenty degrees downwards, and she was glad she'd worn a business suit. She pulled the lapels on her jacket a little closer together, took a deep breath, moved into her professional vibe and spoke.

'In 1957, Hugh Everett wrote a thesis that blew the collective mind of the physics community, putting forward a hypothesis that ultimately became the "many worlds' interpretation". He postulated that when faced with quantum choices, the wave function doesn't collapse but continues on, splitting into multiple universes. What we observe here in this reality is simply one of those outcomes.

'In 1995, when Ed Witten presented on M-theory, he brought five separate versions of string theory together by adding yet another dimension. He felt that if we moved to ten spatial dimensions and one dimension of time, then each of those five versions could be absorbed into that one theory, coming as close as anyone yet to finding a theory of everything.

'If we combine both these theories, then we can assume that the wave function continues on into the other dimensions that Witten postulated. We don't know this for sure, as our place of observance is in this dimension, though we might assume that particles move between dimensions and there's a way in which we can follow them, due to the fact that we're entangled with them. We simply need to find out how to do so.

'Then we can take this one step further and have another look at Heisenberg's uncertainty principle. His general concept is that if you can measure the mass of a subatomic particle, you can't accurately measure its velocity. Same the other way around; the more accurate the velocity, the more you lose the certainty of its mass. We even see particles wink in and out of existence.

'If we look at all this through new eyes, then we might just see that these particles reach a certain vibration and move between dimensions. They only need mass in this 3D physical realm as they adapt to that environment. What drives them to move? How do they "choose"' their movements? Do they have free will? Are they moving to these other dimensions envisioned by both Everett and Witten?

'Then we ask the big question. The macro realm is completely constructed from the subatomic world. What does this mean for us and our own reality? Are we ourselves multidimensional, and can we access other realms?'

QB took a somewhat condescending tone. 'I have two questions: first, how can you conceptualise that this is even possible in the first place? Second, how would you be able to show experimental evidence to support your hypothesis?'

Celeste remained cool and focused in her response. 'In response to your first question … the language of the universe is mathematics, whether we're looking at the golden ratio, Planck's constant or even $E = MC^2$. All have served us for a century. Even Newtonian physics was able to use force = mass × acceleration once we measured acceleration due to gravity. I feel that the maths in this dimension can help us to know that the other dimensions exist. Witten showed us this with M-theory. The maths only works if we use eleven different dimensions. Maths is either right or wrong; there is no wiggle room. To say that other dimensions don't exist means Wheeler was wrong, Witten was wrong and maths is wrong. This just isn't possible. Even Heisenberg was right. He was just using the wrong reference point, though it was 1927, after all.'

Schrodinger chimed in. 'Thank you, Celeste. I'm more interested in your second answer. How do you make all this measurable with data?'

'Indeed, Dr Nicholson, that is so pertinent. Though let me divert just for a minute if I may and challenge the status quo.'

Out of the corner of her eye, she saw Dr Bart form the smallest smile and felt encouraging energy coming from his direction.

'I am putting myself forward as a PhD candidate in the field of theoretical physics, a doctor of philosophy no less, a field that goes back in time to the musings of Socrates, Plato and Aristotle. I believe we can imagine things into existence and that we perpetually intrude on reality without knowing it. One of my favourite Einstein quotes is:

> *"Imagination is more important than knowledge. For knowledge is limited to all we now know and understand, while imagination embraces the entire world, and all there ever will be to know and understand."*

'I follow the great thinkers, rather than those who collect data to prove a point. Those thinkers blaze new trails for humanity. As a PhD in theoretical physics, my contribution to extending this field of endeavour will be through new theories and concepts that help us break the shackles of current thinking.'

QB interrupted. 'So you're yet to work out how to measure the data that validates your concepts?'

Celeste responded with more confidence than she felt inside. 'That part of the project is still coming together, and I have some leads, though it's too early to discuss them at this time. I know the data is there and that all I've postulated exists. I simply need the means to retrieve it.'

In response, QB got up on her high horse. 'This university has a solid reputation in the field of physics. We could never support a doctoral thesis that was outside the parameters of accepted practice. You need to show us an experimental component and hard data to support your wild ideas. Attaching your thinking to some of the legendary names in quantum physics is not a path to credibility.'

Dr Bart spoke. 'I, for one, am enjoying the interweave of some of these key concepts that we've known all our academic lives. New thinking brings life into our chosen field, and no matter how long we've been around, we should always appreciate the courage and vibrancy of those who challenge accepted practice.'

QB pursed her lips, and Dr Bart turned to her. 'How about we give this a chance to evolve and see where it takes us?'

Some more questions followed and administrative details were covered, though the energy had settled somewhat following Dr Bart's supportive interjection.

'Okay, so we have a way forward?'

Schrodinger nodded, QB did also, though begrudgingly, and Dr Bart closed the meeting. 'Thank you for your time today, Celeste; can we see a status update in three months, please?'

'Of course. Thank you all for your time today.' Celeste smiled, steeling herself as you do when standing at the foot of a mountain, just before you start climbing.

The professors left, but Celeste stayed in the room for a

little while, reflecting. She would find a way to gather the data she needed. Her father's voice in the background of her mind reminded her to 'Stay open …'

Chapter 3

Celeste, feeling just a little dishevelled after the meeting, was about to leave campus when her phone pinged. It was a text message from Dr Bart:

Coffee at the usual place?

She smiled and typed a quick reply:

On my way.

Nico's, one street from the campus, had the best coffee in Kensington. When Celeste entered the café, old Nico was shrouded in steam, hands busy. He smiled when he saw her and nodded in the direction of the garden. She'd had some wonderful conversations here with Dr Bart over the years, and she needed another of those right now. He sat under the usual tree in the corner, sipping a cappuccino. A few people sat dotted around at tables, though he was the only one not glued to a phone. He rose as Celeste approached—an echo of an older world. She'd always valued his wise counsel and easy company, even more so since her father had passed.

He gave a reassuring smile. 'So how did we go?'

'As expected, I guess. Shrewberry still wants the data, and I think Nicholson follows her lead, though I guess they're just doing what they are supposed to,' she replied, as a cappuccino with oat milk arrived at her elbow.

Nico still remembered. He winked at her as he departed.

'Nicholson is all right,' Dr Bart said. 'He's malleable and is marking time till the end of next year. His health isn't great either, and retirement can't come soon enough for him. If you can find something that looks "data-ish" with some grounded conclusions, you'll get him over the line.'

'Perhaps he'll look me in the eye, then?' Celeste enquired.

'Yes ... well, he's always been like that. When he was younger, he was even worse. He's one of those types of people who's in perpetual danger of becoming a dirty old man. He had a reputation back then and an even worse nickname.'

'What was that?'

'I'm not sure I should tell you. It's probably not in the best interests of your relationship with your review board and may be a little inappropriate as well.'

She knew he was teasing. As usual, he was making her dig for the information she wanted. The humorous sparkle in his eye betrayed his mock seriousness.

'How long have I known you, Dr Bart?'

'Long enough to drop the doctor tag. Maybe twenty years.'

'I'll drop the doctor tag when I become one too,' she replied. 'I think it's best I know the board members as well as possible so I can present my thesis to an audience I completely understand.'

He sighed in mock resignation. 'Okay, then. Back in the old days, he was working on particle physics and mapping the properties of light as a wave function. He had a known fetish for female anatomy, so we used to refer to him as "the double tit experiment".'

After the morning she'd had, Celeste was ready for a laugh, and it burst forth with great enthusiasm. 'That's actually hilarious!'

Dr Bart grinned, then became more serious. 'So how are you going to get the data, Celeste?'

'I know those other dimensions are there, just beyond reach. I know we're physical beings in a metaphysical landscape. Once we realise that, then we too, become metaphysical. The subatomic world does weird things—just look at quantum entanglement. You move entangled particles thousands of kilometres away from each other and they still have an instantaneous relationship. Einstein called it "spooky action at a distance", though I sense he knew it was simply the universe in action.'

Dr Bart smiled. 'Still quoting Einstein, I see.'

'Who better? He had as much to say about life as he did about science.'

'Agreed. I have a suggestion.'

'I'm open.' *Wow,* she thought, *there's my father again.*

'One of my favourite lines from Einstein is about solving problems. Do you remember it?'

'Of course. "*We can't solve our problems with the same type of thinking that created them.*"'

'Right. You also remember the power of his rocking chair, where he sat for hours on the porch and then came up with a profound thought or idea?'

'Yes; he was a deep thinker, and that helped him relax his mind.' Celeste nodded, enjoying the conversation more as it unfolded.

'What if that wasn't what was happening?' Dr Bart continued. 'I've always wondered if he was tapping into the quantum field of possibility. Finding what he needed and bringing it back into this reality for further exploration? I'll quote Einstein to you for a change: "*I think ninety-nine times and find nothing. I stop thinking, swim in silence and the truth comes to me."*

Celeste nearly spilled her coffee. 'You mean to say that you think he was going into the quantum field to find the ideas? That would've made him a conduit, and his thought process wouldn't just have been the development of ideas but, rather, him moving through the field to find the piece he needed. He thought he was exploring his brain; perhaps he was exploring the universe instead!' She'd come alive. 'If I can do that too, maybe I can find what I need.'

'Yes, perhaps you have to do this differently from normal data collection. Experimentation should be different also. If you want to break new ground and blaze new trails, you need to imagine a destination that has never been reached before.'

'So how do you think he got himself into that state?' she asked.

'Hmm.' Dr Bart looked to the sky, as he often did when he was thinking. 'It may be as simple as the rocking of the chair. That type of repetition can induce a trance state. It's why the shamans used drumming in their ceremonies and to journey into other worlds. I saw it on a trip to Peru once. Einstein may not have even realised what was happening; his process just worked for him.'

They sat in companionable silence, reflecting on the possibilities of what they'd just discussed.

After what seemed like an aeon, he broke the silence. 'Oh my, I have a class in fifteen minutes,' he said, looking at his watch. 'I have to go. Let's have a Zoom call next week and chat more about this.'

Celeste jumped up and gave him a big hug, one of those that you bring out for a favourite relative you haven't seen for a while.

'Thank you so much!' she said, and he was gone—a great mentor dressed exclusively by chaos theory, returning to the landscape of university life.

She watched him go, knowing that she'd received an important clue that could change everything.

CHAPTER 4

The train ride back up the mountains provided time for Celeste to reflect, Einstein's experience in the rocking chair on her mind. He was well known as one of the greatest minds that had ever lived, but perhaps there'd been even more to him than people realised. She'd always prided herself on her own strong intellect and had been drawn to others like herself. Conversations with these types of people had sparked her curiosity, inspired her passionately and led to countless moments of insight. But what lay beyond that?

The train stopped in Glenbrook in the late afternoon light, the shadows already stretching. She alighted and walked down to the carpark. Jeeps sat where she'd left him, like a faithful hound awaiting her return. A stickiness beneath her shoe distracted her as she approached the car, and she paused, leaning on Jeep's front end, while she investigated. She'd stepped on chewing gum. Cursing her bad luck, she removed her shoe and took a tissue from her bag to try to wipe the gum off. She flashed back over twenty years to when her father had bought the car he'd always wanted and Jeeps had become part of the family.

He'd taken her around the front and said, 'See the grill, Lesty?' She'd nodded.

'It has two functions, one practical and the other philosophical. Firstly, it protects the engine, particularly the radiator. Having a grill also means air can flow through the engine as it runs, which helps keep it cool.' He was in lecture mode.

Celeste grew bored, hoping the story got better. It was about to.

'The grill has seven slots,' her father continued. 'It's said that's because the Jeep can be found on all seven continents, but because they're all the same, no one knows which slot reflects which continent.' Her father paused.

'Have I missed something?' she asked.

He'd nodded and continued, 'You need all seven slots to make up the grill. None are more or less important, and if any one was missing, the grill would be incomplete. It's like life; even when you think something doesn't have worth, it does. You just haven't found the value it offers. Sometimes, you find valuable information from unlikely sources …'

In a flash, she was back in the carpark at the station with something on the edge of her awareness, doing its best to drop into her line of sight. Suddenly, it crystallised, and she exclaimed aloud, 'Oh my God … unlikely sources … the gum. I have to talk to Abbey.'

CHAPTER 5

Abbey had been the misfit at school and had lived further down the same road as Celeste in Glenbrook. Having gone to different schools, they'd never met during their primary school years, but they both attended Blue Mountains' Grammar School for high school. 'Grammar' was in the upper mountains, so travel was necessary. Celeste's mother had driven her the first few days, then put her on the train.

The first morning, Celeste stood on the platform alone, feeling a little lost and anxious in the busy crowd. She felt a tap on her shoulder and turned to see another Grammar pupil in the distinctive uniform standing there grinning at her.

'You must be new,' she said. 'I'm Abbey.' A lifelong friendship began in that moment. Abbey had done her primary school years at Grammar and had been catching the train since she was ten years old. She was the perfect person to meet.

They say that opposites attract, and this was certainly the case for them. Celeste, the deep-thinking introvert, and Abbey, the energetic extrovert, who just blurted out her thoughts even before they were finished. Celeste was studious, particularly in the sciences where she quickly excelled. Abbey often forgot her homework, though it was usually doubtful whether she'd done it at all. Celeste was drawn to astronomy, Abbey to astrology. It was a case of the periodic table versus the Ouija board, science versus spirit and science textbooks versus books on past lives. Somehow, they clicked into the precious energy of 'besties' and were there for each other through those exploratory years of first kisses, first drinks and other important rites of passage from girl to woman. Over the six years of high school, they debriefed their lives as they travelled to and from school, an hour each way. The trip always seemed twice as long when the other wasn't there.

Celeste wept in Abbey's arms at her father's and mother's funerals. Then when Abbey's sister was taken early by lymphoma, they swapped roles of comforter and comforted.

Since school, they'd gone in different directions, though always connecting for birthdays and an occasional drink or meal together. It helped them remember where they'd come from and that old friends are sometimes the best ones. Abbey had become a social worker, doing her best to rescue people from a societal system that didn't work for them. She was the one to rescue lost kittens, homeless dogs and birds with a broken wing. She did some 'healing work' on the side and had learned something called Reiki, where she brought energy to people who needed it.

Then there was the gum.

It seemed that Abbey's purpose in life was to keep the producers of chewing gum in business for as long as she walked the planet. She only stopped chewing for two reasons: to consume food or to talk to her social work or healing clients. Celeste believed she probably chewed gum in the shower and possibly even when she made love, and that may have been one of the reasons why a marriage in her early thirties didn't work out.

Celeste called Abbey, and they met for lunch at the Lapstone Hotel, or 'The Lappo', as it was more affectionately known, where there were good vegetarian options for Abbey. It worked for Celeste too, as she was becoming increasingly inclined in that direction.

After a huge bowl of Penne All'Arrabbiata and a glass of red wine each, the talk started in earnest. Abbey always asked about Celeste's projects and, on occasion, even had an insight or two to share.

'How's the doctorate going? Is that old bat still giving you a hard time?' Abbey asked.

'Yes, QB is still asking the questions designed to make me squirm. She may enjoy that a little more than she cares to admit. They do drive me forward, though.'

Abbey looked thoughtful. 'Maybe she's jealous of you.'

Celeste was surprised. 'How do you mean?'

'Well, from what you've told me, she's never really shone in your kind of work, whereas you've been the up-and-coming star. You still have your looks, whereas she might have missed that bus long ago.' Abbey let her thoughts bubble out like water from a burst pipe.

'Not sure I'm any kind of up-and-coming star anymore, Abs, but can I ask you something about my research?'

Abbey laughed. 'Sure, go ahead, like quantum physics is my thing, Lest.' No one else called her by that name, certainly not in academic circles. The old school nickname felt warm and familiar.

'I've reached a point where I can't find what I need through traditional, experimental means. I must find a way to get evidential support for my doctorate that comes from a different source. I need to chat to people who have a different view of the universe to me … so I thought of you.'

Abbey was silent for a rare moment of seriousness. 'So what are you asking?'

'For your definition of the universe.'

'Hmmm …' Abbey paused before speaking. 'I believe that the universe is made up of energy … all of it, even us, as we, too, are a part of everything. You already know I offer Reiki to people. That word means 'universal life-force energy'. I become a receiver of that energy and then offer it to someone else.'

'How?' Celeste asked.

'I draw the energy down through my crown chakra as I place my hands on them. My hands become hotter, and the person may feel a sense of warmth and become more peaceful. The energy soothes emotional or physical pain, and they feel better.'

Celeste translated. 'I see … so you draw energy out of the universe, like free energy technology is said to do, and then transmit it to another energy system. We know the energy exists. The evidence is there, given the heat in the hands. The subject has a boost to their own system and then uses the energy for some level of change. What do you do to turn it on and draw the energy?'

'I set an intention to open to the universe, and I invite the energy in,' Abbey replied. She opened her blouse a little and showed Celeste two Japanese symbols that had been tattooed above her heart. 'I got this tattoo done to remind me of my role in bringing this energy to the world. These are the symbols that mean Reiki.'

Celeste was impressed. Most people she knew thought commitment to something was a diploma on the wall. Her friend had taken it to another level. 'So that creation of intention is like your observer effect. Which is followed by the quantum entanglement of two people, who then share energy between them … wow. Does it exhaust you?'

'Not really; it invigorates me, as I get some of the energy on the way through. We both benefit. I'm not using my own energy; I'm using limitless universal energy.' Abbey shrugged. 'It really works, and people feel better.'

'So you're doing what Nikola Tesla was talking about, drawing energy out of the ether. What else do you experience as you do it?' Celeste asked, intrigued.

'Sometimes I get information. I can see what their troubles are, and sometimes I get flashes of their life or even past lives. When you're in that zone with people, it gets a little telepathic.'

Celeste raised an eyebrow. 'How do you know they aren't just random thoughts of your own?'

'More often than not, the information means something to the client. Last week, I saw a lady who was really unhappy, but she never told me why. When I did the session for her, I kept sensing an impression of a dog jumping around her, trying to get her attention. When I told her this, she burst out crying. Her dog had recently died, and she felt this was him letting her know he was all right. It brought her peace and made her feel better.'

Celeste paused and considered what Abbey was saying. Maybe there was something to this. 'So people can tap into information, and it can be validated?'

'Sure!' Abbey's eyes lit up. 'There're stacks of this stuff out there. Near-death experiences, remote viewing, mediumship, and some of it has been proven in various studies of the paranormal. Even contact with aliens!'

This was a bit much for Celeste all at once, though she wanted to know more. 'So where would I start with investigating some of this?'

'You have to be a little discerning when it comes to spiritual people. Some of them are amazing, but there are some charlatans around. Why don't you have a chat with my Reiki teacher? She's a medium also and tunes into lots of stuff. She's really good and knows heaps about all this.'

After a remarkable lunch with more to digest than just food, they hugged in the carpark, and then Celeste climbed into Jeeps and headed home, deep in thought.

CHAPTER 6

Celeste realised that thinking wasn't going to help her at this point. She needed to surrender to where the trail was heading. A strong intellect had been her saviour many times throughout her life, but the conversation with Abbey offered a different interpretation of the universe. The best thing to do was visit Abbey's teacher and find out for herself.

Chantelle lived in the town of Windsor, about forty minutes away. Celeste introduced herself as someone wanting to know more about what the Reiki teacher did from a scientific perspective. Though initially reluctant, Chantelle agreed to see Celeste when she discovered that Celeste had been Abbey's best friend at school.

Chantelle greeted her at the door. Celeste observed a lady who looked to be somewhere in her late fifties with a grey bob hairstyle and blue eyes that were sharp and clear. She wore jeans and a top; no flowing garments or flowers in her hair. They took a seat in the lounge room, and Chantelle gestured to a pot of tea on the coffee table. 'I hope peppermint's all right?'

'Fine, thank you.'

Chantelle poured, then Celeste reached for a cup and took a sip. It both warmed and relaxed her. 'Thank you for seeing me,' she began. 'I'm seeking information about other dimensions in the universe and, more importantly, how we can access them. I'm undertaking a doctorate that blends some key aspects of quantum physics. Part of that landscape involves other dimensions that've been proved mathematically, though I'm looking for a more physical validation.'

Celeste paused, realising she may have spoken a foreign language to this person who'd welcomed her into her home and made her tea.

'Okay,' Chantelle said. 'I can see where you're coming from. Perhaps if I tell you how I got into my work, that will be a good place to start.'

'Sure.' Celeste nodded.

'I originally trained as a nurse, and as you know, the medical world is very fact based and evidence driven. The system treats the symptoms and doesn't always take into account other sources of distress that cause illness. For example, if a condition is seen to be psychosomatic, it's written off as a mental health issue, though we as nurses could often see that what affects the mind affects the body. There is no separation. We were sometimes frustrated by medical training that was based on a cause-and-effect model, with no permission to look outside it. I did part of my training in palliative care, and it was there that I realised I could see energy. I'd had plenty of experiences as a kid that my parents had put down to imagination. But when I passed on a message from my dead grandmother, who talked about where she'd hidden the deed to the house, they started to be a bit more open. Nanna had hidden it under some floorboards. I told my dad and he found it.'

Celeste leaned forward. 'Tell me about seeing energy.'

'The first time, I was with an old lady as she died, and I saw a beautiful energy rise up and leave her body. I felt the emptiness of the physical form that remained. Sometimes, I'd see people come into the hospital with a heavy shroud around them. They were the relatives of those about to depart, deep in their impending loss. They would go through the death event and come back out of the room changed by it. Many were lighter, some less so, all having their own unique experience. Other times, I'd get a sense of the person who'd passed standing alongside loved ones, comforting them. I don't see them as clearly as I see you now—it's more of an energetic impression—but it helps people to know that someone they love is still around, just in a different form.

'I wanted to know more about energy, so I learned Reiki and eventually came to teach it. Every day, I meditate to bring the energy of the universe into my being. It's been a long time since I've had any sort of illness, and I turn seventy next year.'

Celeste was impressed. Chantelle looked so much younger than that. If this caught on, it would put cosmetic surgery out of business in no time, maybe even form a new field of 'cosmic-cosmetic surgery'. 'So this ability is something you're born with?'

'I believe we can all tune in to energy, though for some it's much easier. I don't know exactly why some are gifted and some not, though when parents support the gift and don't have their child shut it down, it does make a difference.'

The look on Chantelle's face changed suddenly. 'Celeste, sometimes when I have these conversations, things happen. There's an energy trying to get my attention. I wish to be respectful, though, so if you prefer I ignore it, then that's fine. I have to do that when the timing isn't right. Or if you like, I can explore it a little, as I sense it has something to do with you.'

Celeste felt a chill up her spine. 'Well, I guess you should explore it.'

'All right, then …' Chantelle closed her eyes, and her eyelids flickered a little.

Celeste wondered if this was a performance or a gift. She stayed sceptical but interested.

'Seems to be a male energy, a gentle caring one, here for you. May I ask if your father is in spirit?'

'Yes, he passed a few years back.'

'He's showing me a car, a blue car.'

Well, no surprises there. Jeeps was parked out the front.

'Wait. There's another car, a white sedan surrounded by trees.'

That was significant. 'He had an accident, and the car was in a gully. It had to be winched out of the bush.' Celeste felt decidedly uneasy now.

'He says he's still watching over you. He's proud of you, and he'll help you with your work. He's going now.'

Celeste didn't know what to say, so she just said, 'Thank you.'

'Wait, he's turned back around, and he's saying, "Stay open."'

Celeste burst into tears … and then it happened. The room flooded with a scent that she recognised instantly. It'd been part of every one of his hugs in his later years after she'd given it to him for his birthday. It was his aftershave, *Aqua – Pour Homme,* and in that moment, she missed him more than ever.

Chantelle paused for a moment and then said, 'Is there anything you'd like to say to him?'

Celeste had no idea, so she simply said, 'Tell him I love him, I miss him, and I thank him for finding us such a beautiful home to live in.'

'He's laughing and saying the home is great, but the shed is amazing!'

Then he was gone, leaving Celeste in a bit of a mess.

Chantelle handed her some tissues and waited quietly for her to collect herself. 'Have you had any contact before?'

Celeste shook her head. 'Nothing like that, though I've felt him around sometimes. I thought it was just my imagination.'

'Can I ask you something?'

Celeste nodded.

'He seemed to have something happening with his wrists. They were sort of held in front of him. Maybe he was holding something? It didn't seem comfortable. Does this make sense in any way?'

'Nothing that comes to mind, though I'm not thinking very clearly at the moment.'

'Of course. These things I see are sometimes metaphorical, sometimes literal, though I thought it worth mentioning.' Chantelle smiled gently.

Celeste rose to leave, and as Chantelle walked her to the door, she spoke once more. 'Can I ask if you believe in past lives?'

Celeste answered honestly. 'No, not really, though after today I guess I need to be open to anything.'

'I'll just offer this; I have a sense there's another lifetime that has relevance to your work. That's all I know.'

Celeste nodded politely. She'd had enough metaphysical adventures for the day and needed some time to gather herself.

As she drove back through the country roads, the smell of her father's aftershave lingered.

CHAPTER 7

After arriving home, Celeste sat in the carport in stunned silence for several minutes, taking stock. Her world had been shaken to its core.

There was absolutely no scientific explanation for what she'd experienced. Chantelle couldn't have known about her father's favourite saying to her, that there'd been a white car in the bush, or the fact that he even had a shed. She couldn't even come close to considering the aftershave incident. Her data gathering and research over the years had rarely included the sense of smell.

What would she do about the wrist metaphor, or the fact her father would help her with her research? For the moment, she had to set aside anything to do with him, as it still brought up too much pain.

Celeste switched into scientific mode. For Chantelle to be able to see energy, she needed to be able to perceive things differently to the norm. Celeste went inside, and on her whiteboard in the main living area of the house, she started a mind map of her thoughts.

Most of the electromagnetic spectrum was invisible to the human eye; in fact, visible light was a very small percentage. The rest of the spectrum had remained undiscovered until science had developed the equipment to detect and then measure things like infrared and ultraviolet light, x-rays, microwaves, gamma waves and so on. What if some people had the ability to see a greater range, and that's where these experiences came from?

Likewise with the auditory spectrum. Though people can't hear as well as dogs or even dolphins—who used sonar to find food, each other and alert their pod to danger—Chantelle had heard her dead father speak and had passed on messages. Dolphins were known to read the whole landscape through a variety of clicks and whistles that gave them a sixth sense of their surroundings. What if people had other senses they didn't know about, except for the few who'd discovered them? Over the years, following her father's advice to stay open, she'd read studies on extrasensory perception.

What if her father's appearance at Chantelle's had been possible because she and he were quantumly entangled? She had to be there for Chantelle to detect her father's presence.

What if, when we die, we move into one or a number of the other dimensions hypothesised in string theory? What if we leave the body and become non-local, no longer trapped in three-dimensional reality and linear time? We could surf the multiverse!

Celeste was getting dizzy, and her mind map had filled the whiteboard, though one large bubble at the side seemed to be a dead end—reincarnation. She paused. It was something else entirely, but if true, it would be the exact opposite of a dead end!

Today was the first time someone had ever asked her if she believed in past lives. She didn't, but if she really wanted to stay open, then perhaps she should consider that she might believe in reincarnation in some of her other lives. She shook her head at her growing sense of cosmic humour.

Celeste spent the rest of the day researching the concept of reincarnation, staying as open as she could to something she didn't really resonate with. Her first surprise was to find that several of the world's religions had tenets into reincarnation philosophy. As she went further, she found a survey that showed forty-five per cent of Americans were either believers or open to the concept of reincarnation. Celeste wrote that off, given the small sample size used for the survey.

Then she found the work of Dr Ian Stevenson and the University of Virginia. He'd passed over a decade ago, but the Division of Perpetual Studies still existed today, continuing what he'd started. In short, he'd interviewed children and their relatives who had memories of previous lives. These children knew specific details of the other families to which they'd previously belonged. He'd also noted physical evidence of birthmarks in places where life-ending injuries had been inflicted during the other lives. Stevenson had written something like three hundred publications, including fourteen books on the subject. As an eminent psychiatrist with five decades of clinical work and research behind him, his work carried a lot of weight with Celeste, and she ordered a couple of his books online.

Leaning back in her chair, Celeste eyed the bookshelf across the room. Her parents had been voracious readers, and she wandered over, intuitively looking for something. Her mother's books about art and gardening were interspersed with her father's more scientific titles, alongside her own contributions to the family library—books on quantum theory by the likes of Brian Greene, Fred Allan Wolfe and even a few early Issac Asimovs before he moved into science fiction. She spied one by Amit Goswami PhD called *Physics of the Soul*. Celeste knew the name, as he was a well-known quantum physicist, though he'd also been part of the Institute of Noetic Sciences in the USA, which from Celeste's viewpoint had always been a little on the fringe of science. This book had been one of a number given to her by her parents for Christmas a few years before they passed. She'd placed it on the family bookshelf and forgotten about it. It held sentimental value for her in this moment, as her pain once more seeped into her awareness. She distracted herself by opening the book and scanning the pages. She stopped at page 135. A name leaped out at her as she read:

> *With the quantum memory of a past life helping us, it is now easy to understand the phenomenon of genius. An Einstein is not built via childhood learning in one life; many previous lives contributed to his abilities. The inventor Thomas Edison intuited the situation correctly when he said, 'Genius is experience. Some seem to think it is a gift or talent, but it is the fruit of long experience in many lives. Some are older souls than others, and so they know more.'*

Celeste had to sit down, as she contemplated the significance of this if it were true. She wondered if her scientific view of the world was expanding exponentially or collapsing in a heap of rubble.

She looked across to the whiteboard filled with her own thoughts and noticed 'Reincarnation' on the edge—literally and figuratively. She was almost out of room, and this could lead to an immediate whiteboard shortage and an even more crowded living room.

Over the next hour, she dismantled the Celeste-ial Wall, took down all her certificates and diplomas and put them in a box in one of the spare rooms. She then covered the wall with flipchart paper. Celeste now had a wall where she could mind map in countless directions, even though she needed to stand on a chair at times to write in some of the higher areas or be on her knees to write towards the floor. She transferred her thoughts from the whiteboard onto the wall and, having done that, took a break and walked outside.

A warm autumn afternoon and gentle breeze greeted Celeste. She sat on the veranda near the old chess board, wondering if she should get a rocking chair like Einstein. *That might be an even better method of research.* She looked across the lawn towards her father's shed, half-hidden by heavy bushes. Then her attention turned in the other direction to her mother's studio at the back of the house. Three buildings stood on the property: his space, her space and their family space. When her parents were alive, Celeste also had her apartment down in the city. It was as if the three of them were unique particles that came together to form a wave as a family. Maybe the macro world did echo the quantum realm after all.

Driven to know more about reincarnation, Celeste cleared her mind by breathing deeply—a technique Dr Bart had taught her years ago.

Breathe deeply … clear the mind … and wait in the emptiness for thought to come. Within twenty seconds, the insight came.

A knowing had been just beneath the surface. If she believed in reincarnation, her parents were not gone forever, and one day she would see them again. Emotion welled up in her. Celeste had always advocated no emotional involvement in research … no intrusion from your own observer effect! As that would influence the results, and she had to stay objective.

Sighing deeply, she parked her emotions and headed back inside to continue researching the reincarnation angle as a scientist and not a grieving daughter.

One of the emerging theories of past-life memories that Celeste came across was that these memories were accessing a form of collective memory. This could only be possible if three things were in play:

First, memory had to be non-local, which would mean memories weren't stored in the brain but in the quantum field. Celeste wrote this up on the wall with a whispered apology to the world of neuroscience, where some believed the brain to be the centre of everything.

Second, the quantum field would need to be able to transcend time and space. The linear time issue would have no relevance except in the third dimensional reality, because that was the place from where we observe the phenomenon. There would be just memory information, some of it coming from this life and the rest from the collective. Some events just looked like past lives, as a way for us to integrate them.

Third, everything would have to be quantumly entangled and connected in some way, including ourselves. This was closer to home for a quantum physicist, but there still needed to be a way to retrieve the information.

Something was missing.

Her pen worked furiously as her thoughts started to fill the wall. This collection of experiences had to be held together by some form of infrastructure that could be accessed to retrieve information as needed. If the history of humanity was held in a limitless collection of stories and events—a vast library of sorts—what would the shelves of this library be made of and how would you get a library card?

Another theory behind past-life memory was its similarity to a dream state where we're told a story for learning. The teller of this story is our unconscious state, and the same way that dreams have messages of unresolved complexes trapped in the subconscious, past-life memory was designed to teach or heal us. Celeste thought this theory unlikely, as it embraced the theory of local memory in the brain. Beyond that, there was the well-documented research from Stevenson's team on the physical similarities between lifetimes and the eyewitness testimonies of the families of children who'd travelled across town, walked into a house and greeted all the family members from their last life. In short, dreams didn't create birthmarks in the next body as echoes of fatal wounds from the last life. This theory didn't seem to hold too much credibility, and Celeste banished it to a bottom corner of the research wall.

The final theory was that reincarnation was real. This would mean that the religiously aligned and the researchers were both right. We travelled across the world over a vast number of lifetimes, somehow transferring our immortal identity from lifetime to lifetime, having our memory wiped in between to give us a fresh start. But why would you do that? If it was about resolving karma, then how do you resolve something if you don't know what you are trying to fix?

She returned to theory one and thought about collective memory. Something stirred in her own memory about the work of Carl Gustav Jung, the founder of analytical psychology and the theory of the collective unconscious. If the other areas of research she'd gone down were rabbit holes, then this took her into an underground cavern.

A new stream of information spanned out across the wall with bubbles, arrows and statements heading in many directions. She paused for breath and looked at her watch; it was 9 pm. The whole afternoon had disappeared and materialised as a wall of thoughts, assumptions and connections that had her satisfied and completely exhausted.

Celeste wandered into the kitchen, looked in the fridge and found some leftover pasta that still smelled okay. She put it in the microwave for a couple of minutes, grabbed a fork and headed back to the lounge room, where she sat on the sofa and looked up at the wall. The last several hours of looking deeper into Carl Jung and his life's work had been fascinating.

First, it had taken her into a whole different field of work, not the quantum physics she'd been embracing for over twenty years; and second, certain aspects seemed to fit across both fields of work.

Through appreciative eyes, she saw Jung's evolution as he grew past the theories of Sigmund Freud and went in his own direction. He moved beyond the restrictive nature of childhood complexes into new theories, and she found that fascinating. Jung was a wonderful example of someone who'd stayed open.

One patch of the wall denoted his work on the phenomenon of synchronicity, referring to random events that seemed to have a connection that went beyond coincidences. This had Celeste wondering about the intrusion of quantum entanglement as a source, or even cause of, synchronicity. If there was some form of entanglement at the subatomic level, then this could play out in the macro world in generally observed phenomena that seemed to evidence a connection that didn't make logical sense. It was a lot to digest at this hour of the day.

What made even more sense to her was the theory of the collective unconscious, where everything that had ever unfolded in the history of humanity was out there, stored as collective mental concepts, instincts and characteristics. Jung named them archetypes, and they could be used for analytical purposes to gain insight and make psychological progress for people. Analytical psychology examined a person's relationship to this immeasurable volume of information. They had their own relationship with it, because they were part of it.

Bang! Another insight. What if this was the infrastructure people tuned into when they retrieved past life memories? What if the fact that they were part of humanity, donating their experiences to this repository of information, earned them a library card? That would mean the whole of humanity was quantumly entangled, and all of us had the ability to move beyond time and space to find the answers we seek!

In all her enthusiasm, Celeste spilled what was left of her pasta on the sofa. She was okay with that, though, since the food was a little older than she'd thought.

Pausing, she took stock and reflected on the three theories behind reincarnation.

Collective memory was starting to make sense from a quantum perspective if she considered some of Jung's work, specifically the collective unconscious. It just needed a new angle, not influenced by traditional psychology and more in alignment with the mystical aspects he'd embraced.

The theory of dream state and messages from the subconscious were out due to Stevenson and others' physical and research-based evidence. She hadn't dismissed the idea of the movement of an eternal soul from lifetime to lifetime yet, but it was sounding less likely now.

It had been one hell of a day. She fell into bed, exhausted.

CHAPTER 8

She dreamed a thousand dreams, was in many places and had many faces. Something was starting to open up within her and gently nudging her forward on this journey of discovery.

Celeste awoke early and clear-headed just as the sun rose over the ridge. She dressed warmly in a tracksuit and went outside, feeling the chill in the air, typical of autumn in the Blue Mountains. This low down, they very rarely had snow in winter, though sometimes the dew froze into frost. She wanted to walk more before the winter came. The coolish air filled her lungs, helping her to think. As she headed down a familiar track, Celeste felt the sanctity of the huge expanse of untouched bushland. It had always been a place of solace for her.

A wallaby detecting her presence watched her carefully for several seconds before bounding noisily away into denser bush. Celeste paused for a moment to wonder if wallabies might do reincarnation. It could be a good life to roam the bushland in peace, but then you might get hit by a truck. Did that mean that, karmically, you had to come back as the truck driver next time to balance things out? She'd researched some of the philosophies and religious dogma around reincarnation, and they hadn't resonated with her. Aspects of the karmic cycle seemed a little Old Testament, like an eye for an eye and a tooth for a tooth. She'd even found an article claiming that evidence of reincarnation had been removed from the Bible. The religious rabbit holes she'd gone down the day before hadn't inspired her. After all, she was a scientist and was wary of indoctrinated mindsets, more so than some of her colleagues who had become locked into their own opinions.

Firsthand experience had always been her catalyst for further investigation. Today she wanted to look further into the third possibility—the movement of an eternal soul from lifetime to lifetime—and during her morning walk, she spent time pondering how best to do that.

After returning home, Celeste gulped down a quick breakfast of muesli and fruit. When in this type of focused mood, food was simply a refuelling stop. She showered and spent a little more time than usual with the warm water running over her body, relaxing her and washing away the white noise of a hundred irrelevant thoughts.

Before long, she was sitting on the sofa once more, looking up at the paper mural of her collective thoughts. Celeste wanted to find someone she could grill on reincarnation, someone who knew what they were talking about. The day before, she'd touched on this at a high level and was now drawn to become far more focused. She searched for 'Reincarnation Australia Research' online, followed a few leads and found an article that drew her interest.

A researcher called Dr Paul O'Malley had written some extensive papers on reincarnation. Using hypnotic techniques to retrieve these memories, he'd then undertaken fieldwork to confirm the memories, collecting different aspects of evidence. Now over seventy years of age and long retired, he had a background in psychology and science, and his doctorate had been on Jungian dream analysis. Celeste was strongly drawn in his direction.

It took some time, but eventually she found a reference to where he lived, and she tracked him down and gave him a call.

An aged and deep voice answered the phone. 'Hello?'

'Dr O'Malley, my name is Celeste Kelly. I'm a quantum physicist looking to make sense of some theories and metaphysical experiences, and I'd like to talk to you about your work. I'm currently working on a doctorate, blending together some of the core theories of quantum phenomena.'

'I wish you well with that, Celeste, but please know that I am retired now and no longer do interviews. I've written a few books about my work, and you'd find most of what you need in those, I would imagine.'

Celeste changed tack a little, leveraging what she'd read of Dr O'Malley's background that embraced Jung's work. 'I'm currently pursuing a theory as to whether past life memory may come from the collective unconscious rather than the specific transpersonal memory of a person. Would that be in any of your books?' She felt an underlying importance in connecting with him.

He paused, not answering the question directly, and Celeste could feel the energy change at the other end. 'Where are you doing your doctorate?' he asked.

'University of New South Wales. I've been part of the school of physics down there for twenty years, on and off.'

'Is Bart Kindred still there?' he asked.

Celeste breathed a sigh of relief. 'Yes. He is actually a member of my review board. He's been my mentor for a long time.'

'His father was a dear friend of mine. Is Bart well? '

Celeste took a risk. 'He is very well, apart from his sense of dress.'

It worked. Dr O'Malley chuckled. 'That comes from his father. He got his mother's amiable personality and his father's unfortunate sense of style.'

The ice had been broken. 'I'd be grateful if we could meet and have a conversation, if at all possible, Dr O'Malley.'

'I don't drive much anymore, though I could receive you at home for a short while. I prefer the mornings. You could come tomorrow.'

Celeste spent the rest of the day reflecting on what she'd like to ask Dr O'Malley.

CHAPTER 9

Paul O'Malley had retired to the top end of the mountains in the small town of Medlow Bath. Celeste climbed the hill in Jeeps and drove past the turnoff to Blue Mountains' Grammar School, which transported her back in time to her school days. She glanced up the hill they used to climb to the main gate and remembered lumbering up there in her overcoat, scarf and hat in the middle of winter. It was always such a shock to the system after the warm train ride up to Wentworth Falls station. Celeste shivered at the memory.

Then she smiled as she remembered her favourite teacher.

Mr Haynes had been her mathematics teacher in her middle school years, an enthusiastic and caring person who'd asked her to stay after class one day. Celeste had stayed at her desk until the classroom was empty, thinking she was in trouble for some reason yet to be disclosed.

Mr Haynes came down to sit at the desk next to hers and said, 'Celeste, I've only had a couple of these chats in all my years of teaching. I want you to know that the way your mind works is exceptional. You grasp mathematics better than anyone I've ever seen. I really feel you should consider moving towards advanced maths and blending it with physics in your final two years. I feel that some of the sciences will call to you, and I believe you have a strong future there.'

It took thirty seconds to steer Celeste in the direction of her gifts for science and maths. In her final year, Mr Haynes had been her teacher again, and she'd shone under his guidance as he recognised her unique mind. He told her she had a gifted way of thinking, different to others—which was no doubt why they found it hard to follow her thought processes at times. It worked for her, though.

From there, she'd taken her undergrad degree at UNSW and blossomed into the realm of quantum physics, won awards and worked in CERN. In some ways, her career had all started with that conversation twenty-five years previously.

Medlow Bath lay about twenty minutes further on from her old school. Celeste's destination was well off the main road, a small brick cottage at the end of the street surrounded by gardens. It had an old-world feel, and turning into the drive felt a little bit like stepping back in time. The irony wasn't lost on her. Celeste parked Jeeps in the driveway and walked up the front steps to find an old-fashioned brass bell at the side of the door. It tinkled a welcome as she pulled its string.

She heard footsteps, and an older man opened the door. A kind face with a full head of thick salt-and-pepper hair greeted her. His energy seemed more vibrant than on the phone.

Celeste began, 'Hello, Doctor—'

He silenced her with a hand. 'I'm reliably informed that I'm not supposed to let you in unless you promise to call me Paul.' A twinkle in his blue eyes betrayed his stern voice. 'Bart says hi.'

Celeste reluctantly agreed. So he'd called Dr Bart to check

50

her credentials. Clearly, Paul's lifetime of research was still in play when needed.

'Come in, Celeste. I've made some coffee if you'd like some.'

She stepped inside and found the experience was like walking into a library. Books lined every wall, and many were in various states of being read. The coffee table alone had at least a dozen spread out across it, leaving just enough space for two coffee cups. Paul poured from a metal pot and gestured to a small milk jug and sugar bowl. Celeste settled into what was probably the most comfortable armchair she'd ever experienced.

'Bart says that meeting you will be great for us both. I have no idea why, so how about we kick off by you telling me about your work?'

That was quick. He'd dived straight into her reason for coming. She paused, gathered her thoughts and said, 'I believe we can access other dimensions. We've theorised their existence through string theory and the many worlds' interpretation, though we're yet to experience them fully. I'm starting to wonder if their existence defies time and space as we know it.

'If this holds true, then we live in a metaphysical universe. Concepts like reincarnation become just another part of the landscape. It's not easy territory, though, as it means that most of what we've been taught about science is wrong, that our belief systems about our place in the universe and what life is all about are completely incorrect at worst and hopelessly incomplete at best.' Celeste paused. This was the moment that would determine if she left within five minutes or had another life-changing conversation.

Paul paused for a moment and then leaned forward and put his cup down. 'I thought string theory was more a philosophy since it hasn't been proved experimentally. Aren't those strings too small to be observed?' He seemed to be warming up …

51

'Yes, that's true, but quantum physics is based on the discipline of mathematics. When we run formulas, use constants and make educated assumptions, they all have to be mathematically calculated. I feel mathematics is its own language, and it not only transcends cultural and linguistic boundaries but also has the potential to validate those other dimensions hypothesised. If they weren't there, then the maths wouldn't stack up. Maths has no grey area; it's either right or wrong.'

'So where does my work fit in?' Paul asked, eyes sparkling with interest.

'I want to know more about reincarnation and its ability to confirm the theory of the collective unconscious to show that past-life memories come from there. If reincarnation exists, then it's possible that the information gleaned comes from dimensions other than this one, beyond time and space as we know it, which would prove the metaphysical nature of existence.'

'If you could ask one question about it, that summarised your search, what would it be?' Paul's growing engagement seemed to drop ten years off his age.

'I'd like to know whether past-life memories are information retrieved from the collective history of humanity, driven by our own observer effect—that is, we go looking for a particular something and we find it. Or whether we're tapping into a form of our own personal quantum memory that's held in an energy field of which the body is only one part.' She winced at how complicated she made it sound.

'So you wonder if past-life memories are our own or come from the Akashic record?' Paul simplified—thankfully.

Celeste had seen the term 'Akashic record' in her recent research, so she replied with a simple, 'Yes'.

'Have you considered that the answer might be both?'

Celeste stopped, surprised at the question. 'Well … not at

this point. Should I?'

Paul smiled. 'Mathematics as a black-and-white mindset will only get you so far, Celeste. The whole universe exists in shades of grey. Human consciousness is filtered through belief systems, differing opinions and history recorded in the way a person sees events from their own perspective. Beyond all that, we know absolutely nothing. I have seen things over the years that will never be explained by science, religion, logic or even philosophy. I already know that our view of the universe is hopelessly flawed, and you're right, it's blatantly incorrect.'

Now he was really warming up, and not from the coffee. Clearly, this was the passion and purpose that had driven his work over the years. A trailblazer looking for answers …

'Let me give you my summary of the scientific method,' he continued. 'I come up with a hypothesis within my field of expertise, psychology, probably driven by my own experiences and background. I feel passionate about this concept and set out to validate it experimentally. Chances are that I will, since I'm influencing my own experiment due to the observer effect. At the same time, a colleague may have another hypothesis, which they set out to prove. We both publish papers with each of our theories that are similar but different. We may even peer review each other's papers from our own opinions, and it doesn't go well because we believe more in our own work. A great example in your own field is when there were five different versions of string theory back in the nineties before Witten merged them all into M-theory. But, the whole time, we've missed the point. There are no right or wrong answers, just many different ones, as we exist in a universe of possibility that we haven't even come close to tapping into.'

It was like he was repeating some of her own thoughts back to her. Though much of what Paul said rang true, Celeste wanted to defend science. The time at Chantelle's place when her father appeared had shaken her iron grip on science. She was still holding on with one hand, while she reached out with the other towards new horizons.

'So what would you do differently?' she asked.

Paul grabbed a pen and a notebook. He opened it, drew a rectangle on the page and wrote a word on each side. 'We see life as this box. We're trapped by these four walls made up of our *culture, beliefs, experiences* and *conditioning*. Our education system from start to finish is a great way to build this box, as is the information fed to us through mainstream media and other informational feeds. The box has us trapped, even though we don't realise.'

Paul then moved his pen to the other side of the page and drew a star way outside the box. 'This star represents an event that doesn't fit within the box. It's a new experience that doesn't fit with our beliefs, conditioning or experiences to date. So we have a choice: we can either accept it, and stretch our box out to include it, or reject it. We use our free will to decide. Do we stay in the existing paradigm, or do we build a new one?'

Next, Paul redrew the box to include the star. 'If you measure the size of the old box and the new box, you can see which is the best way to go. We have to stay open and explore the new when it arrives.'

There was that phrase again.

Paul continued, 'I have respect for the scientific endeavours that have brought the world so much, from aircraft to heart transplants, to all the technology we take for granted. Though I see many scientists, even some in my own field of psychology, staying within the comfort zone of their own box. Science was always meant to be exploratory, though we're missing the greatest discovery ever in mainstream science. The breaking news is that we're living in a metaphysical universe yearning to be explored.'

'I had one of those star-type experiences recently,' she said and then shared with Paul her experience of her father at Chantelle's place.

Paul listened quietly and then nodded. 'So you being here is confirmation that you've stretched the sides of the box,' he said quietly.

Celeste hadn't seen it that way, though now she realised that was exactly what she'd done. It gave her some good context to continue. 'When you say that past-life memory is both, what do you mean?'

'I've seen different levels of recall, so let me offer an analogy... Let us say that the entire history of humanity, this repository of experiences and wisdom, call it the Akashic record or collective unconscious, is like a giant library full of books, and it exists beyond time and space as we know it. As a participant in humanity, you have your own book in this library and it represents the story of your soul. There are various chapters in your book, one for each lifetime you've had here. Your book may even sit next to other books on the shelf, which may belong to people you've known from the different chapters in your own.

'Let's say there comes a time when you want to explore your book. Perhaps you may've had a flash of something, a memory, a dream or felt something troubling that makes no sense from this lifetime. If you create an intention and go looking, that will send your enquiry into the library. In order to resolve something, you may have an experience of needing to see another chapter or chapters. It may be helpful to know of a skill or talent from another chapter that could serve you now. It may even be more helpful for you to be shown something from another part of the library that isn't in your book. Your intention will create the experience you most need. What you call the observer effect, I call the creator effect. You create the experience you most need from the intention you set. Your intention affects the library and draws the answers to you, sometimes from your book, sometimes from beyond it.'

Celeste digested the analogy, then nodded. 'I understand.' She glanced at the thousands of books around her. *Wow, this guy really loves books.* It was like she was sitting in the Akashic library at that very moment.

Paul finished his analogy with a final comment. 'Life changes for us when we realise we are the book ... and not the chapter.'

'How does it change?'

'Well, for one, knowing that our consciousness continues, we lose our fear of death. If the greatest of our fears no longer matters, that has a ripple effect into our lives in a very significant way. Second, we realise that we're a spiritual being having a human experience, not the other way around. And third, grief is merely a parting of chapters ... until books reunite. The list goes on ...'

The third one caught Celeste's attention.

Paul continued, 'I feel it's the experience outside the box that shows us our true potential. An unexpected past-life echo, a near-death experience, spontaneous astral travelling, a lucid dream, an alien encounter or a psychic experience. Any of these events that unfold in a completely unexpected way gives the person concerned the ability to stretch the box both for themselves and when they share the experience with others, for humanity as well.'

'So what would you advise me to do?' Celeste asked.

'Well,' Paul replied, 'I guess we could always have a little past-life experiment now, if you're up for it?'

'I thought you were retired.'

Paul shrugged. 'I am. It just seems that we should do this. I have a feeling it may be helpful for you somehow.'

'Okay, but I've never done anything like this before.' Celeste wondered what she was getting herself into, but it seemed she could trust him. Perhaps due to the connection to Dr Bart.

'If you have no expectation and just let the experience flow, it'll be easier. You can stay in that comfortable chair, and I'll move beside you.' Paul came around the coffee table and moved an old wooden chair next to her. 'All you have to do is relax and follow my guidance.'

He worked a lever on the side of Celeste's chair, and a footrest came out as the chair tilted back to recline her into a relaxing position.

'Now close your eyes and take a breath … and release it …' Paul's voice slowed, stretching the words out. His tone was one of peace, and Celeste felt her mind clear and her body go heavy … and so began the dance between their souls.

Celeste listened to the words and the energy they created and felt her awareness drifting across time and space. Realising she was in the company of a master of his craft, she surrendered to the experience. Before long, she was travelling back decades, recalling times she hadn't thought of for years or never consciously remembered. She remembered sitting in German class at school and how easy and natural the language was for her. She remembered the excitement of Christmas morning and the presents under the tree. She strongly recalled the feel of her new puppy, Tilly, in her arms. Each time Paul peeled back another layer of time, she found herself actually there, in that moment, able to describe what was happening around her.

Then he steered her further back, to before she was born. She felt the sensations of her mother's womb, her mother's excitement at being pregnant, and she heard a deep, muffled voice outside the body in which she resided. She recognised that voice as her father's, felt an excitement for the life ahead and looked forward to the challenge. It felt purposeful somehow.

Then Paul's voice came into play again, lifting her from her mother's womb and holding her as she floated across the lineage of her soul to be 'drawn to a lifetime that is helpful for Celeste to see and has a connection with her life today …' She moved out further across time and space, scanning for such a lifetime. Naturally and inexplicably, a light in the distance drew her, and she slowly moved into that light …

Paul's voice seemed to reach her from a long way away, though was also still right beside her. She heard him whisper, 'Be there now … in that place that has called you. Details are gathering … easily and naturally … you are there and can describe where you are and what is happening.'

Celeste spoke as if in a dream. 'I'm walking along a path among some buildings. I'm looking up at a tower made of stone.'

'This tower that has drawn your attention … describe it, please.'

'It looks … gothic. Like a church, but it's not a church. There are arched windows and four spires on the corners. I've passed it now and am moving on further … I'm on my way somewhere, and I know I can't be late. It's somewhere important.'

Paul drifted her further into detail. 'It's okay, you won't be late. Time has stopped just now. Move outside your body and look back at yourself; describe what you see.'

'I'm a young man, maybe mid-twenties. I'm wearing an old-fashioned suit and tie. I'm carrying a leather satchel with papers in it.' Celeste's voice seemed to change, taking on a more urgent tone. 'He's here, he's here … oh, I so want to meet him.'

Paul noted this comment for later and turned on a small recorder sitting on the table. 'Move forward now; you've reached the place you were going. Where are you?'

'It's the lecture hall, the large one, and I've never seen it so full. So many people. I'm pushing my way in so I can get closer to the front before everyone takes their seats.'

'Does your satchel have a name on it?'

'Yes, it was a gift from my parents, but it's quite old now and the print has almost rubbed off.'

'What can you still read?' Paul asked.

'*Isaac M* is all that's left.' Celeste screwed up her eyes as she attempted to read the old print in another time and place.

'Is it all right if I call you Isaac?'

'Of course,' Celeste replied. 'That is my name, but most people call me Zac, so that's probably better.'

'Zac, I'd like you to remember when you last looked at a newspaper.'

'That was this morning.'

'Just be back there again for a moment and tell me, what is the date on the paper?'

'May ninth, 1921.'

'Thank you, Zac. Now, this lecture hall … let me know its location.'

'It's in the main part of the campus, not far from the library,' she replied, not quite sure what Paul wanted.

'Allow yourself to know the name of your campus or school.'

'We're not just a school.' Celeste sounded a little indignant. 'Princeton is a place of higher learning, and one of the greatest minds in the world has come to visit and speak to us.'

'Move forward in time till this person is speaking and describe that to me.'

'Herr Einstein is speaking in German about relativity and his theories of motion. As he speaks, a lady is taking notes and hands them to one of our own professors. He is then making summaries of Herr Einstein's ideas in English for the audience.

His translation is poor and many of the people are confused. I can understand perfectly, though.'

'So you understand German?' Paul asked.

'My mother is a German Jew and my father is an American industrialist. I grew up speaking two languages. Many of the greatest books on physics are in German, so it's an advantage to know that language. Germany is the centre of the world when it comes to physics! I'm taking notes in German, so I can capture Herr Einstein's thoughts in the best possible way.'

Paul continued, 'Let's move forward now to the end of the lecture and tell me what happens next.'

'It's nearing the end, and people have already started to leave, as they can't fully understand what's happening. It's good for me, since the more who leave, the closer I can get to the front. There are only a handful left around him now. Very few people speak German, so they can't really converse with Herr Einstein. I'm moving forward. I feel drawn to meet him.'

'Tell me what happens—when you're ready ...'

'*Herr Einstein. Entschuldigen sie bitte, ihr vortrag war inspirierend.*' Celeste moved easily into fluent German.

'As you speak in German, you communicate with me in English, please, Zac,' Paul directed.

'I'm telling him that I found his lecture inspiring, and he smiles at me. I feel he's pleased to have found someone from Princeton who speaks German. We start to speak, and he warms to me and asks about my family. I tell him my mother was born in Munich, and he says he grew up there. He knows some of the same families in the Jewish community as my mother. He asks about my position at the university, and I tell him that I'm a senior and that I have read almost all of his works in the original German versions. I'm hoping to go into research, as my father has the resources to fund me. He says he would like to keep in touch with me, and he says he may return to Princeton. I write down my address for him. We shake hands, and I leave the lecture hall. I think this is the greatest day of my life!'

Paul offered Celeste a few moments to feel the joy of Zac's experience, then continued the journey further. 'Drift now to the next important thing that happens … Tell me when you're there.'

'It's some months later. I'm in the library, reviewing some of the undergraduate papers for my professor. His assistant comes to me and says I must attend his office urgently. I do so, and he ushers me in. He holds up a letter. It's from Herr Einstein, and it mentions me!

'He's asked if I can join him on some trips abroad as an assistant and translator. He wants me to represent Princeton University in that role also, which strengthens the connection here when he travels to America. It's a great honour for both Princeton and for me as well. Mr Hibben, the president of Princeton, has given his personal blessing to this idea. They want me to leave in two weeks' time to meet Herr Einstein in Europe. I can't believe it!'

Paul pauses again and lets the news sink in. 'That is wonderful, Zac. Congratulations. Move through those preparations now and tell me how they go …'

'The first few days are exhilarating, as so many people congratulate me. I contact my parents by telegram to tell them, and they reply, saying they are very proud. But it's all a bit too much, and I start to get sick. I have a high fever and take to my bed for a few days to rebuild my strength …

'It's getting harder to breathe, so they send for the doctor. He comes to examine me. He sits on the bed now, and his face is really sad. He tells me I have the Spanish flu, and while the worst of the epidemic is over, there are still some cases. They will watch me carefully over the next few days.'

'Move gently through time now, Zac … allow yourself to know what is happening.'

'I'm looking down from the ceiling … I've left my body … Oh no … I think I've died. I can see my mother holding my hand and weeping. My father is standing by her side with a hand on her shoulder. I'm drifting away into the light … Everything is bright, and I feel a sense of being welcomed home … There are people around me.'

Celeste moved into a state of deep peace, and Paul allowed her to rest there for a moment. He realised she was somewhere between lives and framed his next question accordingly. 'What are the messages for Celeste that come from the life of Zac?'

In a tone that came from another world and emanated a sense of wisdom, Celeste said, 'Isaac was unable to fulfill his potential, so it falls to Celeste to continue his work. She will help many and breathe new ideas into the old ways. Now is a time when this is needed most.'

'What else does she need to know?'

Celeste's other voice spoke again. 'She has what she needs for now. There will be more another time.'

'Thank you,' Paul said.

Ever so gently, he brought Celeste back to waking consciousness. It took some time, though he was in no hurry. Paul recognised the significance of what had just unfolded.

CHAPTER 10

Celeste sat there stunned, unable to speak or move. Paul sat quietly, holding space for her and with a glass of water for when she was ready. After a full minute, her eyes focused on him, and she asked, 'What just happened?'

He took a deep breath before saying, 'Something that you were ready for. Take your time; there's no hurry.'

'It seemed so real; it was like I was actually that person. I remember leaving my body at the end and feeling an incredible wave of peace. What was that light I went into?'

'Many people talk about that light and the reunion that unfolds. I always take them to the light, so they know that something awaits them after this life,' Paul said. 'I've made some notes and a recording for you. I have to say that it's rare for an experience to be as connected as yours was, and almost never on the first time. Your recall of detail is exceptional.'

Celeste asked the inevitable question. 'But, surely, I made all that up? I'm a great admirer of Einstein, so if I wanted to imagine a life like that, I'm sure I could.'

Paul smiled. 'I guess that is possible, or perhaps you admire him in this life *because* of your contact in Isaac's life. You realise you spoke fluent German for a moment before I asked you to translate to English?'

'It felt completely natural. I learned German at high school for a couple of years before moving into the sciences. But that was twenty-five years ago. Hardly a word since. Apart from working in Europe some years back.'

'Do you remember what you said?' Paul asked.

'No, it seems to be fading, but the feeling is still there. I was very nervous interrupting the conversation at the front of the hall.'

They debriefed a little more until Celeste was grounded and completely back in her body. Though similar to the experience with her father at Chantelle's place, she was shaken to her core. Science was now just hanging by its fingernails.

'I need to do some research about all this.'

Paul nodded. 'I expected that. Look for the signposts that join the dots. Remember Jung's synchronicity definition: "Connections that go beyond coincidence." Let me know how you go.'

CHAPTER 11

On the way home, Celeste turned off the main road and went to the lookout near Katoomba known as the Three Sisters. She needed to clear her head, and, as always, the bush was her place to do so. Standing at the guardrail, she looked out across an expanse of endless bushland and mist-filled valleys. The landscape seemed to mirror the feelings of expansiveness that still pervaded her consciousness.

To her left, the Sisters rose out of the ridge, immovable and ancient, still identical to when Isaac had his life in the USA around a hundred years ago. *If, in fact, that's true*, said the scientist in the back of her mind.

Perhaps she was heading down a false road just to try to heal the loss of her parents. Knowing they weren't gone forever would help her heal.

Celeste was caught between worlds now. She took a deep breath and headed back home, looking for answers.

The drive was pretty much downhill all the way. It occurred to Celeste that if she couldn't marry these two competing worlds together, her career as a physicist would be going in the same direction. Until this time, she'd had the macro physical world behaving as it should, and she had the subatomic world behaving in a weird way under quantum principles. Now the macro world was starting to behave weirdly as well. Where would she find certainty? Was it even possible? Did she have to reframe her view to that of an ever-unfolding metaphysical universe and just live with it? She'd wanted to prove other dimensions existed to finish her doctorate, not be thrown into them herself and start living them.

She made it home and headed inside. She had no idea what time it was, though her stomach rumbled enough to let her know she'd missed lunch. After grabbing a banana and an apple, she headed to her computer and sat munching the fruit as she drew her thoughts together.

As it was part of undergrad work in most physics curricula, she knew Einstein's theories of relativity well enough. She remembered also that he'd moved to Switzerland, then worked again in Germany. He'd emigrated to the United States in 1933 when the Nazis came to power. She remembered him being in the USA in the early 1930s—no doubt to have discussions about that emigration, but 1921 was a decade or so before that. Perhaps her past life memory was inaccurate, or even made up, since she was about ten years adrift.

She didn't know much about Princeton University, though she'd collaborated on projects with a few physicists there over the years. She'd never visited in person—perhaps not for a hundred years, anyway.

She clicked on the university website and dug around to get a feel for the place. It was somewhat austere, rather traditional, and the website seemed as complex as its history.

Then she saw it.

Her jaw dropped open.

Celeste blinked and tried to comprehend what she was looking at.

A photo of Holder Tower filled her screen, a gothic-type structure with arched windows and four spires in each of the four corners. The photo was taken at roughly the angle that Zac had described, and a familiar feeling came flooding back. She felt like she'd been there.

Rocking back on her chair, she started to rationalise. It was a common architecture from earlier periods in Europe and had been reproduced over the years. She was sure it could be found across older establishments in the USA, used to denote importance and wealth, and she remembered Zac's comments about the reputation of Princeton.

Next, Celeste confirmed that the president of Princeton University from 1912 to 1932 was indeed John G Hibben. There was no way she could've known his name.

As she continued to dig, she came across an article from 2021 celebrating the one-hundred-year anniversary of Einstein's first visit to Princeton. It was in the alumni magazine and described how he'd lectured in German, a stenographer had taken notes, then passed them to one of the faculty, who translated from German to English. The lecture was held on the ninth of May, 1921, in the large lecture hall.

That was the moment she almost lost it completely.

Her box of perception didn't just stretch, it disintegrated, and she was left to build another from the splintered remnants of the old one.

She rose and wandered aimlessly around the room. How do you add to a wall of paper a bubble that says, 'Met Einstein in a past life. Got a job offer.'

Celeste then researched the Spanish flu epidemic of 1918–

1920. She found that it had spread around the world after WW1 as soldiers returned home. Over 600,000 Americans died. The number of flu cases returned to normal, though some deaths were still recorded in 1921.

Finally, she went looking for Isaac M. She took out a subscription to the newspaper archives available through Princeton University and started to dig further around the time Zac would've passed. If his father was a wealthy industrialist, then there could be something about it, perhaps even in the death notices. She stopped and thought. Princeton was halfway between Philadelphia and New York, though it was more likely that a death notice would appear in the New York Times, that being the newspaper of status back in the 1920s. Taking a punt, she searched the death notices. After half an hour, she came across a notice that sent a chill up her spine.

> *In loving memory of Isaac William Meredith, only son of Bill and Ruth Meredith of New York. Taken before his time at 26 years of age. A young man who would have changed the universe as we know it. Our hearts are broken, though we know we'll see him again one day. His service will be held at....*

Celeste burst into tears. In this moment of reckoning, she felt the pain of Zac's early passing, the devastation of a mother sitting by his bedside weeping and a father's stoic outer expression, while his heart felt crushed by the loss of his son.

Beyond that, a Kelly family secret was staring her in the face. Something only her parents knew and had sometimes teased her about over the years, her refusal to use the middle name they had given her when she was born. It was 'Meredith'.

Isaac's last name was Meredith.

She remembered Paul O'Malley's parting advice: 'Look for connections that go beyond coincidence.'

CHAPTER 12

Celeste didn't sleep much that night.

She tossed and turned, trying to integrate where she'd been led over the past several days. There was so much opening up, as though her own personal archive of quantum thoughts and experiences from across time and space were spilling out all over the place. It felt like an exhausting arm wrestle between the explorer and the scientist, the conscious and the unconscious.

As always, the bush called her, and she responded at dawn, wandering down the track and blending with her surroundings. The sun peeked through eucalyptus trees dropping dew, and the leaves rustled underfoot as she glided further into the landscape. The sounds of birdlife began, and they called to each other with their early morning song of joy and hope. More than anything, that soothed her fractured energy. Her mind started to clear. She knew she needed advice and decided to talk to Paul again.

When she called him, everything she'd found came gushing out through the phone, more like Abbey than herself.

Paul listened intently until she was finished. 'So give me your best hypothesis,' he asked simply.

'I feel I've personalised my admiration for Einstein into a story. I may have known about some of the details, and they've been buried in my subconscious.'

'Okay, try a little exercise with me,' Paul said. 'Over the phone is fine. Let's do a little comparison between imagination and memory.' Using that slow voice again, Paul said, 'Firstly, close your eyes … and take a couple of deep breaths. Now, remember a significant experience from when you were young, perhaps from the school years. A nice one, perhaps. Tell me where you are and what's happening.'

'I'm in my last year of high school. I'm receiving the science prize in front of the school. Everyone is clapping, and it's a very proud moment for me. My mum and dad are there, and they are smiling.' Celeste was surprised how quickly the memory emerged. Clearly, she was still sensitised to Paul's voice.

'Remember the feel of this memory,' Paul directed, 'and then let it fade.

'Now, imagine you're having dinner in a restaurant with a well-known rock star that you've never met. What are you having?'

'I'm having pasta, and Bruce Springsteen is having a steak. The restaurant is busy and loud. People keep wanting his autograph.' Celeste was a child of the eighties, after all.

'Remember the feel of this scene too … and let it fade. Now … drift back to being Zac and the conversation with the professor when he showed you the letter from Einstein. Feel this once more … and remember that feeling. Now open your eyes.'

She did as he instructed and blinked a few times.

'You know the feeling of a memory and then of imagination from the first two experiences,' Paul continued, 'and they would've been quite different in how they're stored in your energy field. What did the third scene with the professor feel like? Memory or imagination?'

Celeste spoke with certainty. 'It felt like the time at school ... a memory.'

'Okay, so how does this help?'

'Hmm ... Perhaps I need to be more open to the fact that the quantum field holds information from other lifetimes across time and space. I need to seriously consider that the collective consciousness may be real and that I'm a contributor to it, personally. Zac's life felt deep and connected. It felt like my own and not someone else's contribution. I'm close to accepting all this, but I'm not quite there yet.'

'That's fine, Celeste; do it in your own time. Though I'll offer you one piece of advice: when you accept the metaphysical nature of the universe, you awaken to another level. Things will speed up; be ready for them. I'm here if you need me.' Then he added, 'It's far more interesting than being retired. To be honest, I'd been a little bored till you came past.'

Celeste thanked him, told him she'd stay in touch and returned to the wall of paper. For the section between reincarnation and the collective unconscious, she now had her personal experience to draw upon. Whilst it couldn't be ruled out that she could access other information beyond her own, she now had her own validation of the work of Stephenson and others. Had she experienced one of the dimensions hypothesised in string theory or the many worlds' interpretation? Did Zac's life fit into either or even both?

Celeste's head was in a spin. She needed a break of sorts and someone to talk to about all this. She called Abbey. 'How about lunch at my place?'

'What are we having?'

'Umm ... Uber Eats?' Celeste said hopefully.

Abbey laughed. She knew Celeste's energy when she was in

project mode.

Abbey arrived at the same time as the Uber Eats guy, clearly prepared for lunch—no gum. She brought their lunch inside as though she'd made it lovingly herself and brought it from home. They settled down in the lounge chairs to some still-warm vegetarian focaccias. Abbey's eyes popped when she saw the wall of paper with the lines and bubbles heading in so many different directions. 'Holy crap! Love what you've done with the place, but surely, you've heard of real wallpaper.'

Celeste was happy for the company and a little light relief, and they caught up on less serious things while they ate. After that, eager to share her journey since they'd last met, Celeste shared all that had unfolded at Chantelle's and then Paul's place, walking in front of the wall of paper and pointing to some key points as she spoke.

Abbey followed her, absorbing everything. When it came to the information on Zac's life, she baulked a little at the name on the wall. 'Isaac Meredith?' She raised her eyebrows. 'Isn't that your middle name?'

Celeste's eyes widened. 'How could you possibly know that?'

Abbey looked a little sheepish. 'Well, your mum was missing you when you spent that time in Switzerland. I came round to cheer her up one time, and we opened a bottle of champagne. By the end of it, we'd decided they had more chance of finding the God particle than getting your middle name out of you. We were laughing for hours, but it helped us both deal with you being so far away. "Meredith" sort of popped out that day. I was sworn to secrecy.'

The circumstances took the sting out of Celeste's reaction to Abbey's confession, even more so when she continued. 'You know, of course, how the ripple of one life turns up in another, don't you?'

'Of course; I've already realised that being so interested in Einstein's work in this life probably started with Zac.'

'Yeah, great. But I'm not really talking about that.'

Celeste tilted her head. 'What, then?'

'Well, it's more than just a continued interest, isn't it, Einstein?' Celeste remembered Abbey's eye-rolling tone from her teens. 'You are so driven in this life to make up for Zac's being cut short. Also, the name "Meredith" reminds you of that life. That's why you hate it so much.'

Celeste felt her breath catch. Abbey had nailed her to that piece on the wall of paper. She flopped down on the sofa and looked at her friend. 'Wow ... I'm still new at this. Guess I missed that one, but it hits home.'

Abbey smiled. 'I've been dabbling in this stuff for years, Lest. You have an awesome mind, but with this stuff, that won't always get you there. Give the head a break and let go a little. Mind maps are great, but sometimes the mind isn't enough. Sometimes, you're better to stop thinking, so you can go beyond it.'

And there it was again: valuable information from unlikely sources. Abbey had things to offer that Celeste couldn't see for herself. All for the cost of a toasted focaccia. All she had to do was transcend her mind. It was that simple, though perhaps not for a scientist.

'So where do I go from here?' Celeste asked.

Abbey shrugged. 'No idea, but just keep going forward, I guess.'

Abbey left a while later and, looking for inspiration, Celeste wandered down the bush track and surrendered to nature once more. She closed her eyes and merged with the familiar trees, listened to the wind through the branches and did her best to empty her mind. A wild idea came in from nowhere, and she wondered if this was her version of Einstein's rocking chair.

Over the following forty-eight hours, the idea formed and gained momentum. It became an obsession, holding its place in her line of sight.

It was time to call Paul again.

CHAPTER 13

'You want me to what?' Paul sounded incredulous at the other end of the phone.

'Take me out of my body and toss me into the collective unconscious,' Celeste repeated in a matter-of-fact tone. She felt this was the best way to follow Abbey's suggestion to go beyond her mind, even though she probably sounded more like a mad scientist than a quantum physicist.

'Okay, I need to understand where you've gone since our last conversation,' Paul said.

'Okay, here's my theory. I understand the whole Akashic library analogy. I've looked into my book and glimpsed another chapter. I want to know what's beyond the library. I've been researching near-death experiences, and they don't go to other lifetimes, they have other experiences. They leave their body and come back. I'd like you to do something a bit different and take me on an out-of-body experience while I'm still in my body.'

'Hmmm.' Paul sounded thoughtful. 'You realise they're called an out-of-body experience for a reason, don't you? It means you go out of your body.'

'Well, you tell me how it could be done.'

Paul paused. 'I was dabbling in something a bit like what you're describing—some years ago.'

'I'm listening.'

'To truly explore consciousness in an unlimited way, we have to transcend the human intellect and physical body. We have a human personality and an immortal persona. If we can get beyond the intellect and that human personality, they're no longer in the way. We have access to another level of being; some call it the higher self, some the superconscious. We need the human vehicle for the communication, of course, though that ends up a subset of the overall being delegated the task of expressing what we find out there.'

'I think I follow,' Celeste said, 'but can you give me a summary? I need to know that I'll get past my mind.'

Paul obliged. 'Yes … technically you will, though it's more a matter of transcending the mind. Your awareness entangles with the limitlessness of human possibility. The human body is your access point to a state of quantum consciousness.'

The statement hit her in the heart. This was what she'd been seeking. It was like a door opened and a crack of light came through that was simply blinding.

'When can we do this?' she asked.

Paul sighed. 'Give me a couple of days to look at my old work and get ready.' He sounded resigned to the fact that this would happen, as if the horse was bolting and he was hanging on to the reins for dear life. 'Go easy on this old guy … remember, I'm supposed to be retired, though I can now officially claim that my boredom has been cured.'

CHAPTER 14

Celeste arrived at Paul's place, ready for whatever the day may bring.

He greeted her warmly. 'Come on in, Celeste; no coffee this morning, perhaps afterwards.' She entered the Akashic lounge room and stepped around a few piles of books as Paul remarked, 'Why don't you sit in that same chair as last time? It seemed to work well then.'

She sat once again in the comfortable chair.

'I've been reviewing some of my older work to get some ideas,' he continued. 'I feel a path for you could well be moving into a place where you "remember" what it's like to be beyond your body. When people have a transcendent event like a near-death or out-of-body experience, they feel a sense of limitlessness. Usually, it's characterised by leaving the body behind, though I'd like to bring that remembering to you while you're still in your body. If you like, your limitlessness can *include* your body, and I'll steer you towards an expanded awareness rather than take you out of your body or across time and space to other lives. Do you understand where I'm coming from?'

Science girl framed it differently. 'So you're saying that I'm part of the quantum field of all things, anyway, and by experiencing it, I'll remember more.'

'I guess that will do,' Paul said. 'Though it's important to know and believe in your limitlessness and just completely let go of the thinking part. As you mentioned on the phone, in some ways, you move beyond your mind. It begs the question: Who is Celeste? Are you a flesh-and-blood person moving through life, or are you an expanded consciousness pretending to be human so you can have experiences that serve you and others?'

Celeste smiled. 'I had a wonderful teacher at school who used to quote Descartes, "I think, therefore I am." Now I want to add another part to that: and I feel, so I'm even more. Chantelle felt my father in the room that day, and I tapped into the feelings of Zac from this life. A dear friend of mine told me that thinking will only get you so far. So, Paul, the question, "Who is Celeste?" is unanswerable at this time since I no longer really know.'

Paul smiled back. 'Well, I guess we should continue the quest, then. Do you have an intention for us today? To help us blaze a trail into the unknown?'

'I do. I seek an experience that helps me make sense of my reason for being. I know that will help me bring my work further into the world.' This was what she'd come up with after a few days of reflection.

'I really like the sound of that, Celeste,' Paul said. 'Are you ready to start?'

She nodded and leaned back in the chair, the same as last time. Paul's voice slowed and held her in a space that was hard to describe; she felt both floaty and light, as well as super focussed, though guided in a direction different from last time. Rather than take her back through the experiences of earlier years and down into a trance state, he seemed to expand her outwards.

Celeste felt her awareness move beyond her body and fill the room. In that moment, she knew everything in the hundreds of books that filled all the bookshelves. They seemed like her old friends.

Paul expanded her further and moved beyond the cottage. She noticed the tiles on the roof, a small portion newer than the rest. She saw Paul's neatly kept garden and then moved out further, tuning into the bush around the village of Medlow Bath. She saw the local landmark, the Hydro Majestic Hotel, and beyond that, a sweeping view of the Megalong Valley. Expanding further, she felt the magnificence of the Blue Mountains, stretching north and south, extending into the Great Diving Range. She could feel the wildlife and every plant and tree as the great tapestry of Mother Nature, and she was an intricate part of it. She saw farms, coastal cities, bushlands, deserts and then expanding even further, the ocean and the countries on the other sides of great expanses of water. She started to see the curvature of the Earth, and then, at Paul's direction, her awareness turned away from the Earth. She looked out on the universe in all its wonder, and she was in awe. There was a sense of being part of the incredible silence beyond the busyness of humanity … as she floated and drifted beyond time, beyond space and beyond the physical dimension.

Paul's words took her further on the journey: 'As the layers of the human self fall further away … your natural state of being is free … as you continue to expand …

'You are pure consciousness, gently embracing your divine state of being, beyond all human knowing and imagination …

'And you are always this …

'In this moment, as this is remembered … the gentle surrender to your magnificence is felt easily and naturally ….

'Everything else falls gently away ...

'You are a vibrational being in a universal symphony of light ... flowing freely through all dimensions and realities ...

'The knowing of this sets you free ...'

And it did set her free, in a way she'd never experienced before. He held her there with his voice while her senses adjusted to a new level of being, absorbing the experience that was unfolding in a way that could never be described. She truly felt part of everything.

After what was probably a short space of time, but felt like forever, Paul started to move her further on the journey.

'We seek now the experience that helps Celeste understand her reason for being ...

'You are drawn further into that experience ... and it is unfolding around you in all its magnificence.

'Take your time, and when you're ready ... share with me what you're experiencing.'

Celeste remained silent for a few moments, then said, 'There's a light coming towards me. It's golden white and very bright.'

'Tell me more,' Paul said.

'It feels welcoming and familiar, and it's paused right in front of me.'

'Offer greetings and thank it for coming.'

Celeste did so. 'I'm now receiving a wave of love ... it's just beautiful.' A tear ran down her cheek.

Paul paused for a short while, allowing Celeste to experience this wave. 'Ask the being to take shape and form, so they may communicate with you,' Paul directed.

'Okay. A being has stepped forward, looking a little more human. He takes the shape of a male about sixty years old. He has long hair and a beard and says he's been waiting to connect with me for a long time. He says that he and others like him want to work with me and that we can help a lot of people.'

Paul had already turned on a small recorder and was taking notes as well. 'Does he have a name he'd like to be called?'

'He says … he has a name that's a sound that can't really be translated into our language. It's like he's sort of telepathing me. I hear his thoughts. He's saying to call him Bob. *Bob?* Really? Are you serious?' Celeste was taken aback. This was like no other Bob she'd ever met.

'Ask Bob how he wants to work with you,' Paul suggested.

'He's saying that connection will come during meditation. I should set up a place at home where regular communication is possible. He's saying that I'll have the information I need, and he'll help. In return, he asks that I share what I learn with others, and between us we'll make a difference to humanity.'

'Ask Bob why he wants to work with you specifically.'

'He says I have a basic understanding of the universe through my work as a quantum physicist, and he wants to use that as a start point. He says he'll teach me more from there. He's speaking about you, too, Paul; he says there'll be times when you're helpful also.'

'Tell Bob I'll help wherever I can. Why are you being asked to help now, though?' Paul's intuition told him there was something significant about the timing of this meeting.

'Bob says that I've shown myself to be ready. He's using some of the language from the first conversation you and I had. He says I'm now willing to stretch the box to absorb my new experiences. That means I'm ready for the next one. Ahhh … he's showing me something I did. He's referring to the time when I built the wall of paper at the house. He said that by removing all my academic qualifications and mementos from the wall, I showed that I was ready to move beyond those mindsets and open into new territory. That was the time that Bob and the others knew I was ready. Apparently, it was quite symbolic.

'He's saying that they need someone with certain personal qualities to work with. A mind that thinks at another level and is open to the possibilities, someone who won't give up. Looks like Bob might have a sense of humour; he's saying that determination is great, but sometimes stubbornness is even better when pointed in the right direction.'

This was a moment of significance, and Paul knew it. He'd seen weird and wonderful experiences over the years, and he could sense the importance of this particular moment. He expanded her even further to access her greater being, referring to Celeste in the third person, before finding the answer to his next question. 'Let's pause for a moment and simply absorb all that has been offered in this conversation with Bob. Now feel into Celeste's intention for today, to *make sense of her reason for being.* Does that intention resonate with Bob's offer to work together?'

Celeste paused and felt into it. 'What's coming to me now is that I feel that working with Bob is actually a big part of my reason for being Celeste.'

Paul wanted to be sure. 'So you are happy to proceed?'

'Yes, I am.'

'So be it,' Paul said. 'Ask Bob what he'd like you to do next.'

'He again says I should set up the communication space at home. It needs to be done vibrationally and energetically. I'm not sure I know how to do that.'

'Ask him how.'

'He's saying nothing; he's just eating or something.' Celeste smiled. 'Very funny, Bob. He's pretending to chew gum, so I'll ask Abbey.'

'Is there anything else he wants you to know for now?'

'He says, "That's it; see you soon." Now he's gone.'

Paul very gently brought Celeste back into her body. There

were a few minutes of silence, somewhere between the wow factor and the what-the-hell-just-happened energy, then Celeste sighed. 'I'm struggling with this, Paul. I really need your take on what just happened.'

He smiled with genuine warmth. 'Celeste, my view of the universe has been formed from my experiences, not by my academic background, the dominant societal view or my research of quantum mechanics as a point of interest. It helps at times like these.' He took a breath and continued, making sure she was ready. 'We simply must accept that we know nothing about the universe. We're told there are around a hundred billion stars in the Milky Way, and we only know one of them reasonably well. Our sun is the source of life for this planet. That's only in 3D. We also know there are other dimensions. Your father's spirit had to come to you from somewhere.'

He moved closer to home for Celeste. 'Even in your own field, we talk about eleven dimensions in M-theory. Time is simply one dimension. You slip out of that one dimension and we can time travel to other moments in life and even other lifetimes. If we pull a snapshot of a limitless universe together by adding in the other dimensions, it's mind blowing. The cosmic joke is on us as we go looking for the 'theory of everything'. We believe that even if we found it, we would be able to understand it with this human intellect that's like a grain of sand on a beach that never ends.' He paused then, realising he was almost on a rant. 'That's my take.'

'So who do you think Bob is?' Celeste asked, hoping for an answer that made sense as the certainty of her old life and scientific conditioning disintegrated even further.

'Most models of consciousness have an evolutionary path. As we move higher in consciousness and wisdom, we want to give something back. For example, people who move into retirement sometimes do charitable work or volunteer to help others. It would make sense that if you had a galactic model, then benevolent races would want to help others who are further back on the same path.'

He continued, 'Bob initially appeared as light, which may mean he's not physical as we understand it, though he was able to change shape and form into a person to aid with communication and give you a focal point. Seems he has mastered the art of form, which probably means that his state of being is more fluid than ours. I suspect he's from elsewhere and has something to do here.'

'Well, he seems to have a rather impressive set of skills, so why doesn't he just get on with it? Why on earth would he need me?'

'I've been told in client sessions over the years that advanced civilisations can't interfere with those races who are still maturing. There's some form of "non-interference" law of the universe. It's as though they can support people who are ready to listen, but if they were to turn up in numbers with spaceships or pop out of a portal, there would be bedlam. The vast majority of people in this world have no idea about all of this and aren't ready for the conversation.'

Celeste absorbed every word. 'How do you know all this?'

'When I started investigating past lives, a few people went to non-human lives. At first, I thought they may have read too much science fiction, though more of them continued to come. The information was consistent, and in the end, I came to understand that most of what we've been told about this world and our place in the universe was rather incomplete.'

'So am I imagining all this? Have I read too many astrophysics papers or seen too many movies?'

'Go and try out what Bob suggested,' Paul replied. 'He has

tested you today, and it looks like you passed. Now test him and get some validation, make sure you're comfortable with this each step of the way. Like I said, once you accept these experiences, the journey speeds up.'

Celeste remembered something from her session. 'Paul, are there some new tiles on the roof at the back of your house?'

'Yes, a tree came down last year.'

'I noticed as I went past …'

Paul nodded, unsurprised.

They chatted a while longer, then Celeste left. Instead of heading down the mountain, she went the other way to clear her head. She drove up through Blackheath and on to Mount Victoria, watching civilization dwindle even further while drawing the fresh air into her lungs. It had been so long since she'd crossed the mountains to the other side.

Her stomach began to make noises, so she stopped at a roadside café and wandered inside. Celeste ordered a large coffee and a sandwich to take away.

The young woman behind the counter gave her a smile and said, 'Here's your lunch. Have a nice day. Thanks for coming to Bob's.'

Celeste started, then wandered outside and looked up at the sign she hadn't noticed before: *Bob's Café.* 'So this guy is following me around now?'

She finished her sandwich at an outside table, downed her coffee and got behind the wheel. Jeeps took her in the direction of home.

She called Abbey.

'Hey, Lest, what's happening?'

'I've been surfing the universe, had a chat with a guy called Bob who probably comes from another dimension and he wants to work with me to help humanity.'

There was silence at the end of the phone, apart from the sound of Abbey chewing gum, then, 'Umm … okay then …'

'Can you help me create a space where I can set up some form of ongoing metaphysical contact through meditation?'

'Umm, sure. Are you saying you want to clear a part of the house of old energy and tune into something from elsewhere?'

'I guess so; it's more your area of expertise than mine.'

'Okay, what if I come past in a couple of hours? I need to get some things.'

'Thanks so much, Abs, I'll see you then.'

'Hey, Lest?'

'Yes?'

'You are the weirdest scientist I know, even though I don't really know any others. That's coming from someone who is already weird. I just never thought you'd get into this stuff.'

'Me neither. See you later.' Celeste settled for the drive back down the hill. She was miles away in her thoughts, but Jeeps knew the way home.

CHAPTER 15

Abbey arrived with a bag, took out a dried bouquet of herbs, a pile of rough rocks and a small metal bowl with a stick.

Celeste smiled. 'So I guess this is a Reiki tool bag?'

'It's more "space clearing for all occasions". This is a house call, by the way. It's gonna cost you a lunch.'

'What is all this?'

Abbey picked up the bunch of herbs. 'This is a smudge stick. We light it and move through the area that we need to clear. The smoke cleanses the space and purifies the energy.' She picked up the rocks. 'These are pure quartz, unpolished. They go in each of the corners of the space you're claiming as your own meditation sanctuary. They hold a high vibration and offer supportive energies. Crystals are alive too, you know. These will be your new friends.'

Celeste wasn't sure about that, but after recent events, she was open to almost anything.

Abbey picked up the bowl. 'This is a Tibetan singing bowl. When I strike it with this carved stick, it sends high vibrational sound waves into the surrounding area. You can use this before you start to meditate.' She demonstrated, and Celeste felt as well as heard the pure tone of the bowl. 'All we have to do is choose the space and set you up.'

'Okay, what's the best kind of place?'

'Well … peaceful, quiet and out of the way. Maybe even away from the house, since you do some of your work here. What about your mum's old studio?'

'It still has furniture and her old art materials in there. It's a bit of a mess, I'm afraid.' Celeste felt a little guilty that she hadn't cleaned out that space yet.

'How about the shed?' asked Abbey.

Her father's message from the day at Chantelle's came back to her; *the home is great, but the shed is amazing.*

She shrugged. 'Let's take a look.'

Abbey followed her out onto the veranda and into the garden. A bougainvillea vine, which gave an incredible display of crimson flowers every summer, half covered the shed. Summer headed into autumn now, but a few of the last blooms remained.

Celeste hadn't entered the shed for some time, and the dust had settled on a few old pieces of furniture. This had been her father's domain, and even though it was roughly the size of a bedroom, he'd managed to store a lot of his building materials in there. There were pieces of wood, roof tiles for the house and quite a few tools scattered around an old workbench.

Abbey turned to Celeste. 'Lest, are you okay if we move this stuff out?'

'Sure,' she replied. 'Glad for the help.' There was something that didn't need to be said, given their long friendship, though they both felt it.

Over the next hour, they moved the building materials, tools and bench out to the carport. Between lifting, carrying, huffing and puffing, Celeste told Abbey about the experience of meeting Bob. Abbey took it all in her stride.

They returned to the shed with cleaning materials and attacked the inside thoroughly, knocking down old cobwebs and polishing the one window that looked out on the garden. In the end, just the four wooden walls and floor, rafters and open, airy roof space, and the small pot-belly stove in the corner remained. Her father had needed the warmth in winter for his shed time. The sole decoration was an old Persian rug used as a wall hanging on one wall, an old favourite of her father's. Though faded now, it still had presence with its swirls of blue, green and red. Celeste left it there to keep her company, and that felt right.

Abbey took charge. She lit the smudge stick and walked around the small room before handing it to Celeste and asking her to do the same. Then she directed Celeste outside to do a full circuit of the shed. It seemed bigger out there because she had to negotiate the bougainvillea, growing almost out of control. Abbey then showed Celeste how to place the large crystals in the corners of the shed's interior, even using a small stepladder to reach up and place another four in the top corners where the beams joined. The scientist undertook all instructions in a bemused way, whilst the little girl within enjoyed playing 'cubby house' for the first time in thirty years.

'Okay, one last thing,' Abbey said. 'Pick up that bowl and bring some sound into the space, but before you do, state some sort of intention. What do you want to say?'

Celeste was outside her comfort zone but gave it her best shot. 'May this shed become a place to access the quantum field?'

Abbey met that with the dual display of a laugh and an eye roll. 'Funny way to set up a meditation space, but that'll do. Say it again like you mean it. Intention is everything.'

Celeste had heard that before from someone else. She spoke

it with purpose, closed her eyes and brought in the sound. It echoed from the wooden walls and bounced around the inside of the shed.

They went back to the house and found some floor mats, scarves, lamps and small tables and took them out to the shed. A couple of old armchairs came from her mother's art studio. They decorated the room together, Abbey's feel for the esoteric bringing the old shed to life. The finishing touch was a few old abstract paintings from a local artist that added another layer of vibrancy and colour.

Finally, they stood in the shed and admired their efforts.

It felt like something really important had been done, and Celeste acknowledged her friend. 'Bob was right; you do know what you're doing.'

Abbey smiled. It was four in the afternoon, and they'd forgotten to eat. 'What's for lunch?' she asked.

CHAPTER 16

Dawn broke clear and crisp in the mountains. Celeste rose early, dressed warmly and headed for the shed across a lawn still wet with dew. Streaks of orange still faded on the horizon, echoing the dawning of another day.

Abbey had written down a few suggestions for meditation, and Celeste held them in her hand. She'd prepared the pot belly stove the day before, and all she had to do was strike a match, drop it inside and close the door on the front. The kindling did the rest, and she heard crackling as a few pieces of wood caught alight. Even hearing the noise helped her feel warmer.

Abbey's instructions were completely unscientific and a little all over the place, though still helpful. They included that Celeste play the bowl for a few minutes before starting and suggested that she sit in a chair, rather than in a cross-legged lotus position. Having not sat on the floor since primary school, Celeste felt comfortable with that. Abbey had also recommended some deep-breathing exercises to get her relaxed and that she imagines the person she wanted to converse with appearing in the other chair in front of her.

Celeste played the bowl, then made herself comfortable in the armchair with several cushions and started the breathing. For the first few minutes, she felt silly. For the next five minutes, she felt more relaxed and started to expand a little. Her mind was still active. She wasn't analysing but drifting to events of the previous day when they'd set up the shed. Then they jumped to meeting Chantelle ... the message from her father ... meeting Paul ... the journey to Zac's life ... and then, finally, to the white-gold light that had arrived in her awareness during her second journey. It felt as though she surrendered to it once more and it engulfed her, lifting her into a place of wonder ... then she focused and felt a presence. Keeping her eyes closed, she focused on the other armchair in front of her and had a strong impression of Bob sitting there, smiling at her. He was dressed the same and portrayed himself as the older man once more.

It is nice to see you again. Bob's thoughts appeared in Celeste's mind.

The connection from the session at Paul's had re-established easily.

Hi, Bob. Thank you for coming, Celeste replied, remembering the formalities Paul had used.

Bob chuckled. *Have you accepted that we are communicating and that this is a real exchange?*

Yes, Bob, to about ninety per cent, but a scientific part of me still wants some physical proof.

Okay. Bob nodded. *It is that mindset that will serve us in many other ways. I'll arrange that for you, though you need to promise that when you see the evidence, you will embrace these experiences fully.*

I'll do my best with that. What'll you show me? she asked.

It will be a surprise, but you will see an unexpected natural phenomenon.

Okay. Celeste imagined a black cat crossing her path or even a talking owl.

Shall we commence?

Sure, Bob; I'm open. Celeste smiled.

You have a theory that other realities, other dimensions and other worlds exist? True?

Yes, but I can't prove it.

Where do you think I come from?

I guess somewhere else, but I'm not sure where, Celeste mused.

Let me explain a little of that in a way that may be helpful. Bob exuded eternal patience, and Celeste figured that would come in handy in the times ahead. *You understand already about the first four dimensions, three of space and one of time, that make up your 3D reality. What you don't understand is that when you move into a fifth dimension, the first four become fluid.*

Okay. Can you expand a little on that? In her mind's eye, she leaned forward, though her body remained still in the chair.

If you are in the sixth dimension, you have fluid creativity over the five previous ones. If you are in the ninth dimension, you have creativity over the eight previous ones and so on. Do you understand?

It seems to make sense, though an example would be helpful for my human brain.

Bob obliged. *A phenomenon you understand is known as Heisenberg's uncertainty principle. Sometimes, particles even seem to wink in and out of existence. Correct?*

Yes, I was talking about this just the other day.

Yes, we heard you.

Celeste wondered if she should be closing the bathroom door, even though she lived alone.

What is happening in that moment is indeed what you theorised. The particles are reaching a vibration where they pass a threshold and move into the next dimension. Then, when someone goes to look for them, they may reappear.

Yes, I've suspected that. I was thinking they changed form, and we can't see them until their vibration returned to what it was originally, then they come back.

That is close, though incomplete, Bob said. *There is a reason they come back; they actually choose to.*

Huh? Are you saying that these individual particles decide to return?

I am, Bob replied. *What happens is that they have moved into the fifth dimension, though when someone in the fourth wants to find them, they choose to return and be found. They are aligning with one of the cosmic laws.*

ONE of the cosmic laws? Celeste almost shouted—as much as you could in a meditative state of being. *How many are there?*

A number; we will get to them all eventually. The one I am referring to in this instance is that the particles return from 5D because people in 3D want to find them. The particles respond to that request, serving the beings in lower dimensions. He made something very complicated blissfully simple.

But if those particles have free will to do that, then they must be conscious.

Of course, everything has consciousness. The universe is a multidimensional, vibrational structure, and we journey through it by use of frequencies selected by our consciousness.

If ever there was the perfect T-shirt slogan, that was it. Perhaps this was the answer to all of it … the theory of everything in one sentence! Celeste had never believed the answer to everything was forty-two. Her mind activated at the thought, and the quantum physicist began to emerge, so she took a moment to return to her breathing.

I have a question, Bob.

He nodded his encouragement.

In 2012, they discovered the Higgs-Bosun, the so called 'God particle'. It looked pretty much like it was expected to look. Was that an example of this cosmic law?

Of course.

Celeste nearly fell out of her meditation chair at his answer, but she composed herself and continued, *They then discovered that it didn't solve the issues of the standard model for quantum physics, as some had speculated. Why was that?*

There were two reasons, Bob said. *The first one is easy; they forgot to ask for it. There was confusing speculation. Some believed it would solve the standard model, some didn't. In the end, the particles were responding to the strongest intention sent from the lower dimension—simply 'to be discovered'—and so it happened.*

Though her physical body remained upright in the chair, energetically, Celeste became a puddle on the floor. *What's the second reason?* She was almost too afraid to ask.

Bob smiled. *The standard model is incomplete, Celeste. It will take more than the discovery of a new particle to find out how the universe truly works. It is the scientific mindset itself that is holding things back. To understand scientific endeavour, we must move beyond science. Do you remember that quote from Einstein?*

Einstein again, always popping up. Of course, she knew the quote by heart. *'You can't solve a problem with the same type of thinking that created it.'*

Can you see how that comment embraces cosmic law? Bob asked.

I can. When you're close to a problem, you can't see the solution. When you take a different view from a higher perspective, you can often find the answer.

This is how the dimensions work. We serve others in the lower dimensions so they may one day join us and then help others too. I wish for you to know also that the dimensions are not a hierarchy, as many on Earth believe. They are more a path of progression that we all take. The universe needs all of them to be complete. We have deep empathy for all beings, as we have existed in their dimension also as part of our own journey.

Celeste's mind drifted back to Jeeps and her father's comments. Seven slots in the grill, one for each continent, and it wouldn't be a complete grill without all of them. *Which dimension are you from, Bob?*

He just smiled. *That may be revealed in time.* After a pause, he continued, *This has been a wonderful second conversation, though that is enough for now. Perhaps we could meet at the same time tomorrow? I'd like to offer you a personal experience of what we have discussed today.*

Sure, that sounds fine. He'd read her well. Some of her understandings of the quantum universe had been shaken to the core; other wormholes had opened and were beckoning. She needed some time. Bob faded away, returning to wherever he came from.

After she returned, Celeste sat in the chair for a while. She had no idea what to do next, so she decided to allow her mind to wander for the rest of the day. The shed was warmer now, but strangely, the stove had started to cool.

Her eyes widened when she looked at her watch. It was eleven o'clock, and she'd entered the shed at seven. Realising how hungry she was, she stepped outside into the bright autumn sun and headed for the house. As she crossed the lawn, she glanced back at the shed and stopped in surprise and disbelief.

The bougainvillea that covered half the shed was in full and explosive bloom, even though the day before, it'd been heading into hibernation for the chilly winter months in the mountains. An incredible wave of glowing crimson seemed to fill the yard.

'I guess that's what an "unexpected natural phenomenon" looks like,' Celeste said to herself as she headed to the kitchen to find food.

Bob had kept his promise.

CHAPTER 17

Reflections brought inevitable questions, of course. That was the way Celeste's mind worked. Pieces of the puzzle were still missing, and she always sought completion.

The next morning, she sat in the shed with the fire crackling, creating a cosy environment and warming her body against the morning chill. She had no idea what Bob had planned, so she simply let go, wondering what a 'personal experience' would be like.

She breathed into the space they'd created and gradually felt herself leaving her body—even easier this time. In her mind's eye, Bob appeared in the chair in front of her. Celeste opened one eye to a slit, peering back into the physical realm, and noted that the chair remained empty. She closed her eye again, formed the image of the chair in her imagination, and Bob was there. 'Just a little more weirdness,' she said to herself.

Good morning, Celeste, he greeted her. *You have questions …*

It was a statement. Of course, he knew.

There was a time distortion of four hours yesterday when we met. To me, it seemed like about thirty minutes. How do you explain that? she asked.

You and I exist in different dimensions. In order for us to communicate telepathically as we are now, your awareness has to leave 3D and move to a vibration beyond that. This allows us to connect. Your body and intellect are still in 3D, though your awareness is beyond in a vibrational state that I can match. It is as though we can step through a doorway to a place where we can meet each other. Meditation is a great way to shift your vibration into that state when you are alone. You won't always have someone like Paul close by to assist.

And the time distortion?

As I told you yesterday, when you move into the next dimension, you have fluid creativity for the ones below. I adjusted your time for two reasons. The first was to give you more of the physical evidence you have such a focus on. The expression on your face when you looked at your watch was significant. The second reason was that we must respect the laws of the dimension in which we are working. I needed time to honour nature and create the flowers on the vine outside, Bob added. *Know that time distortion is a characteristic of multidimensional work. You will have to get used to it. Next question ...*

Celeste nodded. *After we met the first time, I drove through the mountains and bought lunch at a roadside café called 'Bob's'. Was that your doing?*

Yes and no. I made some very small visual and auditory adjustments that were fast and easy to do, just to make a point.

How so? Celeste asked.

There actually is a café there; it is called Don's. I placed a hologram over the sign outside to change "Don's" to "Bob's". When the woman behind the counter thanked you, I changed one word in her sentence, otherwise you wouldn't have looked up at the sign outside.

So … you didn't have to work with nature that time. Celeste thought it ironic that the only time she'd received flowers in living memory was from someone in another dimension doing cosmic party tricks.

Small immediate things like that are possible as long as they meet a higher purpose, Bob said.

Which was what in this case?

Assisting to enrol you in service to humanity and help you find a deeper sense of purpose for your own life.

Something resonated for Celeste when he said that, echoing a long-forgotten memory or deeper meaning lurking in the background. Perhaps even both. *What happens if you do something that is outside this cosmic law?*

First, I never would, as it is my role to uphold cosmic law in all I do. Second, if I tried to do something without that high vibrational intention, it simply wouldn't resonate and align with the universe. As an example, the sign at Don's Café wouldn't change. Third, and there are some grey areas here, if something did sneak through, I'd be held accountable by my peers and need to make amends. This is not a conversation for us at this time; I just want you to understand that the cosmic tapestry is both simple and complicated, beautiful and challenging, and, as two of the threads in that tapestry, we each have a role to play.

Bob paused at the completion of that thought, so Celeste knew that particular subject was closed for now.

I understand, she said, feeling hopeful. *So my personal experience of what we discussed yesterday, what does that look like?*

Bob smiled. *Yesterday, we spoke about how the higher dimensions serve those below, as part of the cosmic order of the universe. When you move into an expanded state, your awareness moves outside 3D into a higher dimension. You still have access to the dimension where your body and intellect remain. You can bring to it the fluid creativity I mentioned earlier. This is where cases of spontaneous healing come from, and it is also the reason why people can heal through meditation. It is rarely studied or pursued, just written off in most cases as a medical anomaly. We wish to change all this.*

Hang on, Celeste said, *are you saying that when we expand ourselves beyond the body into another dimension, we can access the cosmic law to heal back in the lower dimension?*

Yes. That's correct.

So in a nutshell, you wish to change the medical model of society to a completely different approach? Celeste felt more alert now, in a gentle, meditative way.

That is a start, yes. We also want to rid the world of vibrational disorders which affect the emotional landscape. Changing the perspective of what you call mental health.

So you want to make our medical and psychological models inert and offer something as a replacement.

Bob smiled. *Correct.*

But all those are based on years of science, billions of patients and have saved countless lives over many decades of allopathic medicine.

Bob nodded. *That is not entirely true; though, yes, there have been some benefits.*

How would this work? You said you'd help me with my doctorate. I'm just hoping you realise I'm not that kind of doctor candidate.

Yes, that is what makes you the right person. You know science, but have shown it to be a stepping stone to other ideas and concepts. We simply want you to be you, Celeste.

I'm seriously missing some context here and starting to wonder what you're on about.

Bob's eternal patience presented itself again. *You remember Einstein's quote about mindsets. When your medical system sees a physical issue, they offer a physical solution. Often, they will operate on or medicate people in an attempt to heal them. Sometimes it works and sometimes it doesn't. The lack of success comes from the way people are viewed in the first place. The physical issue is a manifestation of a vibrational disorder; it is a message that something isn't right. It shows up in the body as a message that can be heard or seen. Rather than seeking to understand that message, they often diagnose the symptom as an illness. If we solve the symptom, then it comes out elsewhere. The vibrational disorder hasn't been understood and moves somewhere else to send the message again. Then that new message is medicated as well, and the cycle continues.*

Celeste tried to stop her mind racing so she could stay in contact with Bob. *Okay, can you summarise that for me, please?* She noticed that when she thought more, he faded a little.

All physical and emotional illness is merely a symptom of a vibrational disorder. This knowing is fundamental to all physical life in the universe and the basis of healing work on almost all planets, but not this one. The body is trying to communicate through its symptoms. You assume a symptom is the illness, though it is in fact the messenger, doing its best to help.

This has led to mindsets that have driven whole systems into your society, even an academic culture that propagates those mindsets. You revere your medical system and all of its participants, benefactors and researchers, though much of it is based on the original false assumption.

Celeste, please know that I am speaking plainly here, as I sense you appreciate this form of communication. Many in the medical field on your planet are in deep service to the people with whom they work. We know and appreciate this. Know, please, that it is the system that is flawed, not the people. We can build a system that is truly remarkable, far simpler, and we welcome all people to the learning of these new ways.

Celeste didn't know what to say. She didn't go anywhere near Bob's 'almost all planets, but not this one' comment. She just surrendered, the easiest path. *Okay, Bob, what now?*

An experience of this for yourself, Celeste. That has been our pattern up until now, and we see no reason to change.

What do I need to do? I can't think of anything wrong with me. She felt a gentle glow coming from Bob, like a cloud of loving resonance reaching out and enfolding her.

He telepathed to her softly, *You hold pain in your heart from the loss of your parents. It is time for this to heal.*

Her bottom lip quivered, and she felt that old sharp pain along her ribs. The moment of insight came as she finally admitted she'd parked her own grief from the sudden loss of her father to help her mother. Then, six months later, her mother had passed, leaving her empty and alone. By stating it, Bob had gently brought it further into her line of sight.

Do you wish to heal this? Bob asked.

More than anything, Celeste admitted.

The gentle glow from Bob became stronger, and Celeste felt herself being lifted further out of her body. She'd already expanded just enough to be in the place where they could converse, though this was another level again. Another level of knowing unfolded in her consciousness. She felt her awareness fill the shed and could feel the texture of the wooden walls and floorboards. Then she experienced the warmth of the wood stove and observed 'Celeste' sitting motionless in the armchair with a warm rug over her knees. Though she looked peaceful, she could also feel her burden. While she was still Celeste in her awareness, she was also so much more …

Bob's presence remained with her, as though they observed Celeste side by side. *Where does she hold her pain?* he asked.

It's around her heart; it can be seen like a shadow, said a voice that came from her, though emanated from beyond her.

Tell me more, Bob said.

She works with distraction, so the pain isn't so intense at times. Though there is a void that leaves her hollow and lonely.

Celeste wasn't sure where the words were coming from. They held wisdom that she'd never before experienced in relation to her earthly existence.

What lies beneath her pain? Bob asked.

There is love, enormous love. The connection to her father transcends time and space, and she will know more of this when the time is right. For her mother, it was about loving service, particularly in her final months. Celeste was offered a choice between career and family and chose to come home, knowing that her career would stall. It was a lesson planned long ago, and she learned it well.

What is the greater purpose of the pain she holds?

By experiencing this pain, she will understand it in others. She will know what they need, so they may transcend energies that are blocked. It has been another important step in her learning.

Is the lesson complete? Bob asked.

Yes. She can still hold the love beneath; that will always be there. Though the pain has served its purpose and can now be released.

Let me know when that has been done.

It is so.

From outside her body, Celeste watched the shadows around her heart dissolve. Only love remained, as if the lights went on in her heart and a warmth filled her consciousness. She also felt it throughout and beyond Celeste's body.

How will her life be forever changed? Bob asked.

She will step into her magnificence with nothing in the way. Others will follow her and do the same.

Is she ready to return? Bob asked.

Yes.

Bob brought Celeste's awareness back into her body to feel her new state of being, one of lightness and freedom. He paused before addressing her again as Celeste, rather than the awareness beyond her human form.

Ask your parents to join us now, Celeste.

Instantaneously, her parents appeared. Seen through her mind's eye, they stood in front of the rug that hung on the wall, smiling, clapping silently and appearing as vibrant and happy.

Tears rolled down Celeste's cheeks, and a huge sob left her chest, like the final exhale of her pain, which had been trapped for so long.

They are here; what would you like to share with them? Bob asked gently.

A thought conversation took place, one like no other she'd ever had. It raced back and forth between them at lightning speed.

They were well, missed her also and loved her very much. They'd been waiting for this day for a long time and were proud of all she'd done. They were always around, supporting her and watching out for her … and one day they'd be reunited in another dimension.

The last traces of Celeste's grief fell away. This would take some adjustment, as her life had been built around distraction and buried pain. Now it was time to move ahead, no longer restricted by her loss.

Before her parents left, her father turned and admired the old rug hanging on the wall. *These things are supposed to go on the floor, you know.*

Celeste smiled—so they do have dad jokes in the other dimensions. After a deep, powerful and life-changing conversation, this lightened her energy even further.

Then just her and Bob remained in the space they'd created together. *Bob, I feel I've had enough for today. I need some air …*

He smiled. *Of course. Let me know when you're ready to speak again.*

She needed to escape to the bush, so she headed out to the carport, where she sat in Jeeps for a few minutes before starting the engine. Something was different now. Jeeps, she realised as she drove out of the driveway, was no longer her father's car; it was hers. Celeste made a mental note to change the registration papers over to her own name. Jeeps seemed to purr in response, and she had a sense of her father sitting in the passenger seat, smiling at her.

Chapter 18

Celeste needed time to feel into her experience and observe the changes it had brought, so two days passed before Bob and Celeste met again.

The day after their journey together, she cleaned out her parents' old bedroom at the front of the house and moved in. The room had more space and access to the veranda, but most importantly, it signalled a change in her energy. Rather than still seeing that room as one to be enshrined, it had become a way to honour her parents and make it easier for her to feel close to them. That thought gave her a warm feeling inside.

The following day, she sat with Bob, not knowing where to begin. Thankfully, he led the conversation.

How are you different now? he asked.

Like I have a new lease on life! I feel a sense of freedom, and the sharp pain in my chest has gone. I can think of my parents without the pain now. I've shed a few more tears and had some emotions, but I feel I'm moving ahead in ways I couldn't even dream of before.

Bob smiled and waited so Celeste could embrace her

own words for a moment before continuing. *Let us debrief the experience as an observable event. I welcome your thoughts …*

Taking a breath, she moved into research mode and summarised her experience. *I felt my awareness change. I somehow became larger and saw 'Celeste' as just a part of me rather than the whole of me. When I was in that state, I could answer your questions very differently. I seemed to have access to more information than usual. I saw the pain as something I was carrying, not something I was. This broke the hold it had on me, and I could see I had a choice—to release it or keep it. Releasing it seemed the only real alternative.*

When you asked how life would be forever changed, I could feel a very different future within my reach. It was right there, and I could describe it as though I was already in it. My life's been very different the past two days, and I'm trying to understand the change in me. I'm enjoying the shift, but a part of me wants to know how it happened so easily.

Bob nodded. *It is important to understand the true landscape in which we exist, as it changes everything. First, we live in a multidimensional universe, so the intention you set sends a message out into that energetic landscape. You did this when I asked you if you wanted to heal and you said, 'More than anything.'*

Second, since you are a part of this universe, you must also be multidimensional, and through this experience, you begin to remember that indeed you are. Third, consciousness transcends time and space. When we embrace your consciousness in the quantum field, we have access to all possibilities. Fourth, we can make changes from the next dimension that serve in this one—if we work within cosmic law. Hence my question, 'What is the greater purpose of the pain she holds?'

Bob paused, waiting as the human part of her tried to comprehend the metaphysical, but the quantum physicist needed a different context. He offered something to help. *Let me say that differently … I hold the 'knowing' that you are a multidimensional being. When we join our energy fields, that knowing transfers to you. We are quantumly entangled, and what affects me, affects you. So you move into this knowing with me, and your awareness moves into another dimension too.*

From there, we observe you back in human form. In quantum terms, this 'superconscious observer effect' can intrude on the experiment—your healing session. Your free will drives the impact of that positive intrusion. You then select a 'vibrational state of being' consistent with the healed self and that echoes your original intention. This changes your vibration back in the physical realm at the point when I ask, 'How will life be forever changed?' And so you've created a new reality for you to step back into. Your awareness returns to 3D, but you hold a different vibration.

He paused and watched the integration of the two aspects of her aligning. *One more thing, Celeste. This is all done in the energy of love and in a way that serves a greater purpose than us both. When both of those intentions are present, the experience can look and feel like a miracle. Do you now understand the limitations of the current medical systems on Earth?*

I'm starting to. We're trying to fix things we see as broken. That approach will usually just attempt to repair the physical symptoms and not necessarily identify the cause. But if we see those symptoms as a message delivered by the physical body and find the greater purpose behind that message, we can free the issue with a deeper understanding of why the message was created in the first place.

Yes, a wonderful summary … and if you were to say it in a way that all can understand? Bob asked.

We move beyond the body to heal the body. There's another part of you that holds the answers? Celeste asked.

That will do for now. Bob smiled, even more than usual.

The debrief was over. Relieved, she asked, *Okay, what's next?*

It is time for you to pass on what you have learned and offer a journey to someone.

What? You think I'm ready for that? Shouldn't there be an online course or something?

The nature of learning in the universe is through experience, Celeste. It has been that way since creation. You have earthly systems that embrace content and information, even doctrine … and people consider this as advanced learning. Often, it is simply opinion on paper, designed to hold you in previous mindsets. You know already from recent times that you learn about the universe by experiencing it.

Celeste frowned. *But there've been great teachers all through time, and they've offered so much.*

Surprisingly, he met her challenge with unexpected agreement. *Indeed. There have been wise beings throughout your history, and we suggest you learn from these teachers, not from the textbooks written about them. Study them and all they offered; let them open doorways for you, sparking your inspiration and excitement for further experiences in the multidimensional universe. These are the signposts on a journey of discovery that lead to the accumulation of wisdom and new hope for humanity.*

It felt as though she was flooded with light. The words touched her heart, mind and soul. In a moment of blinding insight, she recognised she'd always been drawn to great intellects and visionaries, like Einstein, Witten, Everett, Heisenberg and, more recently, Jung and Stevenson. Celeste had always seen the other aspects of academia, such as exams, assignments, protocols and administration, as part of an inseparable package. Now she saw these as a dumbing down of unique contributions into some form of mediocrity. Her passion for the PhD seemed to lose its lustre in light of something far more limitless.

She sighed. *All right, I'm ready. Who should I work with?*

Someone will present. We will meet again afterwards. Then Bob was gone.

Celeste went back inside and looked at the wall of paper. Amazingly, it had grown, overflowing over the doorway to the front hall. The other side of the door contained more of the metaphysical. Perhaps that was a metaphor that a doorway had opened and she'd stepped into a new way of looking at things. Another validation perhaps, or at least a little more cosmic humour.

She turned her phone on and a text message from Abbey came through:

Watcha up to?

Celeste smiled. Bob was right. The client had presented.

CHAPTER 19

Abbey and Celeste sat in the shed. They could feel the energy building.

'What are we doing again?' Abbey asked.

'I want to drift your awareness outside your body and offer you a journey of discovery.'

Abbey grinned. 'You sound a bit like a brochure. But hey, I'm up for anything. I like the new you; she's cooler than the old one.'

Celeste frowned. At least someone was happy about it, even if she was still struggling with the changes herself. 'Is there something in particular you'd like to work with?'

'Can you find me a boyfriend in that quantum field, Lest? I haven't had much happen since Ben and I got divorced. It's been like five years, and I'm over it.'

Celeste paused, trying to relate her own experience with Bob to what Abbey was seeking. 'Do you feel held back or something like that?'

Abbey shrugged. 'I've gone on a few dating sites and looked

around but then just can't be bothered, so maybe?'

Celeste, well outside her comfort zone, fumbled around for the right words. 'If you could ask the universe for something, how would you say it?'

Abbey gave a good response regardless. 'Well … maybe … to be free to be me.'

In that moment, Celeste learned much about setting intentions for journeys. Simple was powerful and opened the door to amazing possibilities.

Celeste did a fair job of recalling some of Paul's words from her last session with him and tried her best to see Abbey as, in Bob's words, a universal multidimensional being.

Eventually, the energy of the room changed, and so did the expression on Abbey's face. It seemed as if she'd moved beyond her body.

Celeste remembered what Bob had asked her, and she used his example to frame her questions. 'Tell me about Abbey … about her being free to be herself.'

After a pause of several seconds, a voice came from Abbey that sounded very different, much deeper in resonance and pitch. 'She keeps her heart safe. It is shielded from further pain.'

Unsure of what to do next, Celeste simply asked, 'Tell me more.'

'Her heart was broken, and she promised herself that wouldn't happen again. She has placed it out of reach to those who would know it.'

That so doesn't sound like Abbey.

'What does she need to do to be free?' Celeste asked, following her intuition. Though she didn't really know what she was doing, she seemed to be getting the hang of it quite quickly.

'She can bring love back into her life, though the heart needs to heal. An open heart brings freedom to all aspects of life, then she can truly be who she came here to be,' came the reply from Abbey.

'How can she do this?'

'Now that she knows the truth, the heart can mend. It is time to let go of the pain as it resulted from the behaviour of someone else and was never really hers to carry.'

Celeste had been the first one Abbey told about Ben's affair with someone at his work. His behaviour had been a pattern even before they were married. She'd chosen to end it between them and move on. Now Celeste watched Abbey transform in the chair. Her spine straightened, as if a weight had been lifted from her, and her energy lightened further.

Celeste frowned, unsure where to go next, then she remembered what Bob had asked her. 'How will her life be forever changed now?'

'Her healing work will expand and be more authentic now that her heart is fully present. Other insights will emerge as the energy is now free to flow. Her intuition will grow stronger, and she will be free to give her heart again when she is ready.'

If she hadn't had her own experience, Celeste might have thought that Abbey was having her on. She'd known her almost thirty years and had never seen Abbey like this. Something incredible was unfolding before her eyes.

'Is there anything else she needs to know?' Celeste asked.

'We have offered other insights to her, and we are grateful for your help today. Abbey is the first of many that you will help. We are complete now.'

The first of many? She was a physicist, not a therapist. The comment troubled her a little, though she parked it for now.

Abbey returned to normality, opened her eyes and looked at Celeste. Her eyes were bright and shiny. 'Oh my God ... what just happened?'

Celeste smiled and, once again, sought information from an unlikely source. 'You tell me. You've been into the energy scene for years, Abs. I'd love your take on what you experienced.'

'Well, it appears I was still holding something from my time with Ben. It was so clear to me that what was left had absolutely nothing to do with me. He was the one who did the wrong thing, but I was still carrying it. When I realised that, it dissolved before my eyes. It was amazing!'

Apparently still in touch with a wiser energy, Abbey offered further insight. 'I wondered at first if you were going to hypnotise me. I've had that done a few times with a friend from my Reiki class. When she did that for me, I felt like I was going down, and I felt heavy in my body. It was like I had access to a deeper part of me ... Abbey.

'This was very different, though. I felt like I was lifted up and away, and I was looking back at Abbey. I was still her, though she was a minor part of a bigger me. It was more a feeling of lightness. It seems more like the out-of-body stuff I've read about.'

Celeste nodded. Again, Abbey was teaching her, both validating some of her own thoughts and giving another perspective, which was so very helpful.

'Anyway, this was really cool, and I'm going to head home and write some stuff about it. What happens next now that you've experimented on me?' Abbey asked.

'I report back to Bob.'

'Yeah, that guy you told me about.' Abbey looked from side to side. 'Is he here now?'

Celeste laughed. 'No, we usually meet in the early mornings.'

Abbey headed off, and Celeste spent a few minutes sitting in the shed making notes. She wanted to talk to Bob regarding her concerns about becoming a therapist. That path didn't feel right.

While heading back across the lawn to the house, she heard

the landline ringing in the kitchen. She ran inside and picked up the phone.

Abbey answered, speaking at a hundred miles an hour. 'Hey, your mobile is still off, but I have to tell you about a thought that popped in on the way home; it's really cool.'

'Sure, go for it.'

'I went to have a piece of gum in the car and realised I just didn't want to. It was weird. So it came to me that when I was about fourteen and my first boyfriend broke up with me, he said, "No one wants to kiss a girl who chews gum." Since the divorce, I've been chewing gum nonstop. I think it might've been to protect my heart by keeping men away. Hey, Lest, I don't have to chew gum anymore!'

Celeste hung up the phone and shook her head. She looked out the window and across the lawn to the shed, then called out at the top of her voice, 'Thank you, Bob!'

CHAPTER 20

Celeste and Bob 'sat' in their respective chairs in the shed, warmed by the fire. At least in Celeste's mind's eye, Bob appeared to be sitting. After many days of practice, their respective consciousnesses connected easily.

They'd completed the debrief of Abbey's session, and Celeste had various mental notes to explore once her awareness returned fully to the physical realm. Bob was stretching her understanding of the universe, and her learning consolidated further with each interaction.

Intuitive as always, Bob asked, *What's on your mind, Celeste?*

She paused and felt into her own energy so she could telepath her feelings accurately. *I'm not sure I want to be a therapist type of person, Bob, just doing one-on-one work. I had a small taste of psychology in my undergrad days before I went fully into the physics pathways, and it wasn't really working for me. Too many statistics and behavioural models that people had to fit into. I found it quite uninspiring, to be honest.*

Bob nodded. *I'm delighted to hear you say that.*

Perplexed, Celeste said, *Tell me more …*

They both smiled.

There are already too many therapists in the world, Celeste. They are well-meaning problem solvers, but most are using models that disempower the people and further hide their magnificence from them. The therapeutic model does help some people, though it places limits on them and gives them the impression that they are broken and need help from another who knows more than them. This is the prevailing culture that we wish to change because this is simply untrue. If I may speak plainly, the problem with your mental health system is its own mental health.

Celeste frowned. *How do you mean?*

The current approach informs people they may have limiting beliefs and hold themselves back from their past experiences. This way of thinking hides their magnificence from them. They believe in their own limitations, as that is all they know. They are unaware of the limitless nature of who they truly are.

Drawing on my own experience, I guess that's true… I'm no expert, but it sounds about right. She nodded.

The people believe in the system in place and remain trapped in those mindsets, unable to escape. The field of cognitive behavioural therapy has its own limiting beliefs about the person before them— they see them as damaged. The old models had flawed perceptions from their inception. Most often, they are not open to alternative approaches, which is why some energy modalities have been neglected or dismissed over time. The system embraces a culture where anything offered outside their model must be challenged.

So you're saying that the system is limited and so it limits the people who enter it?

Yes. Those mindsets permeate the system at all levels, through the educators, practitioners, patients and they also drift out into the collective consciousness of society. Under these mindsets, society will never advance and will always be divided into broken people and those who are meant to fix them. It works like the observer effect of which you and your colleagues know. It is a cycle that continues to be created. It takes someone from outside the system to see the problems of the system and the supporting culture that sustains it.

Bob paused, then continued, *The truth is, people have their own answers already and they are magnificent beyond their knowing. Those answers exist in the quantum field of possibility. People just don't know how to access it themselves, as they have never been taught.*

Celeste frowned. *Too much detail. Big picture it for me, Bob.* Something stirred deep within, and she felt that internal warmth rising again.

This is all about to change at a planetary level, and you have a role to play. Are you ready to hear this? Bob asked.

Try me. You know that if I run away screaming, I'll always come back.

Bob nodded, no smile this time, and more serious than usual. *Humanity is at a crossroads and will soon move through a period of transformation as you learn more about yourselves and your place in the universe. One of the things you will discover is that much of humanity's potential has been limited at both the individual and collective levels. These limitations were installed in most of the systems on the planet. Those of us from elsewhere have been watching for a long time, waiting for this moment, and it has now arrived. You are entering a time of profound discovery, and we are supporting your efforts with great love. Not all are ready for change, and it will not be an easy road, though the support for these changes comes from all corners of the universe.*

Something strange happened within Celeste. An old memory emerged, somehow resonating with what Bob was saying. She felt a sense that she chose to be part of this. *You mentioned I have a role in this?*

The field of quantum physics is about to realise that those other dimensions being speculated about are close by and can be accessed. This will bring unimaginable reforms, not just to science but also to the world at large. In time, this field will be renamed quantum metaphysics. There will be no more theoretical physicists; they will be known as quantum alchemists. This is because nothing will be theoretical anymore; the secrets of the universe will be known. This will all take time, many decades, as a whole generation who have built the old ways fade into the past. The term physics will relate to Newtonian physics and honour that part of your history. Science, which has been moulded to benefit some, will be replaced by metascience. There will be a golden age of advancement, which will include discoveries beyond imagination. We may discuss these as time unfolds, but not now.

Bob paused to let it sink in. Celeste had been right; she was ready to hear this. *You asked about your role. It will include, but not be limited to, being a pioneer in the discovery of access to other dimensions. Your life's work and that of others will be instrumental in moving quantum physics to the new quantum metaphysics. And a new type of civilization will emerge for humanity.*

So you see, Celeste, it is not in anyone's best interests for you to be a therapist. You have other things to do as part of a greater plan.

Celeste shook her head. *How do you know all this?*

It is known outside your time and space, and it is inevitable. We have seen it and also the role we played in supporting its emergence. There are various futures available to us, but as we all play our role in the greater plan, we will reach the preferred destination.

I don't understand; is it locked in as a future or not? Do we have to do something or just wait for it to arrive? Celeste could see the paradox. Schrodinger's cat came to mind.

Bob spoke again. *The universe is continually in motion and everything is connected. We are creators of many different realities. Those creations unfold from the collective intent of many energies. If we create nothing, then we will receive nothing. If we create something wonderful for humanity that comes from collective intent, then that is the highest vibrational outcome for all concerned and for the universe itself.*

You're losing me, Bob.

In your 3D existence, collective intent must be translated into actions that support the direction of the original intent.

Soooo ... I need to understand the end game of what's possible, then drive my consciousness towards it?

Yes, by embracing cosmic law and understanding that you are working multidimensionally to bring it into being.

Celeste nodded. *I think I understand. I run this in 3D, and you support it from another dimension, and together we create this as our desired future.*

Bob smiled. *Yes. That is enough of a definition for the moment.*

At that moment, Celeste surrendered to her destiny. Her mind and, more importantly, her heart were clear of anything that would stand the way of stepping into something remarkable. It was a leap of faith and she took it. She knew the challenges would be many, but she no longer resisted.

She refocused her awareness on Bob. *Okay, what's next?*

We now need to enrol others. It takes a number of particles to create a wave.

CHAPTER 21

Celeste took a week to build a research-project proposal. She created a new paper wall in the house, along with more flipcharts, did more internet research, and had a few chats with Bob and also Dr Bart.

Ready to launch her proposal, she called a meeting of her PhD review board to ask for formal assistance to create the next wave Bob had mentioned. She drove to the station and boarded a train to the city. Plenty of seats were available where she could sit and put her mind to work, drifting into areas where she might be challenged. She envisaged the three members of the board in her mind's eye and read each of their energies.

Dr Bart was already supportive and had been helpful in giving her advice. There would be no surprises there, just encouragement.

Professor Mildred Shrewberry, otherwise known as QB, would love to see her fail. However, if the proposal came off, there would be an elevation in QB's professional standing as a visionary developer of talented resources. If it failed, she'd have the personal satisfaction of seeing Celeste's career ruined and be able to say, 'I told you so.' Ego was the bait here; she needed to be stroked.

Dr William Nicholson was looking for a high point on which to end his career and retire to his inner-city cat farm in the backyard of his cottage. This could be the 'Schrodinger send-off' he was hoping for.

She visualised the presentation and ran it through her awareness, moving ahead in both time and space to practice her delivery. It felt good. She was ready.

Celeste arrived in the meeting room early so she could set up for her presentation. She placed three hard copies of the proposal in front of the chairs opposite her seat.

They all filed in and took their seats, with a curt nod and greeting from QB, a condescending wave from Schrodinger and a wink from Dr Bart.

Celeste took a breath and began. 'When we last met, you asked me to explore options to find data to prove other realities exist. I'd like you to know that I found your challenge to me inspirational, and I'd like to offer a hypothesis that I hope will answer your questions. The quality of a review board should be measured on how they challenge the candidate, and you have done that for me.'

The egos had been stroked. QB and Schrodinger were a little taken aback by Celeste's humility. Dr Bart was not—it had been his idea.

'I believe I can run a research project that proves other dimensions not only exist but can affect this reality with measurable results denoting either a physiological or emotional change in a carefully selected sample of particles.' She paused.

QB spoke first. 'What do you mean by "a carefully selected sample of particles"?'

'I'm talking about a person,' Celeste replied.

Schrodinger frowned. 'I beg your pardon?'

'Each and every one of us is a part of the quantum field, and so we have access to it. We know it's not limited to us and that we entangle with our surroundings constantly, as one collective multidimensional energy field. This being so, then we ourselves must have access to those other dimensions. I propose that we measure both the person themselves and the environment around them in two different ways, then compare both results.'

'Best you describe your proposed method,' QB said, yet to be convinced.

'The experiment will be conducted in the following way. We select a subject who is experiencing emotional distress. They will initially self-assess on a simple wellbeing scale, giving us a score between one and ten, running from low to high. We will then be using two supporting pieces of technology.

'First, we'll measure their emotional landscape through a device that uses heart coherence software. This will offer us a rating of whether the emotional field is in distress, 'dissonance', or more peaceful, 'resonance'. This will be known as the 'quantum field local', as it measures the sample of particles that is the human body.

'Second, we'll track the vicinity outside the body in the same room with a random number generator machine. These will measure disruption in the energy field that is the room itself. Random number generator machines work on probabilities, much like a coin toss, and should reflect fifty-fifty as an outcome for heads or tails. When the system is disrupted, the randomness skews. It's our way of understanding disruption in the room. We'll refer to the room environment outside the body as the 'quantum field non-local'.

'This will give us three readings in total. One is subjective from the client. The other two are objectively measured through the two machines. These three readings will form a baseline.'

Three blank faces looked back at her, two authentically so and one playing a role.

'Third, we ask the subject to set an intention to move into a higher state of resonance, and this becomes their 'personal-observer effect'. Then we move them through a specifically designed set of protocols to a state of being where their awareness expands beyond their body. In essence, we move from quantum field local to quantum field non-local. When this happens, they've moved into their 'super-observer effect'. This is our definition of the expanded state that has been emerging in early trials as something that holds more information than the test subject themselves.

'We postulate that this is actually another state of reality—in effect, another dimensional experience, because their perspective is beyond the physical plane. In essence, we've left 3D. The original emotional distress is then viewed from a different frequency, a transcendent viewpoint, if you like. A quantum mind rather than a human mind, thus leading to a change of state in the subject. The super-observer effect is asked what is required to meet the intention designed as the personal-observer effect, and we receive that information.

'Finally, we return from this state of quantum field non-local to quantum field local and take measurements for all three parameters, then compare them to the baseline.'

No one said anything. The pregnant pause would determine whether she had support or not.

Celeste filled the silence. 'What troubles me, though, is the size and nature of this project, because it has specific spin-off potential. We'll be exploring the possibility of measuring the difference between the personal-observer effect and the super-observer effect. We will also be able to measurably compare the difference between the quantum field local and the quantum field non-local. We may be offering a new view of the human condition as not only a physical being but also a specific collection of particles that has measurable change in consciousness from interactions in the quantum field non-local. We may even be able to map human consciousness within the field itself, though that is outside the scope of the proposal.

'As you probably know, random number generator machines have been used to measure shifts in the magnetic field of the Earth during large-scale events impacting human consciousness. Our intention is to use these machines to measure the environment in the room. To my knowledge, they are yet to be used in this way for this type of experimentation. We're breaking new ground here.

'As a result, I feel that this is bigger than my doctorate. I believe this is an important research subject that has the potential to move into a vast number of other projects over time.'

'So what are you suggesting?' asked Dr Bart.

The other two clearly still didn't know what to say.

'I suggest that this be sponsored as a joint endeavour between my doctoral submission and a university-sponsored project. My thesis would form a component of the project, specific to the original scope I put forward. All the data collected will form part of a UNSW database that can be reviewed, published and syndicated to other organisations that we collaborate with. It would mean that your individual roles would need to change from a PhD review board to a major project sponsorship role, formally recognised in your respective portfolios within the school of physics. I know that many of our alumni would like to know more about this. I'm hopeful that you'd play a role in educating people about our cutting-edge research.'

Silence again. Then Dr Bart stood and moved into the role he'd prepared for. 'Celeste, I think you have some great ideas here, though you're describing something significant that will require a great deal of university resources. How could we ever make these allocations, given our already-constrained budgets?'

Prepared for this question, Celeste replied, 'I'll provide the premises and all the administration. I just need three research contractors for two days a week, perhaps taken from other projects that are nearing completion. They'd still be available for other project work three days a week.'

Dr Bart continued, 'So it won't cost us much at all, then. Well, beyond that, I don't think any of us want to be known as the people who sponsored a wild 'out-there' project that brought new insight to quantum physics. This could go anywhere … I'm not sure UNSW is leading edge enough for this.' Though subtle, his words baited the others. A lifetime of dealing with academic politics served him well and helped Celeste.

She waited for the response from the others, a greater purpose foremost in her mind.

QB spoke then. 'Dr Kindred, let's not be too hasty. We've been reviewing the progress of this doctorate quarterly, anyway. Perhaps we could establish a pilot timeframe for the project component, a six-month period to run in parallel. At that time, we could review progress to date and then make a decision.'

'Hmm … possibly. Dr Nicholson, what do you think?' Dr Bart asked.

'I feel it's worth exploring. We all know there are certain protocols to follow with the establishment of projects for the allocation of resources. Given this is an existing PhD project and resource allocation is minimal, it could probably be established quite easily.'

Bart wrapped it up. 'I concur. So we are agreed on a review

in six months' time, then. What did you want to call this project, Celeste?'

Celeste smiled, pleased they were casting off some of the old ways, getting rid of the restrictive barriers and mindsets. But what name for it? A word came to mind that encapsulated all of it—the place where it all began. 'Let's call it Project Shed.'

CHAPTER 22

Having the resources of the university to draw upon made a huge difference. Celeste was able to second a technical infrastructure for her three researchers. She'd known the technology manager for years, and Phil was a helpful person who managed to get a lot done while swimming through the waters of bureaucracy. She called him and offered to buy him coffee in exchange for advice.

He sipped a giant cappuccino, then asked, 'What are you working on, Celeste?'

'It's a bit out of the ordinary, and complex, though one important aspect is measuring the impacts in the quantum field from changing human emotions.'

'Huh … sounds cool. What do you need?'

'Four laptops with server backup, for a start. But I need it installed in the Blue Mountains.'

'There's some other paperwork for offsite, and we'll need a VPN, but that's easy. I'm sure one of the guys would love a drive up the mountains. What's the site?'

'My place; I'm housing the project in my home.'

Phil chuckled. 'That's taking your work home with you. But no problem.'

'The next bit is weird. Have you heard about random number generator machines?'

'Sure.' Phil nodded. 'The software around those things has gone ballistic. That's what they use behind online gambling sites. It's pretty sophisticated these days. You can have it on the server, PCs or even as an app on your phone.'

'I need the actual machines, though, with a PC interface that tracks the algorithm in real time and holds the data in a way that it can be retrieved to study. I just need to record the anomalies when the randomness of the numbers is affected in the quantum field. I want to measure the disruption in a system.'

Phil said nothing for a minute, apparently lost in thought. 'A few years back, we were playing with some REG kits. That's random event generators, less sophisticated than recent software, but accurate enough to pick up anomalies. The School of Mathematics was using them in some probability studies. It's like a continual coin toss. The machine runs and you get like a fifty-fifty split between heads and tails. They were experimenting with how group thinking affected probability. When everyone wanted heads and stood next to the machine, the probability swayed in that direction; it was the weirdest thing. In short, the software measures the disruption to the system.'

'That's exactly what I need! Do you still have them? I need four.'

'Sure. We have at least that many. We used to play with them sometimes. I can get them out of storage. The software to catch the data was pretty good back then, but it'll be old now. I'll check for the latest version.'

'I need them in rooms next to each other; will they affect

each other's readings?'

'Possibly. You'd be best to insulate. That'll give you a clear reading.'

'How do I do that?'

'High tech, you need a Faraday shield. Low tech, we get quite a few rolls of aluminium foil and line the walls in the rooms. That's how Faraday started, by the way, so that should make it very authentic.' He grinned.

Celeste smiled in return. 'Okay, the next thing I need is to be able to measure the emotional responses in a subject's nervous system. Before and after the experiment, through heart-coherence software. Have you heard of it?'

'Sure,' Phil replied. 'The Hearth Math Institute built a whole PC-based system. They offer the software to universities for experimentation in exchange for a copy of the data obtained. I seem to remember there's a physical interface. I think it's called a finger pulse oximeter or something. It goes on the finger, and it plugs in with a USB connection.'

Celeste shook her head in amazement. 'How do you know all these things?' It was the best value cup of coffee she'd had in a long time.

Phil grinned. 'Well … we do support the School of Medicine as well. Then there's the other reason.'

'What's that?' Celeste asked.

'I'm a nerd,' he replied.

CHAPTER 23

Celeste had a great memory for good people. Even after many research projects she'd either led or been involved with over the years, she could remember the people she'd met and others she'd only heard about.

She looked back now, specifically recalling those who were a little different, non-traditional and even weird—a fair definition of herself these days, she realised. Celeste wanted to build a team that was open to the metaphysical but still grounded. She'd be asking a great deal of these people, and if they ever connected to the big picture of what they were really doing, she hoped they wouldn't freak out too much. As a project leader, she was given access to the personnel files for all available contractors. She went through and found three names that stuck out intuitively, and so began the interviews, which took place on the university campus in the Human Resources building.

The first conversation was with Rashmi, just twenty-two years old and studying part time, working his way through the physics pathways. His file noted that he was born in India and listed Hindu in his religious affiliations. His parents had migrated to Australia when he was young. Celeste felt a peacefulness about him—not surprising, perhaps, since his hobbies had been listed as yoga and meditation. His eyes emanated that peace, and Celeste found it to be a little contagious.

'Rashmi, this project won't be like the others you're doing. It's offsite, and we'll be obtaining data first-hand from real people. You'll be part of a small team working from my home in the Blue Mountains.'

He shrugged. 'Okay.'

'Why do you want to work on this project?'

'In one of my first classes three years ago, you did a presentation about a project you were working on. You said something I still remember. You said that the quantum realm is the real world and the macro just doesn't know how to behave. You said that maybe this macro life is an illusion, and when we finally realise that, then we can change the world and align the large and small.' His eyes lit up as he shared the memory.

'Really?' Celeste was surprised. 'I don't remember saying that.'

'I also know that in your thesis you're looking for other dimensions. I believe they exist and dream of finding them one day.'

Celeste smiled. 'Why is that so important to you?'

'I am Hindu. Our culture embraces reincarnation. If time is an illusion, then these lives exist in parallel. I believe they may be part of the other dimensions, and this project wants to explore that. If that's so, then my spiritual life and my scientific life can align, and I'll feel whole. At the moment, I live in two worlds, and sometimes I feel lost in between.'

It probably wasn't the time to talk about the life of Zac, but maybe one day …

This young man blew Celeste away, and his mindset was

perfect for the direction she wanted to take. Maybe she could even learn from him. He was a good fit, and his resume said he was great with technology. It was the shortest interview she'd ever conducted. 'Anything else I need to know?' she asked.

'I don't drink; I'm a vegetarian; I'm a hopeless cricket fanatic … and my friends call me Raz.'

Celeste extended her hand. 'Welcome to the team, Raz.'

CHAPTER 24

Next, she interviewed Skye, a twenty-eight-year-old postgrad in astrophysics. She wore a flowery skirt and blouse along with some serious crystals—not an academic fit at all. Celeste couldn't imagine her in a boardroom setting. She seemed perfect for what was coming.

'I couldn't help but notice that you're an astrophysicist and your name is Skye,' Celeste began.

She chuckled, her face lighting up. 'It gets worse, actually. My father was an astronomer and my mother an astrologer, so they didn't agree on much. Except my name, of course; that was inevitable. Just to cap it all off, they gave me Venus as a middle name.'

Celeste smiled. 'What drew you to astrophysics?'

'I grew up looking upwards into the universe, and I could name most constellations before I was ten. Somehow, this planet didn't seem big enough for me. Quantum physics looks through an electron microscope, astrophysics looks through the Hubble telescope. It was an easy choice. Maybe I'm looking for home?'

She shrugged.

'Why do you want to work with me?'

'You're different, and I've known about you for a while. You're not afraid to put people in their place or have your say. I like that; it's refreshing. Most university types just continue the status quo. I want to make a difference and shake things up.'

Careful what you ask for, Celeste thought. 'Can you start next week?'

She'd broken the record again with an even shorter interview.

CHAPTER 25

The third member of the team picked herself long ago. Tall, quiet, wise and a few months short of her fiftieth year, Grace had been on the first project team that Celeste worked with almost twenty years previously. No interview was needed, just a simple phone call and a chance to reconnect.

'I was so sorry to hear about your father and then your mother, Celeste,' she said on the phone. 'I reached out at the time and sent my condolences. I hope they were received.'

'I did get your card. Thank you, Grace. I was in a bad place for a while and didn't respond to many people at all. Please forgive me. I'm in a good place now and moving ahead.'

'Nothing to forgive ... Now, tell me about this project.'

'We're measuring human emotions in the quantum field. It's a bit more complicated than just that and different from other things we've done before. It might involve some other dimensional theories.'

'I like it already. I haven't worked for a few months, and the kids have left home now, so I've been hoping something would come along. My last role was analysing data for IONS. We were running some analyses for the Global Consciousness Project.'

A penny dropped for Celeste. 'The Institute of Noetic Sciences? What's that project about again?'

'We analysed the data from the network of random number generator machines positioned around the world and trends in human consciousness that occur just before or after large-scale events. It's been quite fascinating.'

Celeste's jaw dropped. Her team was complete. She felt the synchronicity in the forming of the team and how easily it had come together. She suspected a helping hand.

Under her breath, Celeste said, 'Thanks, Bob.'

CHAPTER 26

Two days later, Celeste woke fully motivated.

At seven she texted Abbey:

Are you working today? I need your help with a project.

Abbey:

itz my day offf, whatss Up?

Clearly, she'd just woken up.

Celeste:

House makeover. Need to build a place where weird things happen. Interested?

Abbey:

Absolutely. Give me an hour.

No typos this time.

She arrived fifty minutes later. Celeste heard her drive up and opened the door to see her friend staring at the large metal waste bin beside the driveway, already two-thirds full of all manner of things.

After greetings, they walked through the house together, trying to envision it in its new state of being.

'The four bedrooms will become the lab rooms for experimentation,' Celeste said. 'I'll have a contractor working in each of the three smaller rooms. The main bedroom will also become my office. Each room will have a small desk and chair, as well as a recliner for their subject. Two new recliner chairs arrived yesterday and are in the rooms already. I had another two out in the studio. We need to put some folding petitions between the lounge room and the dining room and kitchen. The dining table will become a meeting area, the kitchen eating bar, the lunchroom, and the lounge room will be the waiting area for the subjects.'

'Where are you going to sleep?' Abbey asked.

'I'm moving into the studio. It has a separate bedroom, bathroom and a small kitchenette. Though I need your help to shift some more furniture.'

Abbey poked her head into the three smaller bedrooms. 'What happened to the beds?'

'I gave them to charity. Many of the other things I've been hanging on to are in the rubbish skip out the front.'

'I noticed.' Abbey walked up to Celeste and threw her arms around her. 'It's nice to have you back.'

After getting over her initial surprise, Celeste hugged her back with an open heart. 'It's nice to be back, Abs.'

By the end of the day, the house was complete. The lab rooms were set up for Raz, Skye and Grace. Celeste's office-come-fourth-lab room was taking shape. They'd moved the wall of paper in there from the main living area, and it covered all four walls with a few blank spaces left for further thoughts that could emerge at any time.

The one thing they hadn't touched were the bookshelves. They still proudly displayed wisdom from many subjects and eras. Beyond that, all the clutter in the house had been removed, and the energy felt better already. Abbey did her smudge thing and played the Tibetan bowl just as she had in the shed that day.

The transition out to the studio was yet to be completed for Celeste. She'd moved her mother's large unused canvasses and paints into a storage cupboard—it didn't feel right to throw them away. Her bed had been moved out there into the small bedroom, and a compact lounge suite and dining table fitted nicely into the living area off the kitchenette. It would do. She'd be in the main house most of the time anyway.

'Can I buy you dinner at the Italian place?' Celeste asked.

'Hooray, I love Michelangelo's!'

Forty-five minutes later, feeling satisfied after a big day, they were sipping an ice cold Frascati while they waited for their pasta to arrive. Celeste topped up their glasses before proposing a toast.

'Gratitude for you, Abs.' They clinked and sipped.

'Lest, I need to ask you something.'

'Sure, anything.'

'What the hell has happened to us? You're completely different now. If you'd told me even two months ago that you'd be throwing out all the stuff you've been holding on to from your mum and dad, you'd have met with a Reiki teacher, a past-life expert and would be having regular chats with "Interdimensional Bob", I would've said you'd lost your mind or something.'

Celeste nodded and smiled at the name Abbey had given Bob. It was both cute and accurate.

Abbey continued, 'But most of all, it's the change in you. You have your spark back. It's not just you, but me as well. I have a date next week. I finally put up a profile on a spiritual dating site and got three likes on the first day, and I don't even chew gum anymore.'

Celeste paused and considered Abbey's words. 'There's definitely something significant going on with this work, and we've both experienced it personally. It feels like I have a level of energy that wasn't there before. It's as though my spirit was being drained by my emotions, siphoned off into a black hole. I remember my doctor offering me some medication when my parents were gone and I was in a dark place. He told me it would numb the pain, but what do you do? Do you live your life that way from then on?'

Abbey shrugged.

Celeste continued, 'When you see the big picture, the little picture looks different. You see purpose in things you didn't see before and start to realise that there's a large "something" we're all part of. Once you look at life from there, you can't not see it. Things are different from then, and something that previously seemed so big is then put in its rightful place.

'Here's the best example I can think of: I used to hold on to mum and dad's possessions as reminders of them, so I could feel closer to them. Now I realise they're supporting me, and they don't care about all their physical things anymore. Best way to honour mum and dad is to get rid of those things.

'I don't have many answers, but life feels completely different now. I have both a sense of peace within and an enthusiasm to do something for the world. Bob's told me some things that really seem to resonate, though I'm still trying to make sense of those. One day at a time, I guess.'

The pasta arrived, their conversation became lighter, and for the first time in years, they laughed like the teenagers they once were.

CHAPTER 27

The shed had become a place of solace. Celeste had taken to sitting there and letting her mind roam through the mind-blowing experiences of the last few months.

Phil was sending a technical person the following Monday to set up the technology. Raz had already been spending time at the university learning about the two types of software they'd be using. The first would measure the quantum field local through heart coherence software, and the second, disruption in the quantum field non-local with the random event machines. Phil had even found industrial-sized aluminium foil a metre wide, which had saved Celeste from cleaning out every supermarket in the Blue Mountains of kitchen foil. They intended to line the rooms and then hang fabric in front of the foil, so the subjects didn't feel like they were in a metal box, even though they were.

In this moment of peace, Celeste looked up at her father's rug hanging on the wall, enjoying an echo of his presence in the shed that was once his place of solitude too. Their shared energy permeated the shed now, even with traces of Interdimensional

Bob in the background. Abbey had since shortened his nickname to I-Bob, claiming that he probably had an intergalactic iPhone on which he received cosmic text messages.

The swirls in the rug seemed to speak to her, and she remembered her father's comment when he and her mother had stood in front of it during her first journey with Bob: *These things are supposed to go on the floor, you know.*

Celeste rose from the chair and took a step forward. The top edge of the rug had been nailed to the rough plank wall. The nails would need to be removed. She retrieved a hammer from the carport, stood on Bob's chair and one by one worked the large nails loose. The rug dropped to the floor with a thump. As she climbed down from the chair, she noticed a horizontal crack in the wood about two metres off the ground and about a metre long. It ended at two edges of the wooden planks and looked like some sort of panel.

She studied the wall, wondering what might be behind it. Then she had an idea. She retrieved her father's old metallic tape measure from the carport, returned to the shed and measured the dimensions of the room. Square. Five metres in both directions. Then she went outside and measured the first outside wall—a little over five metres. The other wall measured at seven metres.

On the other side of the shed, she found an opening in the bougainvillea vines and poked the end of the tape measure through, just above the ground. Seven metres once again. You didn't have to be a scientist to realise that there was two metres of hidden space. The vine blurred the spatial awareness of anyone looking at the shed from the outside.

Intrigued, Celeste went back inside the shed and tapped on the wall panel. It was so perfectly aligned that unless she'd been on the chair, she wouldn't have noticed the cracks indicating the panel was there. After a couple of minutes of tapping along the wall, she found a point that looked slightly more worn than the rest. Unless you were looking for something, you'd put it down to the imperfections in the rough grain. Beyond that, it'd been hidden behind the rug nailed to the wall. She pressed that place and the panel popped out on a spring-loaded catch. The panel was a door, and it opened out towards her!

Tentatively, she peered into the gloomy interior and smelled the musty environment. She felt no airflow but heard a soft humming noise. Two mini skylights allowed some light to filter through the vines that covered that part of the roof. Noticing a light switch just inside the door, she flicked it on, and light flooded the room.

Celeste stood motionless as she took in the room. It was indeed five metres wide and two metres deep. A workbench stood at one end, with what looked like a writing desk at the other. Handwritten notes were everywhere, diagrams tacked to the rough wooden walls and the bookshelves at either side of the desk. She'd discovered her father's hidden workspace, but what did he do here?

Drawn to the low humming noise, she turned toward the workbench. A small device about half a metre long sat there. A rotating spindle, it resembled a type of rolling pin, cylindrically shaped and resting in a cradle made to size. Though it was spinning, there didn't appear to be a power source, yet it connected to a small amp meter that showed a flow of current. As the daughter of a mechanical engineer, Celeste could see that the kinetic energy of the spinning cylinder was generating a low-level measurable current of electricity, though she couldn't work out what made it spin. Puzzled, she wondered how long it'd been spinning for, given her father passed more than two years ago.

Shaking her head, she turned to the desk at the other end. She made out some plans that looked roughly like the device, finely detailed in her father's small and neat handwriting. The one drawer in the desk was locked, but Celeste knew her father's trick for hiding keys. He loved magnets, and they often discussed the electromagnetic field as part of the standard model of physics versus the quantum field she knew so well. In her mind, she could almost hear one of those animated discussions they'd shared over lunch …

'How can you embrace a standard model of the universe that doesn't include gravity, Dad? It affects everything you know!' Celeste teased.

Her father teased her in return. 'Well … it has to be a constant, then, so as long as we acknowledge that, then it's by default part of the model. Even Isaac Newton knew that,' he retorted jovially, in a good mood. 'I'm an engineer, Lesty; you leave the electromagnetic spectrum to me. You can have your string theory and other worlds as a theoretical physicist. I can actually show you my world; the challenge for you is to show me yours.'

These conversations had guided her slowly towards the journey of discovery that resulted in her PhD thesis, discovering the life of Zac, connecting with I-Bob and then on to the creation of Project Shed.

Looking at this room, she began to understand that her father was more than an engineer. It seemed as though he was an inventor as well. She surveyed the walls and found she could follow his diagrams. It appeared he had the same mind-mapping idiosyncrasies that she did. However, his handwriting and the quantity of paper needed was smaller. Given the size of the room in which she stood, that was a good thing.

Celeste knew exactly how to look for the key. Up under the desk somewhere, completely out of sight, would be a small, magnetised plate. She'd find a key, most likely magnetised, sitting on the plate. The double bond would ensure that the key never fell or was lost. It took her ten seconds to find it and open the desk drawer with a firm tug.

The draw was full of many things, though only one drew her attention, an envelope with one word on the front: *Lesty*. Her eyes filled with tears. No one ever called her that anymore. Only one person ever had, and he was no longer in the physical world.

Her hands shook as she opened the envelope, and several sheets of notepaper, filled with her father's neat and tiny handwriting, fell out into her hand. The letter was dated three years previously, around nine months before his accident.

> *Dear Lesty,*
> *Given you're reading this, I can only say, well done. Once again, you've made me the proudest dad in the world. If you've found the room and then the key to the desk, it will mean that I'm gone, and there are some things I need to tell you.*
> *The first is that I see things in you that you don't see in yourself. You have untapped potential that surpasses your gift for the sciences. You have an ability to tap into the world as few others can. I hope in time these gifts will develop, and I encourage you, as always, to explore them. I know something about them already, though you must discover these in your own time.*
> *The second thing is that I will love you forever, in this world and any other I move to, through these other dimensions that you and I have spoken of before. Know also that I have always believed in their existence and have experienced them for myself. I never told you that because it encouraged you*

no end to believe you were undertaking a journey
to find them for both of us. They are there; keep
looking and stay open.

Now to my work. I'm hoping it's still in
one piece in the room in which you're currently
standing. Here's a short summary; detail will come
another time.

I was experimenting with magnets and an
ionised rod one day and realised that a metal rod
could spin perpetually between two magnetic fields.
The only thing that slowed it was friction; otherwise,
it would spin forever. I discovered that if I encased
it in a magnetic field and then magnetised the rod
as well, the field prevented the rod from touching
the sides of the casing. Basically, when there is no
physical contact, friction is solved. The perpetual
spinning of the rod gives off a charge, which can
be measured and is constant. If the charge can be
captured and stored, then it will be an ongoing
supply of electricity. What you see at the other end
of the room is a prototype I built myself, and, at the
time of writing, has been spinning for almost two
years at the same current. I suspect that a slightly
larger version could power a neighbourhood. The
rate of output is not directly proportional to size but
on an exponential curve. My maths is not as good as
yours, though I estimate that a device the size of a
tennis court could power a whole city.

You may recall that I travelled to the USA in
2017 for a conference. What I didn't tell you was
that I was a speaker there, putting forward what
I'd found. I wanted to test the landscape and see

*if people were ready to hear what I'd discovered.
I'd heard stories about people who'd come up with
free energy devices, who'd then been raided by the
authorities or threatened by corporate interests.
I was a bit naïve, thinking I could fly under the
radar; nevertheless, I chose to keep the success of my
prototype a secret until I knew more.*

*The presentation went well, and the feedback
was positive. I told them my next challenge was to
solve the problem of friction (which I secretly already
had), and I explained how I intended to go about
that, offering three different paths of pursuit, other
than the solution I'd already found.*

*The next morning, I was having breakfast in
the hotel when a young man asked if he could join
me. He said he'd been fascinated by my presentation
and had a few questions. The questions were more
commercially orientated, rather than scientific, and
I was immediately suspicious. He asked how long it
would take for this technology to be available once
the friction problem was solved, as he knew some
people who may invest. I told him I'd be surprised if
it was within ten years and that there'd also need to
be a sensible transition from the dominating fossil-
fuel model of today. I told him fifteen years at least,
but of course it would be nothing like that in reality.*

*Following that disturbing conversation, I
thought it best to leave the conference early and
changed my flight.*

*I was at the airport late that afternoon when
the same man came and sat next to me in the
departure lounge. He said that if I continued my*

research, bad things would happen to me and
the people I cared about. I was stunned, and I
have to say, this second conversation disturbed me
very deeply.

I headed home, realising I had to have all the
appearances of dropping this direction of my work. I
built this room in the shed and continued in secret.
I wasn't worried about myself so much, though I
worried for you and Mum. I retired to have more
time for this project, though more importantly, for
me to drop out of sight.

So given you're reading this, something awful
has happened. I don't know what that is, but I do
know that what I've got to offer the world is in
this room. If I can't be there to offer it, perhaps you
can. I know it's not your area of expertise, so I have
made detailed notes that can be followed by a bright
mind, and that, my dear Lesty, is definitely you.

If you choose to simply do nothing, then that
also is a choice that I lovingly support. Mostly, I
need you and Mum to be safe, and that is more
important than anything in this shed. Please
understand that she knows nothing of any of this.
With her anxiety levels, she wouldn't cope. It's better
for her to think of me as a retired engineer who
spends time tinkering down in the back shed.

In an uncertain landscape, where anything is
possible, there is one bright ray of light. That is how
much I love you and always will.

Dad x

Celeste felt weak at the knees and left the room hurriedly.

She only just made it back to Bob's chair before her legs gave way. You couldn't be a scientist and not know about the alternatives to fossil fuels, from solar technology to wind power and the remarkable work of Nikola Tesla. Her father had raved about him over the years, though he'd rarely mentioned him in the last years of his life. She was starting to understand why.

There'd always been some details of her father's accident that didn't add up, but Celeste couldn't go there at the moment. The possibilities were too horrible to even contemplate.

She closed the panel and sat back in her chair once more. The gentle humming of the energy device in the next room was unnoticeable, and she wondered about nailing the rug back up to hide the panel. Her father said doing nothing was an option. She felt like she was drowning in an ocean of mysterious energy. In an attempt to calm herself, she closed her eyes and drifted.

A wave of loving resonance gathered gently around her, and Bob drifted into her awareness. She felt reassured, and her energy started to settle.

Bob—she directed her energy towards him—*what the hell is going on?*

Your father had a purpose, Celeste. He just didn't get a chance to finish it.

Did you know about his work, and did you know about his room behind the wall? she asked.

Yes, to both, he replied in her mind.

Why didn't you tell me? Tears wet her cheeks.

The universe unfolds piece by piece, Celeste. We find the next thing when we are ready, and we must always honour free will. You chose to look behind the rug today and to then open the wall. Discoveries happen when they are meant to. It was not possible while you still grieved.

I don't know what to do with this now. This changes so many things, and I can't get my head around it, she telepathed.

He did the Bob smile, radiating more loving resonance. *You do not need to, Celeste. This can wait. There are other things for us to do. We didn't think you would find the room yet, though as so often has happened, you have surprised us. Our loving assistance to you goes beyond Project Shed. As other things arise in the years ahead, we will still be with you. My suggestion for you is to put the rug back up for now. That door can be opened when the time is right, though it is not for this moment. There is just one thing for you to draw from today …*

What's that?

That your father was remarkable beyond your knowing and that you will come to discover more of that in time. Bob faded away then and left her to her thoughts.

She sat for a while, and a steely determination built within her. Things were wrong in this world, and she was being asked to help fix them. Somewhere deep inside her, a furnace had been lit, one that held great power. Celeste looked down, realising her father's letter was still in her hand, so she folded it carefully. As she did so, she noticed a few old stains on the paper and realised her father must've shed some tears as he wrote this letter to her. She recognised the marks on the page because of the fresh ones next to them that were just minutes old—yet another bond that held them together across time and space. She placed the letter in her pocket, intending to keep it in a safe place. At some time in the future, she'd need it again.

CHAPTER 28

Celeste spent some time over the weekend in the bush, allowing herself the experience of nature. The calming, settling time helped her prepare for the next week. She'd sought Paul O'Malley's assistance to build the written materials that would help with the experiments. His gift for language and his experience facilitating out-of-body work had proved invaluable.

On Monday, the technology person from the university arrived, installed the computers in four rooms and set up a server for the network. It took him a few hours to cover the walls in all rooms with the foil. Abbey came through later that afternoon and hung coloured cloth over the foil. By the evening, everything was done. Celeste's family home had become a scientific centre for quantum exploration.

The centre was to run five days a week. Celeste would be there every day, the whole team on Tuesdays, then Raz would come on Wednesdays, Skye on Thursdays and Grace on Fridays, working with volunteer subjects. The timetable meant Celeste could interview each subject beforehand as part of the intake process, and then debrief each of her team after the experiences were completed.

The next day, Raz, Skye and Grace arrived within a few minutes of each other. Celeste gave them the tour of the centre and made introductions. They sat around the conference table, and Celeste asked each of them to talk about themselves and their backgrounds. Abbey wanted to be involved and volunteered some time to do admin, so she joined the group this first day. The team had a good vibe, and they seemed to gel quickly.

'Let me say how thrilled I am to have you here,' Celeste said. 'Each of you brings something to the team that is unique, and together we're going to do something that has never been done before. On the scientific side of things, we'll be moving a collection of particles through an observed process into another dimension and then return those particles to this one.'

The team met her with blank looks.

She continued, 'In other words—perhaps a more human angle—we'll be working with people who are suffering from some form of emotional or physical distress and taking them into an expanded state where they can view the distress from a transcendent perspective. Once that moment of insight occurs, we anticipate that the distress may partially or even permanently dissolve.'

The light of growing understanding came on in their eyes, so Celeste continued, 'You will learn the experimental path and the facilitation techniques, and each of you will go through an experimental process yourself before you work with subjects.'

'How come?' Skye asked.

Celeste watched the group carefully as she answered, 'Before you can help them find their state of super observer, you must feel your own, so you know what you're looking for. That way, when you quantumly entangle with them, you show them "the how" in a way that goes beyond the words we'll use.'

Raz's eyes opened wide, Grace smiled and Skye said, 'Coooool!'

Abbey chimed in, 'Celeste did one for me, and it was awesome! So much has changed for me now.'

Celeste nodded. 'I've experienced this as well, and things that were holding me back have now dissolved. In fact, I imagine that I wouldn't be here now talking to you if I hadn't gone through it myself.'

Grace spoke softly, 'Who did you do the experiment with, Celeste?'

Celeste paused before replying. 'Someone who has become a learned friend and mentor for me. Bob's not from around here, though.' It felt strange to say his name to anyone beyond Abbey and Paul. She caught a glint of humour in the corner of Abbey's eye; she, too, realised the team weren't ready to know more about Bob at this time.

'Here's the general approach we'll use,' Celeste continued. 'I've already placed an advertisement in the *Blue Mountains Times* on behalf of UNSW, asking for people who have a condition of emotional or physical distress to volunteer and be part of a study into the connection between quantum physics and mental health. I had the university admin set up an email, and on the first day, we had twenty enquiries, and the university started to screen participants. So, in short, we have fifty people ready to go and awaiting scheduling. We are currently assessing another seventy applications.

'The profile of the subjects for the first test group has been set, and we've decided that this group will be a narrow field. They've all been suffering from emotional disorders, usually depression, anxiety or both for over five years. They've tried a range of pharmaceutical approaches prescribed by their doctors and have experienced minor relief, no relief or have simply given up and no longer take their medication. Some have moved to alternate health approaches, such as yoga, meditation, diet, exercise and herbal remedies. Some have reported that their condition is manageable, though it still exists. In short, these people are willing to try something new in order to heal. Motivation is gauged as high across this first group of volunteers.' She paused for questions; none came.

'Cases of serious mental illness that involve the likes of schizophrenia, bipolar disorder, paranoia and so on have been set to the side for now. None of us are trained in mental health, and we need a solid start to the project for this first stage, which will give us a baseline.

Raz spoke up. 'If we don't have an emotional disorder and we go through the experiment ourselves, does that matter?'

'No, Raz, it just becomes an exploratory experience. Perhaps there may be one small thing that you'd like to explore, though. Life happens along the way for all of us.' He nodded and Celeste continued, 'I'll work with each of you this week. Our subjects will start to arrive from next week. When they do, we'll ask them to complete a self-assessment as to their emotional state. This will be on a graduated scale of one through to ten. The main scores are as follows: a self-score of one means very depressed, sad, anxious or angry; a self-score of five means they're doing okay or managing; ten means they're great, enthusiastic and/or peaceful.

'Where they place themselves on the scale will help us understand our start point. We expect most of them to be in the one to four range. Then I will hand them over to you in your lab room. You'll ask them to sit in the recliner chair, and once you place the finger pulse device on them, the equipment and software will do the rest. They'll track the heart coherence in the subject and the disruption in the environment for the duration of the experiment.

'You'll work with the subject to create a unique personal intention for the experiment. It's important that they engage in this part as it will activate their own observer effect, or intention, if you like. For example, for a subject who feels depressed and heavy, it may be helpful to have an intention like "I will be light and free", whereas a subject with social anxiety may use "I will feel comfortable in all places and situations". We're simply formatting a hypothesis that matches a transcended state to the one the subject has entered the experiment with. They're creating an observer effect for the new reality, not the old one.

'Next, using a specifically worded document, you'll take them on a journey, expanding them into the quantum field of possibility. At this point, they will drift into a state of being beyond the person they came in as. This offers connection to the super observer, and you'll sense the change in the environment. There is every chance that the equipment will reflect this also.

'Then you'll ask that super observer two questions. The first is "What is the greater purpose of the condition?" This will elicit a response that brings insight, made possible by the expansion into this higher dimension. Then we'll ask a final question, "How will life now be forever changed?" Once you have all this information, you can ease them back into this reality. When complete, they come back to me, and I ask them to rescore themselves on the one to ten scale. Are there any questions so far?'

'I'm hoping this makes more sense once we've gone through the steps a few times,' Grace said. 'I get the general idea, though seeing it in action will be helpful.'

The others nodded or murmured their agreement.

By the end of the day, they were ready for the next step—the opportunity to experience this for themselves.

The following day, Raz was first up. He looked like an eclectic mix of excitement and trepidation as Celeste placed the oximeter on his finger. 'Is there something in your own emotions you want to observe, Raz?'

'I don't have anxiety or depression tendencies like the first group of subjects,' he said. 'If I had to find something, it would be about my father. Sometimes, I feel his expectations are hard to meet. Though we get on okay. I'm not sure if that's the kind of thing you're after?'

'How would you state this as an intention for our observer effect?' Celeste asked.

'I'd like to experience his support rather than his judgement.' Clearly, Raz had given this some thought.

'Perfect. Let's begin.' Celeste had been watching the screen on the laptop as they spoke. When Raz stated his intention, the readings calmed. His heart resonance rose and the disruption in the room fell. It was as though the environment within him and around him was responding to his intention.

They both closed their eyes. Celeste did what Bob had done for her. She saw Raz as part of the quantum field and held 'the knowing' that he was more than he knew himself to be. As she connected with him, this knowing passed to him also. Years of meditative practices helped Raz as his awareness drifted outside his body. Celeste then used the words Paul had designed for her to specifically activate the quantum potentials in the field:

'You are one with the field of quantum potential. Everything is within your reach. You are so much more than Raz, and you drift effortlessly to the wisdom held in the field that allows him to experience support from his father … Moving beyond Raz now and looking back at him, what do you sense in the field?'

A voice came from Raz that was somehow similar but different. 'He is troubled, though he hides it well.'

'Tell me more,' Celeste prompted.

'He holds it around his heart. He is sensitive, and his father's criticism is held there. For years, it has grown, and they are now mostly out of contact. The father feels rejected now also.'

'What is the greater purpose of his father's criticism?'

'His father wants him to be his best. He offers what he received when he was young. It is a pure intention, poorly delivered. Underneath the criticism is a love that a father has for his son. The father knows no other way to deliver this message …'

'How will life be forever changed from knowing this?' Celeste asked.

'This offers a new perspective … a deeper understanding. A new beginning … and they can choose to be different together. They will speak of this, and they will heal.'

Celeste paused and glanced over at the laptop. The heart resonance score was at 100%, and Raz had an air of complete peace about him. Most importantly, though, the disruption in the field in the room was zero. It was a moment of complete resonance, and both fields were aligned. The scientist in Celeste wanted to analyse, though that would come later.

Raz's awareness returned to his body, and he opened his eyes. He sat quietly as a tear ran down his cheek. He left it there and looked at Celeste in awe and wonder. 'What just happened?' he asked quietly.

'You found the answer you needed.'

'I feel so much lighter,' he said. 'It's a little surreal. I think I need a moment to understand what just happened.'

'Why don't you go out and sit in the garden for a little while and then we can talk more?'

He nodded, rose from the chair and wandered outside.

Celeste considered what had happened. One of the benefits of Raz, Skye and Grace having their own experiences as subjects was that Celeste had a chance herself to witness the changes firsthand. She'd neglected to use the one-to-ten rating scale for Raz, though they could discuss that later. What was interesting to her was that the closer Raz came to 100% heart resonance, the disruption in the broader field within the room came closer to zero. Did the ratings change as a result of the other, or were they just one field measured differently? She needed more data.

After about fifteen minutes, Raz came back in. They sat in the lounge area and debriefed. 'Can you tell me what is happening for you now, Raz?' Celeste asked.

He paused before saying, 'I'm experiencing a feeling as though a burden has been lifted, I guess. It's weird, as I'd like to actually see my dad. It's like I understand more of why he is who he is. He migrated here to give his kids a better life. I guess he just went overboard in the message.'

'What's happening around your heart?'

'It feels quite clear, though I hadn't even realised that this had been an issue. It's certainly different now.'

Celeste handed him the one-to-ten-evaluation scale. 'What do you think before and after look like?'

'Well ... I think I started at a four or five, as I felt reasonably okay. But I'm certainly up around an eight or nine now. I needed to understand the after so I could know the before, but there's a big shift in me.'

They spoke a little longer, and then Celeste said, 'Raz, would you like to take the rest of the day off and go see your dad?'

'Yes. I actually would, Celeste. Thank you so much.'

Celeste made some notes on her wall of paper in her office and then updated the project materials. Late in the day, she received a text message from Raz:

> *I went to see my dad, and I told him that I knew*
> *he was just trying to help me. I said I was sorry for*

being so distant. We both cried, and he hugged me.
Then my mum cried even more than us. I guess
it was troubling them more than me. I feel like
something amazing happened today, and I can't
thank you enough.

Celeste smiled. The first experiment had been a success, certainly from the feedback offered. Perhaps they were really onto something.

She had a sense of Bob, away in the distance, also smiling.

CHAPTER 29

A week later, they gathered around the meeting table once more but with a different energy, as they'd all experienced being a subject.

Celeste led the conversation. 'I'd like to debrief our experiences into the super observer. I know each of you has personal experience of this now, and I don't wish to intrude on something private. However, in the interests of care for our subjects, the more we can all share now, the better we can support them during the experiment. We'll have other conversations about process and measurement, and those are important for us to establish a standard approach across all subjects. For now, though, I'll ask you to share what you witnessed from the quantum-field super observer looking back at your human presence.'

She paused, knowing the best way to open the group up was to start with herself. 'I'm happy to begin … Around three years ago, I lost my father in a car accident. Six months later, my mother died of cancer, and I nursed her through the final period. For the next two years, I went through the motions of life, unaware that I was numb. It was the only way I knew how to keep the pain at bay. When I moved into my super observer, I was able to see all this as I've just explained it to you. It feels that from another expanded perspective, this reality looks different. It was like being in another dimension, looking back into this one. In that moment of insight, I saw that my pain was a choice. So I made a decision to let it go, and now I'm different in ways that are hard to imagine.' She paused, seeing the group was moved.

Abbey spoke up. 'Can I go next?'

Celeste nodded.

'I thought I was okay 'til Celeste took me into my supergirl, or whatever you guys call it.' Gentle laughs came from all round. 'I could see I was still carrying some old thoughts from a bad marriage. I didn't even know they were there 'til I had a look from outside. I'd just thought I couldn't find the right boyfriend. I'm seeing someone now, and so far, so good.'

There were a few grins at Abbey's down-to-earth sharing.

Raz spoke next and shared the story of his relationship with his father. Words of encouragement from the others followed.

Grace went next. 'I've been lonely since my children left home nine months ago. One has moved to another city for a great job, the other has travelled overseas and wants to work in Europe for a while. As a single mother for so many years, they've been everything to me. I sat in the super observer and saw that instead of my own pain of loss, I could hold in my heart the joy of their blossoming into the lives they deserve. That set me free to explore what's next for myself. I saw that, as Grace, I was holding myself back, and now I'm not. For the first time in many years, I'm excited about what lies ahead.'

Empathy flowed for each other's experiences. They all turned to Skye.

She'd waited until last, and she sighed deeply before she

shared. 'A year ago, my cat, Sunbeam, died. I heard a screech of brakes on the road outside and ran out to find her on the footpath in a terrible state. She died in my arms a few minutes later. Since that time, I'd been having flashbacks, and at night when I closed my eyes and tried to sleep, I could see her broken body. I was diagnosed with trauma and offered medication. I declined and chose to try to heal it myself, and I'd made some small steps. When I went into my super observer, I could clearly see the damaged particles in my body still holding the energy of the event. I decided to heal them, and from that moment, they changed. The trauma was just gone instantly. It's been five nights since my experience as the subject, I've had no flashbacks and I'm sleeping like a baby. I'm literally blown away by this!'

Murmurs of support came around the table.

Celeste gave them a moment before continuing. 'Thanks to all of you for sharing your thoughts. I feel that we're running two fields of endeavour here: we have our scientific interest, and we also have human subjects who're to be supported. We'll find a way to balance our efforts across both spheres, and like the quantum field itself, given everything is connected, we can't make the distinction of separation.'

They all nodded.

'We have our first four subjects coming in tomorrow,' Celeste went on. 'The same number on Thursday and Friday. I'll debrief you after each experiment, though make sure you keep notes for each subject on the server. It'll be great to have the data from the equipment, though I want all details of subjects entered into the database for cross referencing, validation of trends and the highlighting of patterns. Within a few weeks, we'll start to look at some of the data trends.'

The first day went smoothly. Raz took four people through the experiment and captured all data. Each subject was slightly different in the super-observer state and had different intentions set before they started. It seemed like they'd need a significant number of subjects before seeing the common trends.

On the second day, Skye's third subject left her lab room and came out to face Celeste. The woman looked deeply into Celeste's eyes for a moment, then threw her arms around her in a hug that lifted Celeste off her feet and almost popped her spine.

Their eyes met once more, and the woman said, 'Thank you … just thank you.' Then she was out the front door, taking off in her car and leaving behind a cloud of smoke.

Skye came out of her lab room, and Celeste turned to her and asked, 'What was that about?'

'I think we need to debrief this one.' Skye handed Celeste the file.

Celeste looked it over. Amanda Collins, 'Mandy', had been struggling with depression for two decades and had been heavily medicated on and off over that time. She'd been on a mental health plan for the last ten years following a suicide attempt. Her family had a history of depression, and she'd been much worse since she lost a four-year-old daughter to leukemia. That was twenty years ago. Celeste nodded. 'Okay, I clearly see a difficult past. Tell me about the readings.'

'On the subjective scale, she rated herself one out of ten— "plagued by depression, anxiety and can't even get out of bed some days" were her actual words. Heart coherence was close to zero, and the randomisation from the event machine was nearly one hundred per cent—full disruption.'

'What intention did you set for the initial observer effect?' Celeste asked.

'To be peaceful and joyful.'

'Okay. Walk me through what happened.'

'Usual protocols and standard approach. Then all of a

sudden, she went to super, immediately. Heart coherence shot to one hundred per cent, disruption went to zero. It was like she left her body; she was just gone, and no-one was there. Then a voice came, no chance to ask the usual questions. The voice said that she had incarnated into this family line to break patterns of intergenerational trauma that came through both lines. She'd misjudged the sensitivities of this body and had fallen into that same pattern, carrying the burden of generations past. The loss of her child twenty years ago had kept her stuck in the loop. The suicide attempt ten years ago was unsuccessful, as she has work to do to serve others. In the middle of all this, I managed to get one single question in: "How will life be different now?" Her response was, "By bringing this pattern into her awareness, the cycle is broken and it is done." I just sat there, and she came back. She'd seen her four-year-old daughter waving at her and blowing kisses, letting her know she's all right.

'But here's the thing; she stayed at one hundred per cent coherence and zero per cent disruption after she was back. She scored herself a ten out of ten on the subjective scale, hugged me like there was no tomorrow and ran out to see you. I guess you got the same.'

'Yes … and I'm still recovering,' Celeste admitted. 'A remarkable response to the experiment, Skye. I have to say it warms my heart to hear of Mandy's shift. I'm not sure how to record this in the database, but do your best. Flag it as significant on the human dimension. Did you schedule the two and four-week follow-ups?'

'Yes, she had the dates before we started.'

'Okay, let's see how she is when she comes back …'

CHAPTER 30

The information obtained for Project Shed grew, and Celeste continued to refine the processes. One night, she sat in her office, working, when a knock came at the front door. A late visitor was rare, so she was wary.

She turned on the outside light and opened the door, still holding the security chain. A woman stood there, looking somewhat distressed.

Celeste watched her carefully. 'Hello, what can I do for you?'

'I'm sorry to disturb you this late, but I can't wait any longer. My name is Virginia Gregory, and I have important information for you about your family.'

Celeste hesitated, read her energy and noted that Virginia looked somehow familiar, seemed sincere and was in distress. 'Please come in, Virginia.' She led her into the waiting room and, once they were seated, asked, 'What's all this about?'

'I'll start at the beginning,' the woman said, 'though let me first say that I came to your institute last week as one of the first who volunteered for Project Shed. I'd been struggling with

PTSD for a long time and haven't worked for over two years.'
That's why she seems familiar.

Virginia continued. 'I'm doing so much better and now see the terrible thing that happened to me as a turning point. Thanks to you, I have my life back. Before then, I was on a path to destruction.'

Quite an opening. And also a watershed moment in someone's life. She stayed silent, and with a nod, encouraged Virginia to continue. She didn't have to wait long.

'I was a medical examiner for fifteen years, though I left that job over two years ago.'

A chill ran down Celeste's spine.

'I was on shift the night they brought your father in after his accident. I performed the examination and later wrote a detailed report. We met that night when you came to identify him, though I'm sure you don't remember me.'

Virginia was right; Celeste had been in shock. The police had taken her to the morgue at the bottom of the mountains. There, she had identified her father's body. The energy she'd felt that evening came back, and she shuddered at the memory of it. 'Keep going,' Celeste said, steeling herself.

'I did a full examination, blood work and all the usual tests, then the autopsy. I just want you to know that I never found any drugs in your father's system.'

'Then why did the toxicology report say there were?' Celeste felt as if she'd gone a little pale.

'I was working late one night by myself when a man came into my office unannounced. He showed me a photo on his phone of my children with him in the background. He said that if I wanted to keep them safe, I had to change my findings. He gave me a substitute toxicology report and told me to put it in the file.'

'I was terrified and did what he said. Within a few months, I'd had a breakdown and took stress leave. Then I left altogether. I felt it was the only way to protect my family. Ever since, I've carried the shame of what I did and the fear of my family being hurt. Then your work came into my life and has helped me so much. Ever since then, I've been plagued by the deepest guilt.' Virginia collapsed in a flood of tears.

Celeste moved across to sit next to her and put an arm around her shoulders. 'Thank you for telling me, Virginia. A part of me always suspected something like this, though to have you share this with me helps more than you know.'

'I can only imagine someone wanted to damage his reputation, but that's all I know.'

Once Virginia had calmed down, Celeste asked, 'How well do you remember his case file?'

'I have an excellent memory, well trained over many years. When I was in that role, we often had to give evidence at coronial enquiries. Your father's case was also burned into my memory, given what happened.'

A memory came back to Celeste from a few months ago when she'd first met Abbey's Reiki teacher. When her father appeared to Chantelle, she'd said something about his wrists. 'Was there anything strange about his wrists?' she asked.

Virginia paused and searched her memory. 'Yes. There were hairs missing on both wrists. We often see it on men who wore a metal-banded wristwatch; it pulls the hairs away and leaves that area almost hairless. Your father had that, so I assumed he wore both a watch and some jewellery on his other arm. It's rarer in accident victims because they often still have their jewellery on. From memory, your father didn't.'

'When else do you usually see wrist hair missing?'

'In cases of foul play when the victim's wrists have been

bound,' she replied.

'If I tell you my father never wore a watch or jewellery of any kind, what would you deduce?'

Virginia inhaled slowly and then said quietly, 'That it's possible his wrists were bound with tape, as that would pull hairs out. There were no signs of damage to his wrists, so he would've been compliant or already unconscious when he was bound.'

Celeste felt as if the colour had been stripped from her world. 'Virginia, I'd like you to keep this conversation to yourself until I can work out what it means. For now, it's important to leave this just between us.'

'Yes, of course.'

Something unspoken passed between the two women. Virginia appeared much relieved, her guilt no doubt assuaged, and for Celeste, the revelation validated her faith in her father's character. They'd also become co-conspirators in a scenario that neither of them wanted to contemplate. Celeste had absolutely no idea what to do about it.

CHAPTER 31

Several weeks later, the five of them once again took their places around the table. Grace sat at the end with her laptop open and a data show plugged in, throwing images on the wall at the end of the room. 'We've finished the first group of fifty subjects,' she said, 'and initial trends have been analysed. It's a small sample, but the results are very interesting. We've seen already that heart resonance in quantum field local, the subject, and the level of disruption in the quantum field non-local, the lab room, are mirroring each other, validating as opposites. The higher the resonance, the lower the disruption. These are measured by two completely separate systems and targeting the local and non-local fields in parallel in real time.'

They nodded, aware of this already.

'We have seven time points of measurement. We take the first measure when they join us in the room, the second when they set their intention, the third when they relax into their observer effect, then the fourth when they go super. Immediately after the session is complete, we take their readings as the fifth point, then the two-week follow-up and four-week follow-up as the sixth and seventh. These points are accurate because we're using the timestamps in the audio logs.'

Some line graphs flashed up on the wall. 'Let's take resonance, disruption and the self-score one at a time,' Grace continued. 'These are the average scores over the fifty experiments to date. Heart resonance first: when they enter the room, they're at twenty per cent. After the intention or observer effect has been set, resonance rises to thirty-five per cent. Then, as we relax them into the experiment, resonance reads at fifty per cent. Here's the big shift; when they go super, we see a spike to one hundred per cent heart resonance. After the experiment is complete and their awareness returns, they're at ninety per cent.

'The two-week measurement, when they come back and discuss the life they're living following the experiment, shows they have an average of eighty per cent heart resonance. In the handful of four-week readings available, it appears that score has remained stable, though it's too early to confirm. Early data shows that resonance has increased fourfold, or three hundred per cent, in comparison to the subject's original arrival for the experiment. In words anyone can understand, it looks like this: They are four times better off than when they first arrived, and that shift is sustainable some weeks later.' Grace paused for a moment until that sunk in. 'Now let's look at disruption, otherwise known as randomness. Using the same measurement time points: As they enter the room, disruption is measured at sixty per cent for the environment. After the intention and observer effect has been set, we read it at fifty per cent. When they relax into the experiment, disruption of the system drops again to thirty per cent, and wait for it … when they expand into super observer, they drop to zero per cent disruption.' Grace paused for effect.

Celeste spoke first. 'How can this be, Grace? All systems have some level of disruption since they aren't perfect. Zero disruption isn't possible.'

Grace spoke slowly and deliberately. 'It's only possible under a single condition.'

'What would that be?' Raz asked, though Celeste, having worked it out already, sat with her mouth open, stunned.

Grace replied to Raz, 'That which you are measuring has left the system.'

Silence.

'Go on, Grace, spell it out for all of us,' Celeste said.

'When the subject goes super, they have one hundred per cent heart coherence, which means they must be beyond human emotion. They're also at zero per cent disruption, which basically means the system is empty and nothing in the room can be measured. There are also no outside influences, as we're effectively in a Faraday cage. It's too early for confirmation, though I have a working hypothesis: the subject is no longer in this dimension.' She sat back and watched their faces.

'But they're talking to us,' Skye said.

Grace explained. 'The body is relaying verbal messages, even responding to our questions. Though I sense that super is sending those from elsewhere, just like radio frequencies. The super knows the channel to send the message back to us. The subject has become some sort of multidimensional radio transmitter.'

Abbey asked, 'But each of you is in the room with the client as well. Why wouldn't you affect the system?' She looked to Celeste for the answer.

Celeste looked at Raz. 'Tell her, Raz; it was your brilliant idea.'

'We each have our own unique readings,' he said. 'I measured them and recalibrated the system to exclude our own impacts on the experimental environment. This is why we can't use each other's lab rooms. The adjustments are unique to each of us, and it effectively makes us invisible to the system.'

Abbey nodded in understanding.

'Can you tell us more about the "after" readings for disruption, Grace?' Celeste asked.

She nodded. 'As I said, in super the disruption is zero per cent, though when the experiment is complete, the environment comes back to fifteen per cent. Interestingly, that same figure holds at the two-week mark and potentially continues at four weeks. The interesting thing is we have the same margin, given we started at sixty per cent disruption at time point one and fifteen per cent at time point six or even seven. We have a fourfold factor again. Disruption is twenty-five per cent of what we started at. So again, we have validation that they are four times better off than when they first arrived, and that shift is sustainable some weeks later. In short, four times as much coherence and one-quarter as much disruption in relation to the subject's point of entry into the system. The two systems, that are completely separate, validate each other.'

'What about the subject's self-assessments?' Celeste asked.

'On that score from one to ten, where one is depressed, anxious and so on, five is doing okay and managing, and ten is great, enthusiastic and so on, we only have four time points. Immediately before and then after the experiment, then two and four weeks. It's less accurate, though it gives us insights into the subject's personal perception of the change. They usually average around a two before the experiment. Immediately afterwards, they are around a nine, then they settle into an eight at both two and four weeks.

The team watched her with unwavering concentration.

'Those first two time measures are again showing a fourfold increase in self-assessed mood. What is most encouraging is that they're sustaining the change four weeks out. It appears that after they've gone to their super observer to obtain a greater understanding of what's happening in their lives, the original condition being targeted has been completely desensitised. In essence, the subjective personal data confirms the technical readings. Our subjects are noticeably different once they've gone through the experiment. Though apparently there are some side effects that are starting to emerge in the four-week debriefs.'

'Go on. What are they?' Celeste said.

'Subjects are reporting that they have more energy, improvement in close relationships and those who've been self-medicating or using pharmaceutical drugs no longer appear to need or use them. The sense of wellbeing evident in the self-scores is spilling over into all areas of their lives. Bear in mind we're still a smaller four-week sample, though the trend is unanimous. In summary, it's still early days, though what we're seeing is that those who've participated in Project Shed are never the same again. The change in their lives is for the better and on an exponential scale. It appears to be permanent, powerful and is completely measurable on three separate systems.'

'Do you have any other conclusions, Grace?'

'Just a couple,' she replied. 'First, the local and non-local fields are working as one field. What happens in the subject immediately affects the area around them. They're quantumly entangled with the whole lab environment, not just their human body. I suspect we'll know more as the project continues, though evidence is building that we can affect particles in the universe beyond our immediate body.

'Second, the super-observer effect is supporting the subjects. Once they go super, they heal at some level in a permanent way. The super observer is not from this time and space, and the data reflects that. The subject leaves the system, goes somewhere and comes back healed. Some of our subjects have been distressed for decades and are healed in less than an hour. I'm a scientist, so I don't believe in miracles, though if I did, that's what I'd call this.'

'Higher dimensions serve the ones below them,' Celeste whispered.

'I'm sorry, Celeste, I didn't hear that,' Grace said.

'Oh, nothing really, just something a friend mentioned once. Thank you, Grace, for an enlightening status report. Any questions, anyone?'

'Is there anything we need to change?' Raz asked.

'Yes,' Celeste replied. 'We need to pick up speed and find more subjects.'

CHAPTER 32

Later that afternoon, Celeste sat in the shed connecting with Bob. She'd given him status reports until she realised he already knew what was happening anyway. So they just debriefed from time to time, or met if she had any questions. In this moment, she had a few.

What's really happening to these people, Bob?

They are remembering, Celeste. They are remembering their magnificence, remembering that they have a choice for their state of being. They are remembering that there is a greater purpose behind their experiences. They are remembering that they are indeed multidimensional beings, living in a multiverse ... Then they are expressing their free will to be different, and the people they are closest to get them back again as the person they once were before illness or tragedy struck.

What you're witnessing, Celeste, is that these people are moving back into natural resonance. They are transcending the medical and psychological models they have been trapped in.

Celeste nodded. *So where do we go from here? Within a couple of months, I'll have all the data I need for my doctorate. Though that's no longer enough for me. I've already been thinking about what comes next.*

Bob smiled. *You already know that we have to build scale. A wave makes a bigger difference than a particle. This is all part of an ever-unfolding story for all of us, and we all have a role to play. Our conversation is complete; you have a visitor.* Bob disappeared, and Celeste heard gravel crunching on the driveway.

She walked out of the shed and into the bright sunshine. A well-dressed man of around sixty had just got out of an Aston Martin Rapide. Celeste didn't know much about cars, but she knew a large price tag went with this vehicle. This was a man of means.

'Good afternoon,' she said. 'Can I help you?'

'Yes, please,' he replied. 'I'm looking for Celeste Kelly.'

'You've found her.' Celeste waited expectantly.

He moved closer and offered his hand. She shook it, finding it cool and firm. 'Gabe Collins,' he said. 'I'm very pleased to meet you. I'm sorry to drop in unannounced, but I wonder if you could spare me a few minutes?'

'Sure, Gabe.' She directed him to a bench seat on the veranda, and they sat looking out over the garden. 'What can I do for you?'

'My wife is Mandy Collins; she came here to be part of your project some weeks back. She'd been struggling emotionally for twenty years, ever since we lost our four-year-old daughter. Mandy never recovered from that tragedy, and I'd tried everything in that time to help her. After the best doctors in the country told me there was nothing more they could do, we adjusted our lives around her condition. When I saw your project in the local newspaper, I suggested she apply.' His voice quavered a little. 'We were ready to try anything.

'Mandy left the house that morning a broken woman. She was back by lunchtime, completely different. She has healed in ways unimaginable, and after all these years, I have my wife back.' He dissolved into tears of relief.

As Celeste waited respectfully for him to regain his composure, her mind wandered back to Skye's client, Mandy, who had almost crushed her spine with a hug full of gratitude.

'I'm sorry,' Gabe said. 'It's been the strangest few weeks for me.'

'Please, Gabe … it's fine,' Celeste reassured him.

Gabe continued, his voice stronger. 'I'd like to find a way to support your work so you can help others like Mandy. I know you're funded by the university and that this work is experimental, but there must be something I can do to help. I have a great deal of resources at my disposal.'

Celeste's mind raced. She'd already been thinking about rolling out the work further, and Bob had talked about a wave building. 'What type of resources are you talking about?'

'Have you heard of Collins Industries?'

Celeste nodded. 'Of course.' It was a multinational conglomerate across various industries from property development to mining and engineering. They even had a line of farm machinery that was exported all over the world.

'Well … I'm that Collins.'

'Oh …' What else could you say when you realised you were sitting next to one of the wealthiest businessmen in the country?

'Let me make it easier for you, Celeste. What are the problems you need to solve to take this to the world?'

Celeste visualised a few pages from a new wall of paper that had overflowed out to the studio recently. 'Our resources are already stretched. Word has gotten out in these small mountain communities about what's happening for the subjects—sorry,

I mean people—who've come to be part of this. I have three contractors for two days a week, and we have more enquiries than we can handle. I need them to go to five days, and I also need a full-time admin person.'

'Resources are easy,' Gabe replied. 'What are the big issues?'

Celeste paused for a moment, then decided she'd best be really open. 'It's great to have the university behind us, though at times it does come with bureaucracy. Which is sometimes necessary and yet also constraining. I'm trying to find a middle road through it all.'

He nodded. 'There are creative ways around that; leave it with me.'

Celeste got a glimpse of some of what had made Gabe who he was.

'Who are the main people at the university that you deal with?' he asked.

Celeste rattled off some names, and Gabe nodded as he heard some of them, then mentioned some of his own, which included a 'who's who' of senior faculty and university board members. 'We sponsor five scholarships in the engineering faculty and business school,' he explained. 'What's the next issue?'

'Me,' Celeste replied.

Gabe's eyebrows rose in surprise. 'How so? I've asked about you in certain circles and have usually heard great things. I'm also told you know your own mind.'

'I've been in academia all my life, Gabe,' Celeste admitted. 'My world is the realm of quantum physics; the smaller the universe is, the better I understand it. This has been my life for over twenty years. When you start to talk business and strategies to grow scale, I simply have no idea where to start.'

He chuckled. 'Celeste, I know nothing about quantum physics, and I never even went to university! I've learned about business from the ground up. The secret is to find good people and let them lead the pieces you don't know about. You then learn from them. Would it be okay if I gave some thought to what you've said and come back to you in a few days? I need to make some calls.'

'Of course.'

He handed her a card. 'My private mobile number is on this card; use it whenever you need to.' He rose and extended his hand again. 'I think that together, Celeste, we can make a difference to a great number of people.' His tone had an assuredness that came from certainty that it would happen; it was just a matter of when.

He headed down the stairs, then stopped halfway, turned and said, 'By the way, I met your father. He advised my company on a few projects, and his advice made a big difference. I didn't know him well, though I always felt he was a good man. I was sorry to hear of his accident.' Then he was gone.

Celeste watched his car glided effortlessly down the driveway, sensing a little more 'Bob energy' unfolding behind the scenes.

CHAPTER 33

Celeste's phone rang early one morning. What made the call remarkable was that it was from the university president, Professor Robinson. 'Good morning, Celeste, how is it all going with Project Shed?'

Used to the politics involved in these matters, she said, 'Our findings to date have exceeded expectations, and we look forward to sharing them soon. In all, the project looks healthy, and I really feel we're breaking new ground.'

'That's good to hear,' the professor said. 'There have been some developments. A proposal was put to the university board last night by Gabriel Collins. I believe you met him last week. He has been a wonderful benefactor for us for many years. We've accepted his proposal on the proviso that you're comfortable with it, and he has asked to brief you personally. You should hear from him today. After that, I'd like to hear from you as to how you feel about what he's offering.'

'Yes, of course. I'll be in touch soon afterwards,' she replied, a little stunned.

'Thank you, Celeste. I'm hearing great things about what you're doing up there in the mountains.' He rang off, leaving Celeste wondering what he was talking about.

She didn't have long to wait. Gabe rang within the hour. 'Do you have some time to meet with me this afternoon?'

'Of course,' she replied.

Later that day, his car glided up the driveway. Celeste showed him inside, and they sat in her office.

'Have you heard from the university?' he asked.

'Yes, Professor Robinson called me this morning. He said you'd put forward a proposal. That's all I know.'

He took two folders out of his briefcase and handed one to her. 'This gives all the details. I'd like you to review it and let me know what you think. Meanwhile, let me give you the high-level proposal … I'm proposing a research institute be set up as a not-for-profit organisation that expands the work you're doing. It'll be a joint venture between the University of New South Wales and Collins Industries. In short, what that means is that UNSW provides the staff and expertise, while Collins Industries supplies the funding. The brief of this organisation is to undertake cutting-edge research into quantum physics, specifically designed to serve humanity. Whilst this institute will rely on UNSW for resources and Collins Industries for funding, it will function as its own entity with its own infrastructure and be reasonably independent. It will be overseen by a board of six. Two from the university, two from Collins Industries, plus you and another person of your choosing. In short, you'll be asked to function as both a board member and as the executive director of the institute.'

Gabe spoke for another ten minutes, in language unfamiliar to her, about business, though she was smart enough to understand what he was offering. He was building the infrastructure around the work they were doing, which would take it to a much larger scale. He'd kept the university involved, so they would get the research kudos, while Collins Industries would be seen as moving into new areas beyond engineering and doing good things for the world. Instead of just spreading her wings, she was being given a rocket ship.

Gabe continued, 'I know this idea looks enormous, and you may not feel ready; however, just know that we will have people advising you every step of the way.'

Celeste looked him in the eye. 'Actually, I feel I've been getting ready for this all my life, perhaps even longer.'

He chuckled, not realising that she wasn't joking. 'I intend to chair the board myself, and I'll also bring my chief operating officer along, as he has reach across all my companies and resources. The university has nominated the head of the science faculty and also Dr Bart Kindred from the school of physics. They thought he would be a good nomination because he's been across the development of your work already. There is, of course, yourself, and do you have someone else you'd like to nominate?'

'Possibly. I know a research psychologist who has been a little bored of late. I'll let you know.' Paul could bring so much to the table that would stretch the minds of the others.

'So, Celeste, do you accept the role?'

She nodded. 'I do. I'll get to the finer details later.' Something felt so right inside, and she recognised that an incredibly significant moment for this lifetime had arrived.

'Then, let me welcome you as the executive director. What do you need first?'

'On the people side, I'd like to move my three staff to full-time contracts, effective immediately. Also, I'd like to hire an admin manager who will also serve as my assistant, and I have someone in mind. This place is going to get busy, so I need the driveway out front to be extended into a small car park, for, say, a dozen cars. Beyond that, I'd like to have a quiet space in the garden where our subjects can relax following their sessions—many of them are arriving from further away now … Oh, and I need someone to build us a website.'

'Consider it done,' Gabe said. 'One last thing. This research institute needs a name, and we decided that given it's your house being used and this is the work you started, the naming rights should fall to you. Anything come to mind?'

Without hesitation, she replied, 'The Research Institute for Quantum Metaphysics. Let's go with RIQM for short.'

Gabe paused and looked out the window momentarily, as if feeling into her words. 'Hmm … I like it. I like it a lot.'

CHAPTER 34

The Tuesday meeting was interesting. Raz, Skye and Grace were delighted to hear that they were coming on full time. Abbey needed a little more convincing, and so Celeste had a chat with her as they walked in the garden.

'Abs, I need you. You have insights that don't come naturally to me,' Celeste explained.

'Lest, I'm grateful for the opportunity, but my other work is so important to me. Besides, I have to say that "admin manager" sounds incredibly boring, even if the pay is good,' she replied.

'Well, how about if we get you to work four days a week? We can teach you to facilitate some of the sessions for the subjects as well and you can see the changes in them. You may find this'll offer you another form of healing work.'

Abbey tilted her head thoughtfully, warming to the idea. 'Okay, I'll give it a go.'

The team was complete … for now.

The next few weeks flew by. New resources and funding made an incredible difference, and Celeste was kept busy planning where the work would head under the new research institute.

She sat in her office lost in thought one afternoon when a car pulled up on the gravel outside. She peered out the window at the unfamiliar vehicle. Two men emerged, and she recognised one of them as a well-known medical doctor who'd once been mayor of the Blue Mountains. The local paper often quoted him for his medical perspective and expertise on a range of local issues. He introduced himself as Dr Snyders and his colleague as Dr Irons, who he said ran one of the largest psychology networks in the region.

'There is a matter we'd like to discuss with you, please, Ms Kelly.'

The men's energy had a formality that didn't bode well for a collaborative conversation, but Celeste invited them into her office to a small table around which the three of them could sit. 'What's all this about?' she asked politely.

Snyders said, 'For some time now, we've been receiving information about the work you are doing here. It's having an impact on our patients. I've had conversations with many who are now refusing their medications, claiming some form of healed state that makes them unnecessary. I'm not sure you understand the risk of people who need to be medicated not complying. These people move through the general community in a state of unchecked mental illness, which has a negative impact on society.'

Irons then contributed to the conversation. 'I have a large number of cancelled appointments across various clinics throughout the area. People are saying the issues that we've been managing for them no longer exist. When we enquire how this happened, they point the finger in your direction, saying they've been part of an experiment you've been running.'

Snyders continued, 'We have reason to believe that you are

conducting medical experiments on the general population, through apparatus used to conduct something like shock therapy. It is our intention to resolve this amicably before we bring a formal complaint against you.'

Celeste bristled, fire in her belly, and she was about to let them have it with both barrels. She'd had to defend her work before, and she'd always done so with steely resolve, surgical precision and a big energy that defied her smaller human form. Abbey loved to call this a 'full-blown Aries attack', given that was her star sign, not that she believed much in astrology.

Suddenly, she felt a familiar energy at her side, the first time she'd sensed Bob outside the shed. His voice sounded in her mind. *Take a breath. Here before you are examples of the mindsets that we need to replace. These people represent the old system and the old ways. They are simply echoing the mindsets of those beyond themselves. There will be many of these conversations in the years ahead, handle them with skill … in a way that serves humanity.*

Celeste took a deep breath, exhaled slowly, then said, 'I have a few questions, if I may?'

'Go ahead,' Snyders said.

'My first question is: How many of these patients are in a worse condition than before they came here? Has their mental health deteriorated further?'

'Well, some appear to be delusional in that they believe they are cured.'

'Can I see your research on their deteriorated conditions, please? I'd like to compare it to the self-assessments completed by the subjects themselves, and also to our data measuring their emotional state through finger pulse machines for heart coherence. This is the only machine we use on the participants, by the way. You see, I have scientific data showing the opposite of your claims.' She was just getting warmed up.

'Those are confidential patient records and cannot be shared on ethical grounds,' Snyders said.

'Well, you will have some data, of course. Can I ask how many prescriptions you write weekly now compared to before our project commenced?'

Snyders shrugged. 'I don't know that number off-hand.'

'Surely it's fewer, otherwise you wouldn't be here expressing your concerns.' Celeste moved her firm gaze from face to face. The two men were clearly becoming increasingly uncomfortable. She turned her attention to Irons.

'Dr Irons, at what capacity do your clinics run now compared to several months ago?'

'We're running at about sixty per cent of previous levels.'

At least this one knew his business. 'And this is due to cancellations?' Celeste asked.

'Both cancellations and a decrease in new patients. In short, many of my clients who normally come for ten sessions are dropping out and coming here after just one or two appointments with us. After that, we never see them again.'

'I see. I would imagine that the role of our mental health system is to make people better, am I right?'

'Of course,' they replied in unison.

'So your method for doing this is a combination of medication and ten psychology appointments. Do you have a plan to get people off the medication, Dr Snyders?'

'We continue to monitor their progress regularly,' he replied.

'I'll take that as a 'no', then. Dr Irons, how many people are completely cured after ten sessions?'

'What they learn in their ten sessions is how to manage their condition. In many cases, it can't be cured. They learn to live with it, and we help them have a better way of life.'

Celeste nodded. 'Let me see if I can summarise this, then.

You have a system that doesn't really cure people, and you have ongoing medication approaches, risking possible side effects, and you don't have a plan to get them off these medications. So the summary is that chemical suppression and management of emotional symptoms is your preferred method, and this is called the "mental health system". How am I going so far?'

'Your arrogance is astounding,' Snyders blustered. 'Our health systems are the best in the Western world.'

'Yet people don't get cured; they're taught to manage their condition.' She stared him down. 'As for my arrogance, it pales into insignificance when compared to yours.' She didn't stop there. 'So what you're saying is that a quantum physicist running some experiments with volunteers has done more for the mental health of the Blue Mountains' residents in the past few months than the two of you have done with all of your resources and experience over many years.' She raised an eyebrow in challenge. 'One last question, if I may. Is the mental health in our society getting better or worse?'

Irons answered, looking quite distressed. 'It's at an all-time high and getting worse.'

'Then, gentlemen, I suggest you do some soul searching about the roles you're playing in that. I'll leave you with a tip from someone I admire: Albert Einstein. "You can't solve a problem at the same level of thinking at which it was created." I suggest you do something different if you want a different result. It's certainly working for us.'

They stood abruptly and left. As they walked out the door and down the steps, Snyders called out, 'You haven't heard the last of this. You can expect a formal complaint about your little experiment.'

'Actually, we aren't a little experiment,' Celeste replied. 'We're a not-for-profit organisation that is a joint venture between

Collins Industries and the University of New South Wales. You should search the internet for the Research Institute for Quantum Metaphysics. Our website has a lot of information about what we do, and I'm sure our lawyers would love to hear from you.' The last bit was a cheap shot, but it felt good to her.

She came out of her 'Aries attack', wondering what she'd put in motion.

CHAPTER 35

During a sleepless night, she realised just how invested she was in the work she was doing and the purpose behind it. She went to the shed to connect with Bob.

Celeste took a seat, closed her eyes and took a breath.

Bob arrived almost instantaneously. *Hello, Celeste; how are you feeling?*

I'm a little bruised after yesterday's encounter, Bob. Though it was helpful to understand that some of this won't be as easy as it has been so far, she replied mentally. *Yesterday was the first time we've connected outside the shed. Why was that?*

Two reasons, he replied. *First, you needed the support in that moment, and I wanted you to know you won't face these mindsets alone. Second, I had hoped to settle your energy so that you could be both powerful and personable.*

Did I do the wrong thing? she asked.

You exercised your free will, Celeste. They did come to intimidate you and test the water. You let them know what they are up against. They won't try that again. They are defending a system that is in decline, and they are enrolled in it right to the end. It is simply their conditioning, and they believe in what they do. That deeper enrolment blinkers them to the limitations of the system of which they are a part.

So what's the best approach for me, then?

It is best not to fight the old ways. Just build life-changing approaches and invite people to embrace them, exercising their free will. That is in alignment with cosmic law, and so it will always be successful. Remember, when you align with cosmic law, you will prevail.

That sounds like another of those laws you told me about.

It is. Bob smiled. *A very powerful one, and it will take you towards your destiny. Let me offer something else, though.*

Please do.

Judgement is not the path, as it leads to anger and separation, making it harder for you in the long run. Do not judge a whole system by its representatives. They will usually echo the culture of the system of which they are a part; however, not all will feel that way, and in that smaller number comes opportunity.

Celeste frowned. *Spell it out for me, Bob; I haven't had much sleep.*

He smiled again with that eternal patience energy. *The medical system is full of good people who are trying to do the best they can with the mindsets they have been offered. Some of them have come to their own conclusions and supplement their knowledge with other sources. They are the diamonds in the earth and can be found in ever-increasing numbers. The industry is slowly turning back towards openness and true scientific exploration. Those with open minds are seeking a new solution, and we will offer them that.*

Celeste, your human personality is strong, and you chose it specifically for what you will be doing in this life. You are also a scientific purist, and that, too, is important. If something isn't working, what do you do?

Start over in another way, she replied instantly.

And if you come across something that is outside the parameters of experience? he asked.

Understand it, and by doing so, you stretch the box into new territory.

Indeed. That is what true science is—the investigation of new methods and solutions to old problems. It is about seeking new horizons. The medical and psychological models reject new thoughts and experiences, and, therefore, they are no longer following science. They have become a culture, a way of doing things supported by a business model which sustains that culture. By offering true science, you help repair the world. By offering metascience, you will help evolve the world. Celeste, there are many in the medical industry biding their time, waiting for the culture to change. Many joined with the intention to help people heal, and some of them are doing that within a system that doesn't always embrace it. In time, you will bring those new ideas into their line of sight. Your role is to win their hearts and minds, not to move to anger and judgment of those who are anchored in the old ways.

You have a choice to make about the leadership you will offer. You can take the path of the warrior and fight for what is right, or you can lead from an evolved consciousness, which comes from a place of peace and wisdom. I will honour your choice, of course; under cosmic law, though, I ask that you feel into the history of humanity and track the results of the warrior energy across time before you decide the path of leadership to pursue.

Celeste let out a long breath. In Bob's simple way, he'd pointed out the deeper root cause of most of humanity's problems. If they were to build a better world, they needed to do something different. She smiled at the irony. He'd offered her something like the Einstein quote that she'd used on Snyders and Irons.

She pondered a moment, then asked, *When you say I chose my personality with this life in mind, what exactly do you mean?*

Each thread in the tapestry has a role to play; each of those threads are woven in a way that supports the others around it and performs the role for which it was threaded in the first place. Each of your lives is a different thread. Many are close to each other. Others are further away. They are in many colours, though collectively they create a pattern.

What does the tapestry represent? she asked.

You can call it the multiverse, if you'd like. We just call it 'all there is'.

She shook her head, trying to understand. *Okay, back to this thread, then. It's called 'Celeste', and it has a role to play?*

Of course; they all do. Some threads are very important. A particular one can hold many others together and make one part of the tapestry come to life, showing colours that wouldn't be possible without it. These are the lives with the greatest potential, and they are the most powerful threads. As Celeste, you are one of those.

Bob paused before continuing, *Here is the important part; you chose to be that thread before you came into being as Celeste. You could have been others, but you were drawn to this one. There were many reasons for this, and they will emerge in time. Before you came into this one, you existed in another place and dimension. You are here to be of service, and you chose to do so. This follows two of the cosmic laws: to serve the lower dimensions and to exercise your own free will.*

Why don't I remember where I was before I came here? Celeste asked.

In time, you may, though orientation into this physical reality is very difficult. It is easier to forget where you came from. That way, acclimatising here is much simpler, as you just see it as a natural phenomenon known as 'growing up'. There comes a time, though, where you discover a deeper meaning and purpose in existence. This may happen later in life when you have the experience and maturity to discover and integrate what we call 'the remembering'.

What's the remembering?

When you come to know that you are more than you have ever been told, more magnificent that you could ever imagine. You remember that you are a multidimensional spiritual being and that your human form is simply a disguise, divinely created to help you do what you came here to do.

After a bad night's sleep, this was almost too much for Celeste.

Bob seemed to read her mind and paused before explaining further. *Celeste, when you saw the life of Isaac, you realised that you had lived before, proving to you that you exist elsewhere across time and space. When you saw your parents in this shed and interacted with them, you were able to tap into another dimension. Both of these experiences have shown you that death is a myth and that energy continues and simply changes shape and form as needed. You and Zac are the same, though you are also different threads. It is as though you are in the same row of the tapestry, supporting each other. Intertwined, though still separate. Perhaps even quantumly entangled?*

Celeste wasn't sure if Bob was making a joke. She didn't feel like laughing, anyway. *Where do you fit into all this, then?*

I, too, am in a role. I and others like me move through the tapestry, supporting the important individual threads who can make the most difference. The tapestry itself is conscious and seeks to evolve to the highest possible vibration. It is both the tapestry and all the threads … the unique individual and the oneness. It is both the particle and the wave and exists in holographic form. That's another of the cosmic laws … all consciousness seeks to evolve in order to remember its magnificence.

Celeste shook her head. *Hang on there; if we're already*

magnificent, then what is it all for?

We choose to forget, so that during the search we undertake to remember, we touch the lives of other seekers. We touch their hearts, their minds and even their souls. When we do this, we offer them something magnificent. Insight and awareness raise the vibration of the multiverse. Remembering is more powerful from the state of forgetfulness.

In her mind's eye, he tilted his head as if checking to see if she was following him. *Already you have helped so many to remember profound insights about the conditions they carry. Once they understand the higher purpose of their condition, the learning is complete; the need for the condition has been met, and it simply dissolves. They have remembered, and life will be forever changed. Do you not realise that this is what you have been teaching?*

Celest shrugged. *Umm ... sort of. I do like your summary, though ... So what's next?*

Simply share with others what I have shared with you. There are two other questions that may be asked when your subjects move into super observer.

What?

The first is, 'Why did you choose this life?' The second is, 'Why did you choose this family?' Share these with your team and observe the results. Know that this is the important next step in our work together. You are about to help clear the energetic history of humanity and raise the vibration of the 'collective' across time and space.

By asking those two questions? How...?

Remember I said that insight and awareness raise the vibration of the multiverse?

Celeste nodded. *Yeah.*

When someone is struggling with family connections and then understands that they came into a family line deliberately to halt the pattern of trauma that goes back through generations, that act of love sets the ancestors free and, by default, themselves also.

Really? How?

When you enter a family line, you gain access to the history of those particular genetic lines. You are entangled with those who came before. A loving act of service raises the vibration of those with whom you are entangled.

I see. What about the other question? Why did you choose this life?

That answer can be simple or complex, though everyone seeks a reason for their existence. It's a natural part of a person awakening … and draws on cosmic law once more.

Which one? she asked.

He smiled. *All consciousness seeks to evolve in order to remember its magnificence.*

I'm going to have to write these cosmic laws down somewhere.

Perhaps so; though I'd give deeper consideration before including them in your doctoral thesis.

Another Bob joke? She just smiled, said goodbye and left the shed. He'd given her much to think about again; perhaps even too much.

CHAPTER 36

Celeste pulled the team together the next day and told them about the new questions to ask once the subjects moved into super observer:

Why did you choose this life?

Why did you choose this family?

They all speculated on what might come during the next round of sessions, and much banter flew around the table. The team dynamic was evolving and expanding rapidly. Working together five days a week had been helpful, especially given the surge of people applying to take part in the project through the RIQM website. Abbey had started working with a few subjects as well and enjoyed it more than she thought she would.

Celeste paired them and sent them off to try the new questions with each other.

They were all back within a couple of hours, ready to offer their feedback.

The looks on their faces had Celeste intrigued. 'Just share what you're comfortable with,' she said.

Raz leaned forward. 'I'm happy to start. In super, I was told that I'm here as Raz to make a difference to humanity. I discovered that I chose this lifetime to be part of a great awakening, and I have an important role to play. I chose my family to give me open attitudes towards different cultures so I could come to understand that humanity is really just one people. When we all come to realise that, then the world will know peace.'

There was silence around the room, and Grace, who'd been in the journey with Raz, placed a hand on his shoulder.

Skye spoke next. 'I chose this life so I could bring the wonders of the universe to the people of this planet. My 'super' spoke of how too many people look down into the smallness of their lives and no one looks up to cherish the universe in which we reside. I'm here to help people realise that they're part of the heavens. I chose my family because my mother, as an astrologer, and my father, as an astronomer, showed me different perspectives of the stars. I always thought their opinions were opposed; now I see that both hold awe and wonder for the universe, and I've received twice the wisdom as a result.'

Silence again.

Abbey spoke then. 'I'm here to be a free spirit. By expressing that in my life, I give others permission to do the same. I don't follow the rules, and I avoid bureaucracy as it limits my natural state of being. I was told to follow my heart and encourage others to do the same. I chose my family because both my parents are also free spirits and they allowed me to be me.'

Celeste felt something deep inside, an echo of knowing as to why they'd been such close friends. Abbey's company was good for her, and she'd never seen it as plainly as in this moment.

They all turned to Grace and waited.

A tear ran down her cheek. Then she raised her eyes and held each of theirs in turn as she spoke. 'I've never felt at home on this planet, and I now understand why. I come from elsewhere to help humanity at a time when it's most needed. I saw a glimpse of a world that was full of light. My role is to bring that light to this planet in these times and be the bridge between worlds. I chose a difficult family to be born into, so I could practice being in the heavy energies of this place. It was a turbulent path, though it's led me to wisdom. The discoveries I made today have allowed so much to fall into place.'

In that moment, this group of souls moved beyond being scientists by remembering that they were so much more than they believed themselves to be. They each looked around the table at the others with a deeper level of recognition than they'd known thus far. The universe had brought them together to do something remarkable, and they all 'remembered' in unison.

They already knew that moments of insight could change lives; now they discovered that moments of collective insight could change the world.

CHAPTER 37

Everything was coming together in ways Celeste never could've imagined, and she was on a high until Abbey appeared in the doorway of her office with a newspaper in hand and tears running down her face.

Celeste both saw and felt her distress from across the room. 'Abs, what is it?'

Abbey moved into the room and placed a copy of the *Blue Mountains Times* in front of her. It was hard to miss the headline that filled the front page: 'Institute for Quantum Voodoo'.

The shock hit Celeste like a baseball bat; then anger built, and her blood began to boil. She read the article in silence, with Abbey sitting across the desk from her, looking forlorn.

The article centred around an interview with one Dr Snyders, who talked about how people could be convinced that they'd recovered from deeply seated mental health issues through some form of meditative trickery. He spoke of how decades of mental health practice had been ignored and that there was personal risk to the residents of the Blue Mountains who participated in experimental science offered by people who had no idea what they were doing. The article went on, alluding to other aspects and without making direct allegations. It painted a scenario of unprofessional incompetence on a joint venture into mental health by those who knew nothing about it. The article finished by saying, 'The Research Institute for Quantum Metaphysics was unavailable for comment', even though they'd never been asked.

'Gather everyone together, please, Abs, and let's discuss this.'

They gathered on the sofas in the waiting room, and Grace spoke first. 'Of the ten people we had scheduled for today, eight have cancelled. It's the same for the next month or so, as far out as our schedule goes. Most participants are dropping out of Project Shed.'

Abbey spoke next. 'The article was published yesterday, though we only saw it today. I know it's just the local paper, but the Blue Mountains is our home and where we're helping people. Now everyone will see us differently. Can't we sue them or something?'

'I need to get advice on that,' Celeste replied. 'The way it's worded around an interview with a mental health expert makes it not directly slanderous. He's supposedly just stating an opinion from what has been asked of him.'

Abbey let out a big sigh.

'I'll need to inform Gabe and the university,' Celeste continued. 'In the meantime, let's just tidy up our research to date and use this lull to consolidate. We're collecting important information and helping many people, and I'm sure they'll return when this blows over.' Celeste suspected she looked far more convincing on the outside than she felt on the inside. After this, would she still have the university, and more importantly, Collins Industries, supporting the work that was making such a difference? The institute was supposed to be a cutting-edge venture with a positive image.

She picked up Gabe's card and dialled his personal mobile.

He answered straight away. 'Hi, Celeste. Are you calling about the article?' His voice had an edge to it. 'It's just hit my desk.'

'Yes, Gabe. I'm not sure what to do …'

'Do nothing for now, except take a breath. Get on with the work, and I'll give thought to how we respond. I'll let you know.' He ended the call.

Celeste drew heart from the 'we' in his response, though underneath it she felt a pang of guilt that she may have been the catalyst for this attack, given her confrontation with Snyders and Irons.

The mood was sombre in the centre, so she wandered out to the shed. She'd been granted some breathing space, though in other ways her troubles seemed insurmountable.

She sat and reflected and felt Bob close by. She closed her eyes and connected. He stayed silent, observing her.

I guess you are up to date with what's happened? she telepathed.

Of course, we are always watching and supporting, Celeste.

She sighed. *Is there something you can offer me that helps?*

What you are doing has a profound benefit to humanity, Celeste. This will threaten many people, and they will try to stand in your way. Humans are very predictable, and this was expected.

Why didn't you warn me? she asked.

Because as a good scientist, you would've managed the risks and, in doing so, become smaller. Fear contracts us, but passion and purpose expand us. You would have stayed wary and further away from the potential of who you really are. You would not have found new horizons with one eye looking over your shoulder, waiting for what may come.

So travelling at high speed and then hitting a rock on the road is better?

Yes. The faster your speed, the less noticeable the rock can be.

Celeste declined to comment about Newtonian physics and other possible outcomes. *What should I do, Bob?*

Difficult as it seems, you should do nothing and allow the universe to move back into resonance around you. Trust that all is well and remember when you align with universal law and a greater purpose, you will always prevail. Bob withdrew, leaving her in a reflective space.

Thoughts formed that brought her a deeper understanding of her feelings. She'd healed from her darkest times and had used that journey to find something of meaning and purpose in her life. She'd enrolled others and started to change the lives of many … and now someone was trying to take all that away.

CHAPTER 38

The project almost came to a standstill, and Celeste had heard nothing from Gabe for two weeks, though she'd received a reassuring call from President Robinson at UNSW.

Early one evening, Celeste sat in her office wondering which of her staff members she would have to let go when her phone pinged with a message. It was Gabe.

Turn on Sydney Breakers now.

Celeste moved to the waiting room and turned on the television. *Sydney Breakers* was a hard-hitting current affairs program that aired weekly in prime time on the free-to-air network.

A female presenter sat in an interview setting with Gabe and Mandy Collins and Professor Robinson. She smiled at the camera and started to speak. 'Welcome to this edition of *Sydney Breakers*. I'm Polly Garibaldi.

'Mental health issues, the subject people avoid talking about, quietly destroys families, affects relationships and often goes unaddressed in our society. Anxiety and depression levels are now at an all-time high. The best approaches we have in the medical and psychological sciences seem powerless to address this surge in community distress. Every single one of us knows someone affected by anxiety, depression or some form of mental-health crisis. These people need help, and many of them are ready to try something different, whether it be alternate therapies, mindfulness or cutting-edge research.

'Tonight, we'll focus on that third option: new approaches that may bring us some light at the end of a very dark tunnel. I have with me Gabriel Collins, CEO of Collins Industries, and his wife, Mandy. We also have Professor Robinson, the president of the University of New South Wales. Gentlemen and Mandy, welcome to *Sydney Breakers.'*

Mandy and Robinson nodded. Gabe said, 'It's great to be here.'

The presenter continued. 'I'll start with Mandy. You've had your own personal journey through difficult times. Can you tell us about that?'

'Well, to be honest, Polly, I was a mess for twenty years. Looking back, I realise it was when I lost a child that things really started to get worse; in short, I just never recovered. Since then, it's been a trail of different medical experts and medications, but nothing really helped. Then I signed up for a research project with the university and everything changed.'

'That would be the Research Institute for Quantum Metaphysics?' Polly asked.

'Yes, they were just starting out then.'

'So how long did you spend there, and what has happened since?'

'I spent just two hours at the centre and came away transformed. It was nothing short of a miracle, after all I'd been through. My husband couldn't believe it. I've become my old self that has been missing for years.'

'Thank you, Mandy. Professor Robinson, how do you explain this? I believe there are other cases, and we'll hear from them shortly, but what is going on with this research you're doing?'

'It's only early days, Polly, though this work shows great promise. Many of the viewers have probably heard of the quantum field of possibility. Putting it simply, we've found a way to access that field and set people free from their troubles from the past that hold them back. We're closely monitoring the work of this new institute, and I want to say, this is about quantum physics and how those potentials can be accessed by ordinary people in a safely controlled environment. The thing we forget so often is that we ourselves are made up of quantum particles. Those particles have a life of their own, and it seems that when we work with them in collaboration, more is possible than we've ever thought.'

'Thank you, Professor. Now, Gabriel, you've stepped in to sponsor this work financially. As a businessman across multiple industries, why are you sponsoring a quantum physics research project?'

'The answer to that is simple. I want other families to experience what I have. To have my wife back after so many years has changed my world. Something has been discovered here that is enhancing lives. As the professor says, it's early days, though this could fundamentally change the way we look at mental health. It might just need a view from outside the current system to bring a breakthrough.'

Polly turned to the camera. 'It all sounds too good to be true, so let's hear from some of the people who've taken part in this experiment ...'

Celeste looked on, lost for words, as a man interviewed eight people either in their homes, under a tree, or in the street. All described their experiences. One lady in her thirties remarked, 'I just felt very light and floaty, and then I heard myself telling me that this was all meant to happen and that I'd grown so much from the experience. I'd carried that trauma around with me for years, and it just dissolved. My children can't believe the change in me. I'm just so grateful.'

A wide shot of a young man in his twenties came on screen, long hair, singing and strumming a guitar as a busker on a street corner. The camera cut to a close-up and a street interview. An off-camera voice asked the question, 'Justin, you've been part of this project, haven't you?'

'I sure have.' He beamed.

Celeste's eyes flew wide, and she stood staring at the television. 'No, please, not this.'

'Tell us a little of your story …' the voice said.

'I'd been unhappy all through my life and eventually turned to drugs. I was pretty messed up and finally got kicked out of home and haven't been back since.'

'And how are you now?'

'I'm in a rehab program, and I'm clean. I found a part of me that didn't need the drugs, and I'm starting to live that now. Those unhappy feelings are gone.'

'Do you have a message for someone?'

Justin turned to the camera. 'Dad, Mum, I'm doing much better now, and I want to come home. I'm sorry for what happened.' A tear appeared and ran down his cheek.

Clearly affected, the interviewer's voice cracked a little as he said, 'Thank you, Justin; I hope they're listening. Back to you in the studio, Polly.'

'So there you have it, from the people who know best, having been part of the experiment. Professor Robinson, perhaps a final comment from you, as I believe you've ruffled a few feathers in the community?'

'We're doing something radical and different, leveraging the branch of science that has unlimited potential. Someone referred to this as 'quantum voodoo', which simply shows they know nothing of how real science works or the incredible potential of a human being. We're making good progress; the early results have exceeded our expectation, and we'll share more of the research when it's appropriate.'

'For anyone who wants to know more, where can you direct them to?'

'The university website has information, including contact details. Please go to UNSW.edu.com to find out more.'

'Professor Robinson, Mr and Mrs Collins, thank you for an enlightening conversation. We wish you well and hope to hear more as this work progresses.' She turned to the camera. 'You are watching *Sydney Breakers*. We'll be back after the break, talking about a new performance-enhancing drug being used by elite athletes that appears to be invisible to detection ...'

Celeste missed the sign-off and the following ad break, where the last commercial promoted the Collins Construction Company. She was running across the lawn towards Jeeps, the echo of the slamming of the front door ringing behind her. She took off in a cloud of smoke, powered by a full-blown Aries attack, and for good reason.

The young musician who wanted to come home. His last name was Snyders.

CHAPTER 39

Celeste pulled up outside Gabe and Mandy's large home in Sydney's north-west. She'd been there before for a social function and was again struck by the size of the place. Mandy opened the door, and when she saw the look on Celeste's face, she said, 'He's in the study; he thought you might come.'

Celeste strode across to the door and entered the room. Gabe sat behind his desk and looked up. 'Hi, Celeste, have a …' He didn't get any further.

As she stood before him, the calm and composed words she'd devised in the car escaped her, and she spoke her mind. 'What gives you the right to do that? To attack a family at their most vulnerable and use it against them?'

He remained silent, so she continued, 'You told me I'd be leading this institute, and you've gone behind my back. How could I possibly be seeing this at the same time as millions of others on prime-time television? This has obviously been carefully planned, and my team and I have been excluded. I promised all people who took part in Project Shed complete confidentiality, and you've showcased our work to the world before it's even ready. How could you do this? What an incredible breach of trust ...'

Her tirade continued a little longer, and she became even more infuriated when he smiled and said, 'Yes, you're right on almost all counts, though I had important reasons for keeping you in the dark. Can you now please sit down and let me explain?'

She landed abruptly in a chair in front of the desk, arms crossed, and said icily, 'Please do.'

Gabe came around his desk and sat in a chair next to her. 'Let me say this first for context. We were attacked and had to respond in a certain way so others won't try that again. This remarkable work we're doing was threatened, and there's an incredible cost that comes with that. If we didn't survive this, all those people you're helping would miss out on having their lives back, and that had to be avoided at all costs. They declared war on us, and when people do that to me, I respond in a way that is both clinical and strategic. Part of that strategy meant you had to be left out.'

'That sounds a little dramatic, don't you think, Gabe?'

'Not really, Celeste. Do you know that Snyders' wife owns fifty-one per cent of the *Blue Mountains Times*? Do you know that she chairs an editorial committee for one of the big papers? Do you know she's on the board of a rival university in Sydney? They were testing the water locally before going further afield. Then there are Snyders' medical industry contacts, which I'm still uncovering, though he's the front person for others.'

Celeste paused, and her energy changed. 'I had no idea about any of that.'

'This is my territory, Celeste. I did some digging after your first encounter and had a sense that something was brewing. Robinson and I discussed it, and we went with the interview for a couple of reasons. We had to push the UNSW brand as a preventative measure, so that anything put forward by a rival just looks like sour grapes. The way to put the Snyders in their place was through their son. Their proposed campaign hasn't been set back, it's now dead in the water. Sunk from within their own family. It's the stuff of good movie plots or bestselling books, rather than real life.'

'But what about confidentiality?' Celeste asked. 'You've broken my promise, and my team's integrity is compromised.'

'No, it isn't,' Gabe replied. 'Mandy had sent a few of her friends your way, and they all wanted to help. One of them knew Justin, and when he saw what his parents had done, he wanted to help too. He came to us. I'm paying for his rehab program, though that was offered after he'd agreed to help, not as a condition of him doing so. I was careful to separate the two, and we've done things like that in the past as a community gesture, anyway. He speaks glowingly of his experiences with your team.'

'Okay, I need some time to digest everything you've told me.' Celeste, having calmed considerably, relaxed into the chair.

'One more thing: I needed to keep you and your team clean and out of sight. We'll need you going forward as the face of this work, and you need to be introduced without any controversy or media baggage. Beyond all that, there was one more thing.'

'What's that?'

'You wouldn't have agreed to this strategy and would've fought me every inch of the way. I felt it was better to seek forgiveness than ask permission. I felt when you knew the whole picture, you'd see reason, but time was of the essence. We had to move swiftly and decisively.'

Celeste smiled, finally. 'You read me well. How did you get such a positive response from *Sydney Breakers*?'

'I bought a million dollars in advertising over the next twelve months for Collins Industries. That's the way of the world, I'm afraid. It's a business investment that will pay off, even beyond what we've achieved today.'

'What about the university?'

'Robinson handled all that and had support from the UNSW board. It was his first time on prime-time television, and he's a fan of the show. That's all squared away.'

She rose to go, and he stood also. 'What happens now?'

'You go and change the world, knowing that I have your back. I promise to bring you in if something like this happens again, but please know I'm good at this sort of thing.'

'Yes.' Celeste nodded. 'I can see that.'

The journey home had a very different energy, and she sat for a while with a glass of red wine, mulling over the events. What a fascinating evening it had been. She wondered how she'd brief the team the next morning and what the reaction to the television story would be.

It was midnight before she made it to bed, and at three in the morning, a text message pinged. She'd left her phone on.

It was Phil, the technology manager from the university.

'I was called into work. The UNSW website has crashed. The application page for Project Shed can't handle the volumes. Will have it fixed by morning. Phil.'

In her sleepy state, she had to read it a few times. She whispered out loud, 'So that's what you meant, Bob. Looks like we're back.'

Celeste fell into a deep, untroubled sleep.

CHAPTER 40

After the segment on *Sydney Breakers,* the Research Institute for Quantum Metaphysics, or RIQM as it was becoming known, gained momentum quickly.

Gabe had made resources available for public relations, social media and advertising, and people came from all over Sydney, and even beyond, to partake in the sessions.

Celeste was asked to write articles about their findings to date, and while she felt it was still too early, she knew that the profile it built was good for both the university and Collins Industries brands. She became very good at creating speculative articles that were more 'exploratory than explainatory' as Abbey called it.

They changed the language they used so that people who came were now 'participants in a research study' rather than 'subjects in an experiment'. Her team members were now referred to as facilitators rather than scientists, and the participants took 'a journey into the quantum field'.

A conservatory now sat at the end of the garden, a place of reflection for those who'd taken the long journey to the mountains. The glass panels on the roof let in the winter sun, and the glass walls gave sweeping views of the grounds. It contained tea and coffee facilities, a number of lounge chairs and had fresh fruit and sandwiches on standby.

Abbey called it the temple, and Skye called it the observatory. Raz had taken to meditating there from time to time, saying it had a great vibe. Celeste used it as a space to connect with, and sometimes debrief, some of the participants. The informal setting encouraged them to share their personal stories if they wished, and Celeste often found their accounts inspirational. They used them in testimonials on social media, which ensured an ongoing supply of participants.

The board of directors of the institute evolved. Dr Bart and Paul O'Malley had renewed an old friendship, and Gabe's other representative, his chief operating officer, Jack Hadley, had become something like a cross between a shepherd keeping the wolves away and a handyman who fixed things even before they were broken.

The one thing that eluded Celeste was the PhD. She still missed a piece about tapping into the many-worlds interpretation, though she had some ideas forming regarding particles disappearing and reappearing. Since her days were busy, she spent evenings on the paper wall, mapping new theories and bringing in more research leads.

While she sat at her desk that morning, contemplating all of this, her phone rang.

It was Jack Hadley. 'Hi, Celeste. Gabe saw a conference coming up in Melbourne on the subject of science and consciousness. He wants you to check it out with a view towards presenting next year. Might be good to get a feel for it and talk to the organisers in the meantime. Are you free the weekend after next?'

'Nothing I can't clear in my schedule, Jack.' Having not much of a social life beyond Abbey was helpful at times. It would be good to get away, and she hadn't been to Melbourne for years.

'Okay, watch your inbox.'

Leading a research institute meant more public-relations commitments were coming her way. Meeting people who were exploring the fringes of science and consciousness could offer interesting conversations.

Within an hour, her flight bookings, accommodation and conference information had arrived by email. She looked at the speakers on offer, some of them close to her comfort zone, some far beyond it. It made for a fascinating read, and she reflected on the world she was heading into. A lot of fringe science was emerging, and she was part of that in some ways and not in others. Some of her old colleagues at the university were talking about how she'd disappeared down a wormhole, and they weren't sure where she'd pop out again.

Celeste was interested in the speaker from the Institute of Noetic Sciences, who had an update on the Global Consciousness Project. They had over two decades of data from random number generator machines and were offering an overview of the impacts they'd observed in the magnetic field of the Earth from global events.

A neuroscientist would talk about how the use of shamanic processes to resolve trauma affected brain chemistry. Given what she'd witnessed from the super observer effect, she wasn't drawn in that direction.

Another speaker was to talk about the field of astro-consciousness, which might be interesting. Various other speakers would cover subjects such as near-death experiences, medical research into spontaneous remission, and the connection between specific cancers and their relationships to particular trauma histories.

After spending twenty years going to conferences and listening to one physicist after another, this line-up looked interesting.

One particular speaker jumped out at her: Dr Carlo Lancaster, based in Melbourne. The subject of his PhD in his profile sparked her interest. The title of his thesis had been 'The dreamwork of Carl Jung as a way to enter the collective unconscious'. It looked like he divided his time between lecturing and overseeing a large private practice focusing on dream interpretation, truncated psychoanalysis and art therapy.

Celeste looked at the bio photograph and thought he seemed familiar. He appeared to be late forties with dark hair greying at the temples. She wondered if she'd come across him whilst researching the work of Jung some months back. Either way, his first and last name seemed a terrible match. She made a note to attend his lecture on 'The Pauli Effect—a new interpretation'.

Ten days later, she walked into the reception of the Novotel on Collins in Melbourne, ready for the weekend conference. As she checked in, she noticed many people gathering with that 'conference feel' about them of nervous expectation and excitement. Celeste settled into her room, at first glad to have some breathing space after several busy months. However, being Celeste, she was bored within an hour.

She thought she'd try an experiment. The room had two chairs, and she arranged them so they faced one another, then sat, closed her eyes and thought of Bob. He was there in the chair opposite her almost instantaneously.

So you do travel, she telepathed.

He smiled. *In ways that defy human understanding.*

Can I ask you something, please?

Of course, he replied.

I understand enough of our work to know that I must be here at this conference for a reason. Can you tell me what that is?

No, Celeste, I'm afraid I can't.'

Why not?

I can assist behind the scenes, though we must still work within the guidelines of cosmic law. This honours your free will. For example, you said yes to Jack and made time to be here. Over the next two days, you'll choose the speakers to whom you'll listen. Intuition will guide you to what you need over the weekend. And whatever path you take will be of your own volition. Remember, there are no wrong turns, just different paths.

She'd become used to Bob's elusiveness. At times, it seemed to hold wisdom; in other ways, she just found it annoying. Since they were already chatting, she decided to push a little further. *The institute is running well. As you know, we've helped hundreds of people now, and the data we've collected is remarkable.*

Yes, we are delighted with the progress made, and we have worked well together. There is more to come, and our intention to serve humanity together is advancing well.

Celeste nodded. *I agree, and the people I work with are just amazing. There's still a piece missing for me, and it has to do with the many worlds' interpretation. I need to know where that fits and how I can access it.*

And you will. It is just not time yet, Bob replied. *Your final pieces of research will emerge very soon; I promise you. We have an agreement that serves you, us and the rest of humanity. It will not be forgotten; it is merely that we must groom the energy of circumstance to stay within the guidelines of cosmic law. All will be revealed in time, but please know that everything is progressing wonderfully.*

She realised she wasn't going to get much further. *Okay, Bob, thank you.*

Then he was gone.

Celeste had a restless night, wondering what the next few days would hold.

CHAPTER 41

By 9 am the next morning, the conference was in full swing. Celeste kept mostly to herself so she could absorb the information being offered. She was looking specifically for something to validate their experiences of the super-observer effect, a strong characteristic of the work at RIQM.

Gabe's people had organised some business cards for the conference. They had a new logo and her title of Executive Director—The Research Institute for Quantum Metaphysics. Still unsure of the landscape, she handed them out sparingly. She found the speaker on near-death experiences interesting. He spoke of consciousness leaving the body completely and moving into a wiser state of being, as if it journeyed elsewhere, usually by accident, and then returned later. Celeste's experience was that the super observer remained very much part of the research participant's landscape, as they always heard what the super had to say. There was still a connection, a quantum entanglement, between the participant and their super—perhaps an interdimensional bridge.

Having spoken at many conferences, she understood the speaker placement strategy. Ideally, you aimed for a speaker's slot just before a break, so people had time to approach you afterwards. You never wanted to follow a great speaker, and you never spoke in the 'snooze sessions', right after lunch or after dinner, especially when there'd been a glass of wine with the evening meal.

Celeste looked at the program and realised that Dr Carlo Lancaster was the last speaker of the day. That, too, could be a strategy, finishing on a high note and leaving people with something to think about overnight. The energy of the last speaker stayed with the audience until a new one replaced it the next morning. Alternatively, it may have been the only slot available to him … though it was soon clear to Celeste that what he had to say would definitely stay with her.

Carlo was around 188 cm, or six foot two in the old scale, taller than she'd imagined. Athletic-looking and with a charismatic presence, he stood for a moment after being introduced and surveyed the three hundred or so people in the auditorium. His deep, resonant voice caught Celeste's attention.

'I have been fascinated by the work of Carl Jung since I was a teenager. Over the thirty years since then, I've seen his work come to life in ways that have inspired me, challenged me, brought me frustration and, most important of all, given me cherished moments of blinding insight. You see, Jung was not just the founder of analytical psychology; that was his disguise. He was a mystic, a philosopher and a spiritual teacher of great power. What Nikola Tesla was to science, Carl Jung was to consciousness. Now, around sixty years after his death, many of us are coming to understand the hidden gifts in his life's work. Today, I'll share with you just one aspect of that, the work he did with Wolfgang Pauli, a theoretical physicist from Austria.'

221

Bang! Carlo had her attention. *That Pauli!* she thought, remembering the exclusion principle that had won him the Nobel Prize for Physics in 1945. Pauli had been nominated by Einstein himself. All that Celeste had researched on Jung regarding the collective unconscious came flooding back, and she leaned forward in her seat, as did others in the audience.

Carlo continued, 'Pauli was not only a leading quantum physicist, but he also possessed a strange ability to affect electronic equipment just by being present. In the end, he was forbidden to enter certain laboratories in case he affected the experiments. He really took the observer effect to a whole new level, and it came to be known as "the Pauli effect".' Some chuckles bubbled up from the audience.

'The collaboration between Jung and Pauli was profound. Jung introduced Pauli to the collective unconscious, and Pauli introduced Jung to the quantum field. They collaborated on Jung's theory of synchronicity, I believe, through the analysis of Pauli's lucid dreaming. I sense that together they were bringing information through from other dimensions. One of the greatest-ever consciousness explorers and one of the most remarkable quantum physicists of his day came together to open portals to new ideas and other realities. Together, I believe they created a type of 'quantum consciousness'. In short, they came to understand the oneness between the collective consciousness and the quantum field.

'I believe Pauli was a genius in his field. I know Jung was also. When the two of them got together, they fertilised each other's minds, broke old paradigms, and the universe took shape and form in new ways. They lifted each other into realms of possibility never before seen in history, and that's always wonderful for the evolution of humanity.'

Celeste was riveted. So much began to fall into place,

given her experiences in recent times. Pauli had been a lifelong friend of Heisenberg, and Einstein referred to him as his own intellectual successor and spiritual heir. He also had an enormous personal impact on the non-local quantum field, and this, more than anything, grabbed her attention. Her mind reeled. She felt the journey to Melbourne for the conference was all about this presentation.

Carlo continued, 'I believe what gave these men access to this quantum consciousness was a loss of current reality, an existential crisis, if you will. For Jung, this happened in 1913. While riding on a train, he saw rivers of blood everywhere, and it propelled him into a deep state of personal crisis. He believed he was going insane, and in relation to established ideas of the day, this appeared to be so. He was only thirty-eight years old at the time, and he came to believe this event to be a personal prophecy of The Great War. If this was accurate, then he must have accessed something outside this dimension. Some called it hallucination, though I refer to it as information from beyond time and space as we know it. I believe he fell into a state of quantum consciousness.' Carlo paused, and the audience leaned forward a little more.

'Similarly, Pauli had his own existential crisis at around thirty-two years of age, following his mother's suicide and the breakdown of other personal relationships in his own life. His lucid dreaming and subsequent recall were already evident at that time. He sought the therapeutic support of Jung, who, having been through so much himself, could understand what was happening to Pauli. It was the start of an incredible collaboration.

'Ironically, together the two of them personified synchronicity. Both had accessed information beyond themselves, had their views of normal reality challenged and were trailblazers of new thought. I believe this was enabled by an existential crisis in their thirties for each of them. I see this as a rite of passage that ultimately offered a connection beyond themselves.

'I believe that the hundreds of Pauli's dreams that showed many shapes, patterns and even lifelike events needed to be interpreted by Jung through his archetypes, art forms and mandalas to bring greater clarity to the life's work of both men.

'In 1945, when it came time for Pauli to accept his Nobel Prize in Physics for his exclusion principle, he's said to have stated that he wasn't sure where the idea had come from. In fact, he postulated the existence of a subatomic particle yet to be discovered, and it was, some time later.'

For the next hour, Celeste sat bolt upright during Carlo's presentation. He covered the connections he saw between quantum entanglement and synchronicity, and the merging of science with consciousness in a number of different ways.

At the conclusion of the presentation, the audience applauded Carlo enthusiastically, and a number of people moved to the front to speak with him. A small crowd gathered around, and he answered questions patiently. The crowd gradually thinned, and she finally had her turn.

'Thank you, Dr Lancaster, for a remarkable presentation. My name is Celeste Kelly. Our institute has been doing research into the quantum field to find connections to other dimensions with the use of human participants.'

'Ah … Celeste. I know of your work. I've heard you have upset most of the psychologists in the western areas of Sydney by curing their patients of mental illness. I believe your work is impressive.' He offered this with a collaborative smile and genuine interest. 'We all know the mental health system needs shaking up, though few in my field are willing to admit it.'

She read him as sincere, so she poked a bit further. 'Don't you run a mental health practice, though?'

He paused. She could tell he was considering what to say next. Then he relaxed. 'I do indeed. Though just between you and me, the work we're doing is different from what many people think, but please don't tell the psychology board.'

She was intrigued. 'I'd like to know more.'

The lights dimmed in the auditorium. 'I'd like to hear about your work also. Are you free for dinner?'

'Yes, I am,' she replied.

'Great. Would you like to share a meal in the hotel restaurant in, say, half an hour?'

'Yes, I'd like that.' Celeste smiled, feeling the importance of that dinner conversation building.

CHAPTER 42

Celeste arrived ahead of him, still in the conservative business suit and white blouse, her uniform at science conferences. She was shown to a table and made herself comfortable. Carlo had intrigued her with his comment about the work he was doing, and she sensed he'd be interesting company. Visionary men with powerful intellects drew Celeste, and real ones were hard to find. She was yet to assess him that way, though the conversation could be interesting, given his presentation.

He entered the restaurant and headed in her direction, having traded the suit for casual beige trousers and an open-necked, white shirt. He moved towards her with a confident, athletic gait.

'Thank you for meeting me, Celeste,' he said. 'You called me Dr Lancaster in the auditorium before. Please, I'm Carlo.'

'Okay. The name doesn't fit, anyway. You don't look like a "Lancaster".'

He chuckled. 'I get that a lot, though I'm not quite sure how a "Lancaster" should look.'

'Sounds a little old-world British,' she offered.

'Well, my father was an English banker and very old world. Fortunately, my mother was Spanish, descended from gypsies, in fact. I resemble her side of the family for appearance and perhaps a more open viewpoint on life.'

Celeste detected the very slightest of accents, almost untraceable. 'So you grew up here or elsewhere?'

'We travelled the world when I was young. My father was posted to Spain. That's where my parents met. He took a new job and settled here in Melbourne when I was eight years old. My mother was close to her family, and so I spent a lot of time in Spain over the years. My parents eventually divorced. She lives in Madrid with her sister now, and my father remarried and lives in London.'

'Do you have family in Melbourne?' she asked.

'I have two children in high school, one in university here, and a father-in-law who funds some of my research projects. He's a property developer and needs the tax deduction, so it works for both of us. But surely that's enough of my life story. It's your turn, and tell me what isn't on the internet. I looked there already.'

'Sure, though I need some context first. Tell me what your clinic really does?'

'Okay, we can start there. But let's order some drinks first.'

They ordered two glasses of red wine. Then he continued, 'We have a range of services that we offer the public. We do Jungian dream interpretation, truncated psychotherapy, and art therapy. Each of those disciplines is done in a non-traditional way.

'The dream interpretation is more than just archetypes and metaphors. We believe that the subconscious communicates with the patient by sharing important messages. My team takes them back into the dream and facilitates the translation of those messages in collaboration with their patient's higher self.

'Truncated psychotherapy is just another name for age regression through hypnotherapy,' he continued. 'We track and release trauma from the formative years directly in the subconscious. We've discovered that trauma is stored in the subconscious as a memory in the alpha range of brain wave patterns. The resulting anxiety, PTSD, etcetera, is an unconscious safety system, not a mental illness. Cognitive behavioural therapy is offered in beta brain-wave patterns, not alpha, and so they simply can't get to it. We can. It's known as 'truncated' psychotherapy because we only have to do a single session using hypnotherapy, and the trauma is dealt with.'

In a light-bulb moment, Celeste recalled her spirited conversation with Doctors Snyders and Irons. 'Is that why mental health is getting worse?'

'Absolutely, they're looking in the wrong place. Trauma is embedded in the subconscious, and they're trying to fix the conscious,' Carlo replied.

'What about medication for these people?' Celeste took a sip of wine.

'I believe it chemically suppresses the emotive responses from the trapped trauma in the subconscious. It doesn't actually fix the initial issue, which most often arises from childhood. People may feel less anxious, though they lose their zest for life. It lessens the emotional troughs, though we lose the heightened peaks too. We're designed to feel love, joy, anger and fear. That's what being human is all about. I have strong views that pharmaceuticals for emotional issues rob us of being completely human. It's better to go looking for the source, find it, release it, and take your life back. That's what my team does. Like you, I've become unpopular with doctors and other psychologists.' He paused to drink some wine.

Celeste could have hugged him. She felt validated that she was on the right track. 'Good to know I'm not alone.' She smiled. 'Dare I ask what you're doing with art therapy?'

'Sure, that's much less complicated. We put people into a trance state and then give them paints to create the solution to their issues. We ask them to paint their healed state, and then we work with them to create strategies to bring it into their lives. It is all about the future and not the past. It works best in a group setting, and our 'art classes' are booked out months in advance. I have to say, we go through a great deal of paint, given the state of society.'

She laughed. He had a sense of humour.

'Your turn,' he said. 'What are you really doing up in the Blue Mountains?'

She drew breath and thought for a moment that given the audience present, she could probably describe Project Shed differently than she usually did. 'We've stumbled on something profound,' she began.

It was his turn to lean forward.

'We started looking for connections into other dimensions, and now it seems we've moved into not just that, but something more. I'll give you the scientific snapshot first. We're connecting with another layer of human existence that we've called the super observer, which exists in another dimension. It's like a bridge to a different place where information exists as to the root cause of a person's specific issue or condition. As that information is provided by the super observer, a moment of insight happens, and the condition dissolves. The person returns to their present state of consciousness without it. We've been measuring the human body and the environment around it during these processes, and there's a significant change in both the human physiology and the environment of the room itself. The participant's awareness actually leaves this dimension, though the human body remains as a bridge for the information. I believe that the human aspect and the super are in a shared union that's stronger than just quantum entanglement.'

'What's the other snapshot?' Carlo's gaze on her face never wavered.

'My metaphysical summary is that people are naturally multidimensional, and this is something we've never been told. We have resources available to us that we don't even know about. We live in a multilayered universe with limitless potential, and all of it is within our reach.'

He exhaled and leaned back. 'I believe that too. Your super observer sounds a bit like the higher-self work we've been doing—the wiser part of people. It's been emerging in the dream research. We take them back to the memory of the sleep state and receive messages from the patient. They often come through in another voice.'

They looked across the table, each validating the other's work, and a tangible energy could be felt. They were co-conspirators in a world that didn't understand them, both flying under the radar of the establishment and serving humanity in different ways. It was good to finally meet a kindred spirit.

Celeste continued boldly, feeling the safe space to do so. 'There's more,' she said, then paused as the waiter came to take their order. They hurriedly perused the menu and ordered their meals, and then Carlos asked her to continue.

'We've started to ask other questions in the super observer state,' she said. 'We ask about why the participant chose this lifetime and why they chose their family. When the greater purpose of that is known, something else shifts in the participant. They have a more conscious awareness of what they're supposed to do in this life, and many have found they've incarnated into family lines to stop the pattern of intergenerational trauma. They actually talk about setting their ancestors free as a result.'

'Just a moment, Celeste,' Carlo said. 'You said "this life". Are you talking reincarnation of the soul or ancestral lines here?'

'Both,' she replied. 'Do you believe in reincarnation?'

'I've seen enough in our clients to be a believer. Jung came to align with it also later in life. His publisher suggested he take the mention of it out of his autobiography, as it would've discredited much of his other work. The world simply wasn't ready!'

Carlo took another sip of wine before continuing. 'Some of the dream sequences we investigate at our clinic take us to events a long way back in the past that we've subsequently validated through research. I believe all of this information is coming forward so it can be healed or resolved. It's led to a theory I have about the evolution of humanity.'

Fascinated, Celeste asked, 'Tell me about that!'

He paused. 'I'm conscious that I'm talking to a scientist about this, and it's really out there. Are you ready?'

She thought he might be teasing her, perhaps even testing her out. 'Carlo, after the last year of my life, I pretty much live "out there".'

'Okay, here it is. I believe there's a major clean-up of the collective unconscious happening to get humanity ready to move to a new level of consciousness. I've had clients who claim to have incarnated here into this life to be part of a great awakening. This clean-up happens in two ways. The first is from people incarnating now to complete or heal any karmic patterns left in their soul lineage. The second is for souls incarnating into troubled family lines to change the ancestral legacies.

'There's also a third group, those who carry the energies of civilisations from other planets or dimensions in their soul lineage. They are now incarnating into human form to bring something new to the world and be a catalyst for further change.' He paused, searching her face for a reaction. Their eyes met and something connected deeply in the synergy between them.

Celeste nodded. 'I'm seeing some of this too. It's good to get another angle, and it's giving me more to think about. In short, everything you say resonates, and we're coming across similar themes.' Beyond the conversation, Celeste had been given deep insight into her own team.

He breathed a sigh of relief. 'How have you discovered these things, Celeste? Through your work or personal experience?'

'Both, Carlo. I've had what one may call a very metaphysical year.'

He smiled as if he understood. 'I've had experiences that are hard to describe and have received support from elsewhere that has stretched me and my belief systems. It's been happening for a couple of years now.'

She really went out on a limb then. 'Are you in touch with someone from another dimension who is kind of but not really human?'

'Yes.' He paused. 'She's a female form called Wal, dresses like a priestess archetype, though has nothing to do with religion. She advises me on our research from time to time. Given you've asked, can I assume you've had similar experiences?'

Wow. May as well completely open the kimono. 'My guy is called Bob, and we usually meet in my shed at home, though he was in the hotel room for a short while yesterday.'

They looked at each other for a moment, then both burst out laughing with a sense of both amusement and relief. It was good to be 'doing crazy' in the company of another.

Carlo raised his glass. 'To our unseen friends!' he toasted.

The meal came, and they relaxed with good food. Celeste felt herself letting go more and more, as though she were in the company of an old friend. The alignment of their experiences brought them closer. She asked about Carlo's team and whether he'd had the same good fortune to have found great people. As she told him about her team, like most, he laughed at Skye, the astrophysicist. She shared stories about the synchronicity in her work that had led her to where she was. The one piece she didn't mention was about the secret room in the shed and the mysterious circumstances of her father's death. She'd need to know him far better before moving into that subject. A shadow moved behind her eyes, and she buried it once more for the moment. Carlo seemed not to notice.

He then shared how the right people had dropped into his life at the right time to work alongside him. In all, he had twelve people working at his clinic. The funding from his father-in-law allowed them to provide some services pro bono to those who couldn't afford them. The conversation then moved to amusing stories that had unfolded over the years with his clients and her projects. Carlo was impressed that she'd worked at CERN for a while. By coincidence, he'd lectured from time to time at the Jung Institute in Zurich. '*Aber, mein Deutsch ist nicht gut genug, um Vorträge zu halten,*' he said.

'So your German wasn't good enough to lecture then?' she commented.

He looked impressed. 'You speak German?'

'Picked some up along the way, I guess.' Whilst that was true, she was aware that her life as Isaac had bubbled up to the surface just for a moment. Since her session with Paul, she'd felt his influence from time to time seeping through from that other lifetime.

Time flew, the meal was soon well complete, and they were the last table left. Celeste sensed the staff hovering, wanting to call it a day. They left and soon realised they were staying on the same floor.

They paused at her door. Celeste understood the Spanish custom of a kiss on each cheek, though as Carlo stooped to do so, it seemed more natural to turn her head towards him. Their lips met and held, neither wanting to break the magic unfolding moment by moment.

Surprised, he pulled back just a few inches, though magnets beyond time and space drew their lips, soft and warm, back together. Their mouths opened in unison, and the gentle kiss was in deep contrast to the fires building in their bodies.

Her key card had been in her hand already, and she moved it behind her while her other hand cupped the back of his head. The door unlocked, and they half stumbled, half glided across the threshold. Something awakened in her that had been dormant for so long, and it was like an explosion in her soul.

He held her gently, though she could feel his own reaction building.

They blended together, uniting their energies in ways so few ever experience. Their clothes fell away, and they lay gently on the bed naked, looking into each other's eyes. Their bodies moved together as though they'd been designed for each other in a transcendent moment across time and space. The universe was theirs.

They drew breath and lay entwined, each time complete, before a touch of his hand or the feeling of his strong arms encircling her united their passion once more.

It was well into morning before she dozed peacefully on his chest, unsure of where her body finished and his started, surrounded by a feeling she'd never known, sensing somehow that everything until now had brought her to this exact moment in time. A resonance in the depths of her being felt like home, and Celeste fell into a deep sleep.

Chapter 43

She stood on the ancient wharf, crying, and looked up at the man who was the centre of her existence. A true warrior, tall, broad-shouldered with a mane of dark hair halfway down his back. His clear eyes and plaited beard held a noble bearing, echoing his station as the commander of the city's defences.

He spoke urgently to her. 'You know I must go, my love; the Norsemen have come to Frisia again. We must stop them before they reach Dorestad. There is news of the burning of monasteries and the murder of children.'

Through tears, she said, 'These men are the most evil we know. How will you return to me unharmed? Our child comes in the spring.'

He smiled at her. 'We have planned well, and my men are true swordsmen of great skill. Brute strength has power, though a skilled swordsman is worth three of them. We will take them at night and burn their boats on the river. They won't be expecting us to leave the defences of the city. Without their boats, they will never reach us. It is a better plan than waiting for them to come.'

He kissed her and jumped down to the boat, where his men were waiting. His long cloak billowed behind him as he landed like a cat and jumped up into the stern to wave his goodbyes. The other hand held the rigging of the sail.

He was almost beyond earshot when he called across the water in a clear voice. 'I promise that I will return to you, my love.'

She stood forlorn with her hands over her swollen belly, a feeling of dread coursing through her body.

Each day, she visited the dock, willing him to return. She stood there a week later as the first sails came around the bend in the river, her hopes high as she looked across the water. Three long boats came into view, and her heart chilled. She turned and ran along the dock, screaming to anyone who would listen, 'The Norsemen have come! Hide your children!'

Her heart sank, and she began to panic. The city had few defences now, and the commander's mission had failed. Far worse than any of that was the knowing she had lost the love of her life.

CHAPTER 44

Celeste awoke abruptly from her dream with tear-stained cheeks. Carlo breathed next to her, deep and rhythmic, and she could smell the mix of his body's scent, their lovemaking and a faint aroma of yesterday's aftershave on him. It blended beautifully. She crept into the bathroom and splashed water on her face. It was five in the morning, and even though she'd had little sleep, she couldn't return to slumber. The feelings that came with the dream troubled her, and she still felt them intensely. It was one of the strongest dreams she'd ever known, following one of the strangest nights of her life.

She returned to the bed and lay looking at the ceiling in the pre-light of dawn. The naked man beside her drew her attention. He'd stayed athletic into his middle years, and she still felt the echoes of last night's passion.

The rational part of her kickstarted a whirlwind of thought. How could this happen? This wasn't like her. She'd never had a one-night stand in her life! This man had a family; there was no future in this for either of them. She had no idea what to say when he awoke. Though she didn't have long to wait.

Carlo called out in his sleep. 'No! It can't be. No …!' He moved around in spasms and cried out in unintelligible words.

Wanting to comfort him, she put a hand on his chest. 'It's okay. It's just a dream.' She'd chastise herself later for saying something like that to an expert in dream analysis.

He woke and looked at her, disoriented at first. 'Celeste … what time is it?'

'Just after five,' she replied.

'I had a terrible dream,' he said.

'Tell me, if you like.'

'We were sleeping on a riverbank, many of us, some kind of ancient soldiers with swords and shields. Men with horned helmets, like Vikings, took us unawares. There were so many of them coming at us from the forest. I remember wondering what became of the sentries we posted. It all happened so quickly. I was thrown to the ground in the attack and someone stood over me. All I could think about was that I was breaking my promise … and then it was over.'

He was visibly shaken by the experience, though not as shaken as Celeste, given what she herself had dreamt. It was all too much for her, and she felt herself starting to close off. A part of her had been set free, though another part of her wanted to just run and keep going. The experience had her terribly confused, and she desperately needed time to think.

'Carlo, at this moment I'm not really coping with what has happened. It all feels so surreal, and I need some time to process it.'

He looked into her eyes. 'Celeste, this has never happened to me before. It felt so right. I know this is something we can work out together.'

'There isn't a "we". You have a family, a life, and I'm not sure what to do. Can you please leave? We can talk more later.'

He paused. The look on her face must have shown she needed space. 'Of course,' he said. After dressing, he turned towards her. 'I'll call you later this morning.'

She waved at him from across the room, and he left, closing the door gently.

Celeste thought she'd feel better for him leaving, but she felt worse. Her heart felt as if it were being ripped from her chest.

She'd had enough of the conference. The remaining speakers had no pull for her, so she packed her bags and headed down to the lobby, worried she might see Carlo. Part of her wanted to hide, though another part wanted to throw her arms around him. After settling her account, she headed out onto Collins Street. Celeste turned and looked back into the lobby just as he was coming out of the lift. Their eyes met for a split second and held, and then she jumped into the taxi. 'Airport. Can we please just go?'

Carlo stood inside the glass doors, shrouded in sadness, as he watched her. Celeste was lost in the irony of this being the reverse of her dream. It was her turn to leave.

CHAPTER 45

Three hours later, she was back in Sydney, walking to the terminal carpark to where Jeeps had been waiting for her since she left. She sat in the driver's seat and checked her messages. There were four missed calls from Carlo, and a long text message followed:

> *Dear Celeste, I feel like I've been waiting to find you my whole life. Something happened to me last night that I never saw coming, and now that it has, I can't stop thinking about the deep and amazing purity of our connection. Please call me.*

She knew she'd have to answer or he'd keep trying. So she wrote back:

> *Carlo, I felt it too. But to end this now is the only possible path. You have your family and your work. I have my work, and it's my reason for being. It has*

*always been that way, even before now. And now I
have even more reason to continue, knowing that
there are others like me making a difference. I can't
express enough how valuable that is for me to know.*

His next message came through after ten seconds. 'Seriously!
Who types that fast!' she muttered to herself.

*Please don't shut me out. Take some time. There's
so much we share and can offer each other. I
understand this is so sudden. Talk to me when you're
ready.*

The pain in her heart intensified as she wrote a final text with
tears falling.

Carlo, I just can't do this. Please don't contact me again.

She blocked his number, placed her phone in the cradle
on the dashboard and said, 'Jeeps … please take me home.'
She started the engine and drove out of the carpark. Twenty
minutes later, she was on the expressway heading west towards
the mountains. Thankfully, it was Sunday, and no one would be
at the institute, or as she still called it, home.

Celeste spoke at her phone. 'Hey, Siri, text Abbey.'

'What would you like to say?' Siri asked.

'Hey, Abs, need an ear. Come over in an hour, bring wine.
Lots of it.'

Within a minute, a text message had appeared:

I'm already there.

Celeste pulled into the driveway, and Abbey came out onto
the veranda to welcome her. Abbey watched her crossing the
lawn to the house, and Celeste knew her friend was reading her:
the dishevelled suit, the ruined eye makeup and the stoop of her

shoulders as she dragged her bag along.

'I'll run you a hot bath and breathe a nice red,' Abbey said as Celeste stepped onto the veranda.

Celeste dropped her laptop in her office and her suitcase out in the studio. Ten minutes later, she entered the bathroom to find candles lit and a bottle of red with two glasses on the bathroom sink. She sank thankfully into the hot water. Abbey sat on the floor cross-legged on a towel and looked at her friend over the rim of the bath. They'd been doing this for twenty years, though more often than not, it had been Abbey in the water.

'You look like crap, Lest; what the hell happened in Melbourne? You're home a day early.'

Celeste took her time, unpacking the events of the day before. She told Abbey about Carlo's presentation and the incredible work he was doing. As she shared all that had happened at dinner and afterwards, images flashed through her mind. She described the incredible passion and energy that had overwhelmed her and carried her away. She shared details of her powerful dream and of the nightmare Carlo had awoken from …

She talked herself out—the wine helped.

'So, Abs, what do you think? Is it possible for two people who've only just met to have a similar dream?'

Abbey shook her head. 'Seriously, Lest, you are both the smartest and dumbest person I know. Did it not occur to you that it was a memory and not a dream? You probably know this Carlo fellow from another lifetime! Meeting each other—and you sure did that—probably refreshed an old love connection. For both of you, I might add. Remember, Paul said that once you chase this stuff, it speeds up. This guy is open to other lives too, you said. Well, there you have it. This accounts for your reaction too. Maybe this has been waiting for a long time to heal.'

'Heal what?' Celeste still didn't get it.

Abbey rolled her eyes. 'The broken promise, of course. Remember, "I promise to return", sound familiar? He's come back …'

Celeste's brow furrowed. 'Bit of a stretch, Abs.'

Abbey sighed. 'Get out of the bath and I'll show you some Past Life Research 101. You get dry, and I'll get the computer.'

They sat on the sofa, Abbey with a pen, paper and laptop. 'Right, back to the dream you had. What clues do we have so far?'

'Vikings, I guess?'

'There was a town name you mentioned; what was it?'

It was a great time to have an extraordinary memory. 'Dorestad, I think it was,' Celeste offered. 'But I've never heard of it.'

'Anything else?'

'Something called Frisia; don't know if that's a person or a place or something else.'

'All right, that's a start. Let's have a look.'

Celeste sat back, sipping the last of her wine while Abbey's fingers moved over the keyboard. After a few minutes, Abbey did something she never did—she swore. Her eyes flew wide, and she said, 'Well, fuck me!'

Celeste leaned forward. 'What've you found?'

'Frisia is the ancient name for the northern area of the Netherlands. There was a trading township along the river, inland from that area. It was quite a wealthy town and connected different parts of the river network. People traded there frequently. Lest, it was called Dorestad.'

Celeste just stared at her.

'There's more, Lest. The town was attacked by Vikings repeatedly between the years of 834 and 863. That was the ninth century, almost 1200 years ago.' Celeste still stared, so Abbey tried some humour. 'And here I was, thinking you've never really done long-term relationships.'

'But what do I do with this, Abs?'

Abbey took her hand. 'That's up to you. We know from all we've seen through the work here that things usually have a greater purpose.'

'I'll sleep on it, I guess, though I hope I don't have any more dreams like that one.'

The sun was starting to set. 'Dig out a couple of movies from your old DVD collection, Lest. I'll order some pizzas, and we can have a quiet night in.'

All this had stirred up Celeste's energy field, but she did her best to integrate all she'd uncovered with Abbey's help.

They sat in the 'waiting room' on the sofas, watching old movies and eating pizza till late. Celeste was relieved to have the company and noticed, once more, how Abbey was her teacher when it came to the metaphysical.

CHAPTER 46

Early the next morning, Celeste, needing to clear her head of the red wine, drove Jeeps further into the mountains. The Three Sisters called her that morning as a place of peace where she could share in the expansive beauty of nature.

However, it wasn't the day for that.

A crowd had gathered in the carpark, and two police cars and an ambulance parked close by. Police tape surrounded a red SUV, and a couple of officers were holding back inquisitive locals.

Celeste got out and walked towards the crowd. She stood next to a woman who seemed to know what was going on and asked her what happened.

'They found someone in the car about an hour ago,' the woman replied. 'That girl over there called the police; apparently, she saw her earlier.'

Celeste looked at the girl in a café uniform talking to the police.

'Looks like the person in the car killed themselves,' the woman continued. 'So common these days. Not the first one here at the Sisters either. We had another one last year. This place is getting a bad vibe. Maybe we'll have fewer tourists; I'd be okay with that.'

The woman walked away, leaving Celeste looking at the vehicle. Something hovered on the edge of her awareness, barely noticeable. She closed her eyes and let her mind wander. A shard of light came through the darkness, and she was transported back in time … late one night … a conversation about her father, one she'd parked ever since. She remembered looking out the window and watching a red car head down the driveway, driven by a woman she'd helped through Project Shed, who had then confided in her.

The car she was looking at belonged to the former medical examiner Virginia Gregory.

The moment of insight brought shock, but adrenalin cut in. The only person who knew of her father's fake toxicology report was now dead. How could she find out more? She approached the tape. There were police all around, and a young policewoman confronted her. 'Move back, please; we have a job to do here.'

Celeste tried an angle. 'Good morning, officer. I'm a friend of the family, and I'm here to confirm that this is Virginia Gregory's car. They've asked me to check personally.'

The officer softened. 'I'm sorry for your loss, ma'am. You were very quick; we only informed the family a short while ago.'

Celeste pressed on. 'There are thoughts that she took her own life; can you confirm that?'

'Investigations are continuing, and we have more to do on that, though there's no evidence of foul play at this time.'

Suddenly overcome by a feeling of not being safe, Celeste headed back towards Jeeps. Then she noticed the girl who was the witness heading back into the café. She took a deep breath, fumbled in her purse for a business card and found the one she wanted—for an insurance agent called Ashley Murdoch.

Celeste headed into the café. 'Excuse me, miss, can I have a couple of minutes of your time?'

'What about?' asked the girl, looking uncomfortable.

'I'm an insurance agent.' Celeste flashed Ashley's card. 'Just want to ask you about the matter outside.'

'I told the police. Go see them.'

'I'll do that also, but if you can answer a couple of quick questions now, it might save you from coming to give evidence if there's an enquiry.' Celeste was making this up on the fly, copying old movie scenes she'd seen.

'All right, but you have to be quick. We'll be getting busy soon.'

'What did you see?' Celeste asked.

'The lady parked her car and got out and went to the edge of the lookout. Then she got back in. That's all I know till another person found her.'

To Celeste, it sounded just a little bit too rehearsed. 'What time was that?'

'About 6.30 am, not sure exactly.'

'Okay, last question.' Celeste really went out on a limb, and she wasn't sure where it came from. 'Who paid you to lie, and how much are they giving you?'

The girl went white, confirming Celeste's suspicions. 'Get the hell out of here!' she screamed.

Celeste left like a shot, wanting to get out of there as fast as she could.

Her intuition had been accurate. The world was closing in around her, and she had no idea what to do next.

CHAPTER 47

She sat on her suspicions about Virginia's death, partly terrified and partly in denial, so much so that she didn't even raise it with Bob. He'd already know, anyway, so she did her best to distract herself. One thing she did know was that the late-night visit Virginia had paid her may have ended her life.

Celeste felt drawn to attend Virginia's funeral at the church in nearby Springwood. Her husband, Vinnie, and their two daughters sat in the front row. Celeste could feel their pain in parallel to knowing that she was somehow mixed up in this tragedy herself.

On their way out of the church, the mourners filed past the family, and Vinnie thanked everyone for coming. Four loving grandparents held his daughters a little way away.

Celeste looked into Vinnie's troubled eyes and could imagine the depth of his torment. 'I'm so sorry for your loss,' she mumbled, words seeming so inadequate at this time.

Vinnie leaned forward and whispered, 'Thank you for coming, Celeste. I haven't lost anything. My wife and the mother of my children has been taken from me. Most likely by the same people who took your father from you. We should talk …'

She wasn't ready for those words, and they stunned her.

'I'll be in touch,' he said, and then Celeste was past him.

A week later, they sat in the quietest corner of a coffee shop. The lines on Vinnie's face carried the strain of recent times. He looked down into his coffee and spoke softly. 'She told me everything. I've lived this with her these past few years since she left her job. She carried the worries of the world until just a few weeks ago. After she visited your institute, she was different, more alive and back to what she'd been before all the trouble. For a short while, my girls had their mum back. I encouraged her to come and see you, but I now wish I hadn't. What they said about your father was a lie, and we both felt it had to be made right. I'm so angry, and I don't know who to be angry at. I also need to be careful; my girls can't afford to lose another parent.'

Celeste just listened. Project Shed had heightened her listening skills, though given the circumstances, she had trouble detaching from Vinnie's feelings.

'There's more, Celeste, and this is why I wanted to see you. Virginia went to the police. I know you asked her not to tell anyone, but your people helped her so much that she wanted to do something for you. She went to the police and told them what she told you, and four days later she was dead. So don't go to the police. I think this happened because Virginia did that. She'd never take her own life. I know that for a fact.'

Attuned to him now, Celeste asked, 'There's something else, isn't there?'

'Yep, there is. You see, we were inseparable. Vinnie and Ginnie, our friends called us, and we used to laugh about that. We had a saying from an old movie, "Love means never having to say you're sorry." Have you heard that before?'

'Of course. *Love Story* from back in the seventies.'

Vinnie nodded. 'You see, that was our thing; we said it to each other all the time. On the morning she died, I received a text message from her phone that said, "I'm so, so sorry. I love you." That message didn't come from her. She would never have said sorry, and our way of saying "I love you" was different. It was a capital I and U with a red heart in the middle. I told the police all this, and they just wrote me off as a grieving husband. Yep, that I am. But I'm also really angry and want these people, whoever they are, to pay for what they've done to my family.' He took a breath, then added, 'I know you're making waves. We saw the newspaper article and, to be honest, we weren't surprised.'

'How come?' Celeste asked.

'I used to work at the *Blue Mountains Times*. I'm a journalist, and we see so much. Those people are on the take. They print stories for money. I asked too many questions they wouldn't answer; it made them really uncomfortable. So in the end, when I started to uncover some things, I couldn't stay there in all integrity. I left and went freelance. Ironic, isn't it? You have a career where you're trained to ask the right questions and find the answers, and the people you work for don't want you to do that when it comes to themselves.'

Vinnie's conversation then went all over the place in a grief-stricken ramble. Celeste wanted so much to help him but didn't know how, so she just listened for another hour and gave him the only gift she could: her time. When they parted, she thought he seemed a little lighter, perhaps even unburdened to an extent. Celeste walked away with the opposite feeling, with a sense of dread in the background. In some ways, knowing what they knew, neither of them was safe.

CHAPTER 48

The institute was booming, most of it due to the *Sydney Breakers* story. Project Shed was more than back on track. Celeste had taken a role in sifting through the applications for participation, and the workload had become a monumental task. At the very least, it served as a distraction from her troubled thoughts surrounding Virginia's death and her unresolved feelings for Carlo.

One night, she and Abbey worked late, going through a huge pile of paper.

'What about a fear of clowns?' Abbey asked. 'I've got three of them now. What is it with these guys with the red noses?'

'Put them in the not-sure pile, and I'll ask Paul O'Malley for advice.' Celeste leaned back in her chair. 'Abs, I'm famished; what about some takeaway?'

'Oh, thank God,' Abbey said. 'I've been telepathing you my hunger pains for hours.'

Celeste smiled. 'Call the Thai restaurant and order the usual. I'll go; delivery takes too long.'

The restaurant was only ten minutes away, and the food was almost ready when she arrived. A light rain was starting to mist the air as Celeste drove towards home, taking her usual shortcut down one of the older gravel roads—hardly a challenge for Jeeps. During the day, it was a gentle scenic cruise through the bush, but at night in the dark, it needed a little extra care.

Headlights came towards her from the end of the road. The normal approach for the locals was to slow down and edge past, but the closer the other car came, the faster it seemed to go. Then, when it was about fifty metres away, it switched to high beam and extra driving lights. Initially, the lights blinded Celeste, but she caught a snapshot image of a large four-wheel drive with a bull bar swerving to her side of the road and heading straight for her.

On her right was a rock wall, and on the left, naked bush over an embankment. Fear lasted a millisecond before adrenalin cut in, and she assessed the two options, knowing only one of them gave her a chance.

Then a voice came, loud, powerful and male. It exploded in her head and filled her being. 'LEFT, LESTY. FULL TURN. GO FASTER!'

In one movement, she swung with all her strength to the left and put the accelerator to the floor. The gravel at the side of the road sprayed in all directions as Jeeps flew off the embankment and into the darkness beyond, missing the bull bar of the charging vehicle by inches. Celeste felt the car go airborne and the back tyres skid across a fallen tree she would've caught full on had she not speeded up. Jeeps hit the undergrowth with a huge jolt and continued down the hill for another thirty metres before starting to slow.

The voice came again. 'HARD RIGHT ... NOW.' She reefed the steering wheel to the right. A tree came from nowhere and flashed past the passenger side window, and she broke out of the bush onto a fire trail, which gave her enough traction to use the brakes. She sat motionless and shaken, her heart pounding and the ringing of her father's voice still in her ears. She felt warm moisture on her legs and arms and assumed it must be blood from her injuries. Then she realised she was unhurt and was simply covered in a mix of a hot red curry and a vegetarian noodle dish. She flicked on the internal light. The bag of Thai food had flown from the passenger seat and exploded against the dashboard. She was caked in it, and realising she'd survived, could only think of one thing. 'Abbey's going to kill me.'

CHAPTER 49

It was almost unbelievable that no harm had come to her. Jeeps was scratched all over and ended up needing a wheel alignment and a new headlight. The biggest challenge was getting the smell of Thai food out of the car. But Celeste couldn't deny the more sinister aspect of the event. Was Vinnie right about them both being in danger? Was this just some crazy driver or had this been an attempt on her life? She didn't want to expect the worst, though she had to accept that her father had saved her life from the other side. It was a weird feeling, sensing she may be in danger, but also knowing she was being looked after in metaphysical ways.

She was out of her depth and more than likely couldn't trust the police. One person, however, had shown that he had her back.

Gabe picked up on the third ring. 'Celeste, nice to hear from you. How are the applications coming?'

'Thanks, Gabe, I'm getting there,' she responded. 'However, I'm calling about a personal matter; in fact, I really need some advice, and I'd like to see you.'

'Of course. I have meetings till five thirty. Can you be at my office at six?' he asked.

'I'll be there.' She already felt a little relieved.

Celeste left early for the meeting, and when she arrived at the business park in Western Sydney, she sat in the carpark, wondering how to raise the subject of the circumstances of her father's passing, her suspicions about Virginia's death and the recent accident. She eventually steeled herself and headed into the reception area. The security guard behind the desk had a pass ready for her, and she took the lift to the top floor.

Gabe's assistant greeted her as the doors opened. 'Go straight through, Celeste. He's expecting you.'

'Thank you, Lillian.'

Gabe got up from behind his desk and came round to greet her with a kiss on the cheek. 'Hi, Celeste, take a seat.' He motioned to the lounge area of his large office. 'Can I get you anything?'

'I'm fine, thanks, Gabe.'

'Okay, what's on your mind?'

'I'm dabbling in an area I know nothing about. This is deeply personal for me, and I wasn't sure who to turn to.'

'Glad you chose me. Tell me about it …'

'I had a visitor a few weeks ago, and she told me something that has disturbed me greatly regarding how my father died. I was always confused by his accident, and now it seems he may have met with foul play. She supposedly took her own life a few weeks back as well.'

'Celeste, can I ask you to stop for just a moment? I really need Jack to hear all this, though only if you're comfortable with that?'

'Yes, of course,' she replied.

Gabe got up and poked his head out the door. 'Lillian, please ask Jack to step into my office and bring a file. He'll know which one. Tell him Celeste is here.'

Jack came in and sat in another lounge chair, so they formed a triangle. After greetings, she recounted the story of Virginia's visit and the information she'd shared, her trip to the police, followed by her death soon afterwards and her own near miss in Jeeps.

Gabe's eyes widened in horror, then he leaned forward and asked, 'Celeste, what do you know about a project your father was working on at the time of his passing?'

Celeste responded honestly. 'I believe he was experimenting with a type of free energy. But I know next to nothing about it.' She felt it best to leave the secret room in the shed out of the conversation for now.

Gabe nodded. 'Okay, then some of this will be new. Let me start from the beginning. As you know, my life changed the day Mandy came home from being a participant in Project Shed. Even Jack here says I'm much easier to get along with these days.' He looked at Jack, who nodded his agreement.

'Mandy was the one who initially suggested I throw some backing behind the work. However, I'm a businessman, Celeste, and before I was going to put money into something, I wanted to know the landscape. So I had Jack do some detailed research into you, your background, the university, all of it. Please don't be offended by any of that; it's just due diligence.'

'I'm not offended; on the contrary, I'm a fan of thoroughness,' she replied. 'I'm just wondering where you're heading with this.'

'You won't be for long,' he replied. 'By the way, you came up well. An emerging star in the realm of quantum physics, scholarship to CERN, and a go-to person to solve problems that no one else could. I was told you were completely enrolled in your career, apart from bruising a few egos of overrated academics over the years. Did you really call one of the professors a Neanderthal knucklehead?'

'Not one of my finer moments, but yes, I did,' she replied.

Gabe nodded and continued, 'What then came up was your father's death and the speculation around his hidden drug addiction causing the accident and costing him his life. As I said to you when we first met, I knew him, and he consulted on a couple of big projects for us. Life has made me a good judge of character, and the story just didn't ring true, so I asked Jack to have a more detailed look at it. I also couldn't afford any controversy later while on this mission of goodwill. Over to you, Jack.'

Jack opened the file. 'There are a number of things that don't add up about your father's accident, Celeste. I've a friend at the police department, and he gave me a look at the forensic report. Apart from what you've just mentioned about the toxicology results, there are a couple of other things. When they went to fingerprint the car keys and the steering wheel, they'd been wiped clean. Not even your father's prints were on them, even though he was found behind the wheel. Also, there was mud on the foot pedals of the car and none on the soles of your father's shoes, as if someone else had driven the car. My contact said that, at times, the police don't like to make extra work for themselves, so they just let those small anomalies slide as everything else was close enough. This information that Virginia shared changes everything, though, and I'm even more concerned for your own safety following her death and the car incident.' Jack paused and shook his head.

'There's more,' he continued. 'Your father had been to the USA to speak at a conference where he'd shared some of his research on free energy. It received enormous attention, and we wondered if that was also part of the picture. In the end, there wasn't enough to go on, and we were really just looking at this regarding the proposal to possibly create RIQM. We kept all the information, though. Here's the file if you want to see it.'

Celeste flicked through the file. It contained pictures of her and articles she'd written, also pictures of her father presenting in the USA and copies of some social media reactions to his presentation.

'So where to now?' she asked. 'What should I do?'

'You have two choices,' Gabe said. 'You can let it go, knowing your father's integrity is in no doubt. That would be the safest option, given it looks like there's something sinister here. Other than that, you can bring this new information to the police and have them reopen the case, though given that Virginia did that, it could be very risky and needs careful thought. The missing piece here is to find out what happened to your father's research, as that could be the thing that joins all the dots.'

Gabe paused. 'My advice, Celeste, is to do nothing for the moment, though I think we need to have some electronic security put in at the institute. Concentrate on the work you're doing while we wait for the right path to emerge. I'll make you a promise, though; I will support whichever direction you wish to pursue.'

'Me too, Celeste,' Jack said. 'Anything you need.'

'Thanks so much to both of you,' she replied, emotion caught in her throat. 'I'll sit with it for now as you suggest and let you know.'

She left the building and sat in Jeeps for a while. A whirlpool of emotion and thoughts permeated her consciousness. Tears ran down her cheeks, though a fire was building deep inside her. She would never close the door on this, not while there was breath in her body. This was far from over.

It was a good ten minutes before she could compose herself enough to start for home.

CHAPTER 50

Celeste stayed busy analysing data and pulling together a participant feedback survey. They were getting close to publishing another article, and as always, her PhD was bubbling in the background, now relegated to a secondary priority. Carlo had texted occasionally from another number, possibly his work phone. She read the heartfelt messages, and then after these became too painful, she blocked that number too.

Following a board meeting, Celeste asked Paul O'Malley to remain afterwards. Once they were alone, she asked, 'Do you know much about past lives affecting this one?'

'Sure, do you have a few days?' he joked. 'Can you narrow it down for me?'

'We've had a case of a love interest that goes back to ancient times and seems to be causing some real emotional pain for the people concerned. Wondering how to handle it and what advice we can offer,' she said, playing it cool.

'Love is the strongest energy in the universe, Celeste, so these echoes of other times can be very powerful. Often there's more than one life involved. If it's a pattern to be broken in the soul lineage, then it'll emerge so the two concerned can be freed. There's a chance they've followed each other across time and space.'

Celeste frowned. She didn't know whether to be elated or terrified. 'Freed from what?'

'It could be betrayal, separation, loss. The pattern may repeat again to offer access to the energy held in other lives in the soul lineage. In resolving it here, in this time and place, it may also clear the energy for the other lives. Doing so will serve the collective unconscious as well, as it will send a wave of healing holographically across time and space. We're quantumly entangled with our other lives. You, Celeste, know that better than anyone.'

'So heal this one and the others heal also?'

He nodded. 'Yes, an action here can break the pattern or heal the issue for all of them.'

'Thank you, Paul.'

'Celeste, if it's someone involved in the project, then I'll take the case if you needed me to. It wouldn't be the first time you've brought me out of retirement.'

She smiled. He was more intuitive than she'd thought. 'Thanks for your support, Paul. I'll let you know.'

CHAPTER 51

A few days later, she tuned into Bob in the shed. He seemed quieter than normal.

How are you, Celeste?

Well, you know, I'm not doing so well. The work is changing lives; I'm getting the data I need for the university, and the institute as a not-for-profit research organisation is starting to emerge as a credible voice. Though all that's wonderful and inspiring, I'm struggling personally.

Yes … I know.

Of course he did.

I'm open to any advice you may have, she thought-spoke.

Bob nodded. *There is a greater purpose behind your personal pain, Celeste. You feel its intensity more than what one would expect, and that is because of who you are.*

What do you mean?

There are two more things that you are ready to experience … The first is that there are people incarnating on Earth at this time to rebalance humanity. They feel deeply and profoundly and have

261

a challenge distinguishing the feelings of the world from their own. They're sometimes referred to as empaths, and they also often take on the energy of other people.

This rebalancing is happening because humanity has become desensitised to the pain and suffering in the world. People must learn to feel and care more for each other or the new consciousness cannot emerge. Many of the people who have been coming to see your team carry deep emotional pain. As you help them to transcend that, you are giving them permission to feel once more, but without the pain that comes with it. This reopens their feeling sensitivities, and they can take them into their lives more openly. It helps to usher in a new consciousness where people genuinely care about and feel for each other. Many of those you have served are these empaths. They collect the pain of others and hold it as their own. Until you show them the greater purpose of who they are.

You said something about the fact that my pain comes from who I am. What did you mean by that? she telepathed.

When you meet a new person, either professionally or personally, what do you do?

I size them up, I guess.

How?

I get a feel for them, maybe tune into them, Celeste replied

When you recruited Skye and Raz, when did you know they'd be suitable?

Even before I met them, when I looked at their personnel files.

And when you met them?

I knew they'd be okay within thirty seconds. It was intuition, I guess.

To an extent, yes. But you were reading the quantum field of possibilities in them and comparing it to what you were seeking, and the answer was yes.

Where are you going with this?

You, too, are an empath, Celeste. It is why you read people so well, why you have heightened intuition, and it is also why you feel the pain of the situation with Carlo so acutely. There are also echoes from elsewhere in that one.

Celeste nodded. It made sense. *I do feel that greater intensity. Abbey couldn't fix it with red wine and pizza the way she has other times. But if I'm one of these empaths, why do I not feel the deeper pain that others who come here to the institute do?*

In short, because of your father. Both your parents were also empaths, and he taught you how to deal with energy and how to hold yourself in the world. How to rise beyond the energy of others, if you like. He did this mainly by personal example, and you, as another empath, absorbed his unconscious skills in this. He also taught you the power of nature. That is why he moved your family to the mountains when you were born. He could see you'd need to grow up out of the city and closer to the vibration of the natural world. Every time the two of you took walks into the bush, your energy field cleared. You've been experiencing this since you were a child.

And my mother?

She didn't cope as well and took on the energies of the world at large. His energy field held hers together. When he passed, she collapsed energetically and wanted to join him. She was typical of the empaths who cannot cope. They become unwell or depressed or both. Life becomes too hard, and they really need support. Gabe's wife is also an example.

So when you moved home to look after your mother, you were showing the compassion and care typical of the empath. The impact of losing your father was experienced as deep pain, amplified in your energy field as an empath, so you shut it down. That allowed you to look after your mother until it was her time to pass. By this time, the burden you carried was enormous. It was our work together that healed you and had to be experienced personally before you could bring it to the world for others. In some ways, Celeste, you ARE Project Shed.

The pain of Carlo … was that part of this grand plan also?

Yes. You agreed to that long ago as a way to help magnify yourself in this lifetime.

Celeste grimaced. *Magnify myself. What does that mean?*

Discover your magnificence, bring it fully and completely into your knowing and realise that human form is a disguise.

She shook her head. *I'm still working on that one.*

No, you understand it, Celeste. The feelings for Carlo were for you to experience something absolutely profound. You now know that love transcends time and space in the most beautiful way. To find this and then lose it almost immediately has caused you pain, though it has opened your heart more fully. One that allows us to take a final step together when you are ready.

Is this the second thing you mentioned?

Yes. Though it's best if I show you. Bob rose from his chair and moved towards her, offering Celeste his hand. She drifted out of her body and joined him. He turned towards the door of the shed, which usually led out to the garden, but it had become a portal of light. They glided towards it and were absorbed into the blinding light as they moved outside of time and space.

In what seemed like an eternity and also no time at all, they emerged into a landscape of light and found themselves surrounded by ten beings roughly human in shape and made of translucent light. Celeste noticed that she'd also taken this form.

Bob's voice remained with her. *The others have been waiting a long time to greet you, and here they are. It's time for you to know that you're one of us and that this is your home.*

Celeste's human personality was set to the side for a moment. Later, she would rationalise that she was in the home of her super observer, but for now, she felt the deep and profound resonance of her place of origin. It was like nothing she'd ever experienced.

This is the light tribe you work with across lifetimes. We are here as a loving resource for you. One of us takes form in the physical on behalf of all the others, and this time it is you. We stay connected to you at all times and share your experiences. You are never alone; we are always with you. It has taken till now for us to know it is time to bring this understanding to Celeste.

An experience of pure bliss permeated her being. *Thank you for bringing me home, Bob.*

He laughed. *In this place, you are not Celeste, and I am not Bob. I have a different name here.* He offered her the vibration of his energetic signature, a mix of a sound and feeling that held a deep familiarity.

Now there is someone special I'd like you to meet, though in a different form from what you may remember.

Another energy glided forward, and she recognised it instantly as her father. The joy in feeling his presence couldn't be translated into human terms.

Hello, Lesty, he telepathed using his familiar human term for her and leaving no doubt as to who he was. *Let us sit awhile in the garden.*

They were transported to a place with lawns, trees and a bench seat. In this moment, as they sat together, they echoed their human forms, and Celeste experienced it as though they were talking aloud. She remembered enough of her true home to realise this was deliberately constructed to allow her the ability to integrate the experience later.

'You're still in human form at this time,' her father said, 'so you can remember enough to be here in this other dimension, though all cannot be shared. It's not time for you to remember your complete limitlessness. It would simply be too much. However, there are things you're ready to know. For some of the larger tasks we take on, two of us are sent from our light tribe. It makes a job easier if we share human lives as, for example, father and daughter. Both of us came with a specific mission. Yours will be successful now; mine was not.'

'Are you referring to the secret room in the shed?'

'Yes. I was meant to bring a new type of energy to the world. We always knew it was a risk and that many would try to prevent it. They managed to do so, and you've already discovered that. We had a secret backup plan in case I failed. You're that second chance. Already you've found the room in the shed, and we want you to take the work forward, though the choice is yours.'

'My life as Celeste is so full.'

'We'll send others to help. Be patient and all will unfold as we've planned. We're here to guide you, just as the one you know as Bob has so far. That's all you need to know for now; though remember that we'll do our best to protect you. You saw this when I came to you in the car that night.'

'Yes, I know you were with me then, and I felt your love supporting me. I have many questions,' she said.

'They must wait. It's time for you to return now.'

Instantaneously, she was back in her chair in the shed with Bob sitting across from her.

So now you know who you truly are, he telepathed.

Celeste sat, absorbing what she'd experienced. Now back in human form, she missed her father once more. She needed a minute to compose herself. Then the scientist emerged again. *Is there a connection between being an empath and coming from other places?* she asked.

There can be. Many civilisations across the universe use telepathy, shared consciousness and feeling senses in far more advanced ways than here. Telepathy is how these different civilisations communicate so there are no language barriers.

Celeste recalled a book from her youth. *So we don't need babel fish.*

He smiled. *Our light tribe comes from a civilization that is both empathic and from another dimension. You and your father took human form as scientists to serve humanity. His time is complete; yours continues. There are many on Earth now who have travelled a long way to be here. They have difficulty in this form, as they aren't used to these heavy human bodies. You have practiced this across many lifetimes, so for you, it is easier. Humans use the terms empath and also starseeds, travellers, off-worlders, and so on. These are the people we want you to help next, as they begin to awaken.*

So what does this mean for our work at the institute? How can we help them?

You tell me. You were in deep pain when we started to talk today. Now you know about your empath side and where you are from. How does the pain you held regarding Carlo feel now?

It's still there, but I feel I can cope better. It seems like I have an elevated perspective that brings a greater sense of peace. It feels like I've turned the corner, Celeste replied.

Bob smiled. *The pain is lessened, though the love remains. It will be different now.*

They spent some time together, working out this next piece of the project. Grace would specialise in helping the people who presented as off-world types. She'd ask them, after they moved into super observer, where their true sense of home was. Then she'd ask to be shown that world. Following that experience, they would be more connected to their home and become a bridge between worlds.

Abbey would take on the people who were empaths. When they were in super observer, she'd ask them how they could best use their energetic gifts to serve humanity while still looking after themselves.

Before we finish, may I ask a question? Celeste said.

Of course.

I now know your name isn't Bob—though, of course, I did have my doubts about that already. I felt your real name back in the light tribe. Can I ask why you chose Bob?

It's a subject of great amusement back in the tribe. We are all Bob, even when we are not Bob. It simply means Beyond Our Body. We are never just physical. With that said, he left.

It had been a big morning, and Celeste needed some time to absorb it all. The pain around Carlo lingered, though it now felt different, just as Bob said it would.

She made a note to tell Abbey that the nickname of I-Bob might need some kind of upgrade.

CHAPTER 52

Weeks passed, and the Research Institute for Quantum Metaphysics was in full swing. They'd gradually built up to around fifty new participants a week, balanced with the follow-up visits and data analysis, and they took the time to celebrate their 2000th participant in Project Shed.

An emerging trend was that many of the participants now recommended to family and friends that they visit the institute rather than partake in medical or psychological services. This had led to an increase in people coming in with physical injuries, which needed some sensitive handling at times. On occasion, emotions were trapped in the energy field and did present as physical issues that could be understood from super observer. However, as Celeste said to one young woman, 'If you think you may have appendicitis, then you really need to go to the hospital.'

Celeste hadn't heard from Carlo for six months, not since she'd blocked his second number. From time to time, though, she did watch his latest podcast or read an article he'd published. These reminders of him didn't seem to carry the same pain, though it all still felt a little unfinished. As a distraction, she buried herself deeper into her work.

Her doctorate needed to be completed, but some pieces were still required. Celeste wanted to remind Bob of his original promise to supply the information, and one warm summer morning when they came together in the shed, she resolved to do so.

Hello, Celeste, he said when he appeared. *I've been asked to pass on loving wishes from the light tribe. They are following your work with a sense of wonder.*

Thank you, she replied. *We do have something else to complete, though. I need to find my connections into the many worlds' interpretation. I also want to know more about those particles that move into other dimensions and then return. You promised you'd help.*

I promised that you would have all the information you need, Bob replied.

Celeste frowned. *What's the difference?*

I am bound by another directive. A request to be of service in another way.

Can you please explain what you're talking about?

I gave you the information to access other dimensions to find the super observer, and that has been completed. The other two matters must be discovered by you and you alone, Bob replied.

That is not what we agreed to!

It was a very firm directive put in place, he explained.

Who by?

Actually, it was you. Before you took human form as Celeste. I am simply following your instructions. You made it clear to the whole tribe.

Celeste sighed. *Please remind me of exactly what I said.*

Of course. Though here is some background. When we take

human form, we still seek to learn, and many lessons come from taking physical 3D form. You chose a strong human personality with a profound sense of drive and purpose, and you will need that for what lies ahead. You knew that if you were just given the answers, then when it came time to stand before people and share this new wisdom, it would seem hollow.

It will be far more inspirational for you to have solved the problems in human form and then answer questions in ways that change the way people think. These must be your solutions as a leader in your chosen field of work. Not the answers sent to you from another dimension. Remember, under cosmic law, we also cannot interfere. So I can't share any solutions with you.

I have no idea what I was thinking, but unfortunately it makes sense. Can I at least have a hint?

Yes, you put that in place, and I am able to remind you of three things: the power of quantum entanglement, the directives of cosmic law and to use illusion to your advantage.

Celeste sighed again. *That's not much to go on.*

No, it isn't. However, you had great faith in the human expression of Celeste to find a way through.

Okay, Bob, thanks anyway.

He smiled and was gone in the blink of an eye.

She sat in the shed, lost in thought. A few minutes later, she wandered across to the studio instead of back to the institute, as the others were busy there working. Her living quarters were something of a mess, but she still came here to think at times, especially when she needed a break from an institute full of people.

She sat in a lounge chair, looked up at another wall of paper that had overflowed from her office, then rose from the chair and wrote *Quantum Entanglement* on one sheet and *Many Worlds' Interpretation* on the other. The comment Bob had made about cosmic law remained in the back of her mind, and she had no idea what to do with the 'illusion' clue.

So she concentrated on the first two. How could she confirm the many worlds' interpretation through quantum entanglement and work within cosmic law?

A small light came on in her mind and grew like a new dawn breaking over the horizon. Celeste went back to the wall and reversed the sheets. What if she wasn't supposed to go looking for the many worlds but was meant to bring them to her? All she had to do was reel them in through quantum entanglement. She'd go fishing in the ocean and simply pull out the fish she wanted.

CHAPTER 53

Grace sat quietly in the facilitator chair while Celeste leaned back comfortably in the recliner usually reserved for their research participants.

'So tell me again how this is going to work?' Grace asked.

'I already exist outside of time and space. I'm here in the present, and I carry my past and my future with me. We know that we're multidimensional and that time is really an illusion. That is our start point.'

Grace nodded. 'Agreed.'

'Another universe is created each time I make a decision. A continual unfolding of limitless versions of me plays out these decisions. This is Everett's original concept from 1957 and is the basis of multiverse theories.'

'Agreed, again.'

'I'm connected to each of these versions of myself, across time and space, given we've all come from the same collection of subatomic particles before the decisions made split me into two realities. I'm actually deeply entangled with these other versions

273

of me. So technically, I should be able to communicate with them and either ask for advice or exchange information.'

'You'd think so,' Grace said, furrowing her brow.

'If we use the analogy of the radio dial, all the stations are in the airwaves, and you adjust the dial to find the one you want. We'll be doing the same thing. I'll be searching my future states to find the one I seek. This should collapse the wave function into a specific reality and contact will be made.'

'How do we know which one? What do we use as a radio dial?' Grace asked.

'My observer effect. That's how you collapse the possibilities into one reality. So I create an intention of seeing a particular version of me and ask her to come.'

'How do you know she will?'

'If I set an intention to meet a version of me in a higher wisdom, then she is technically in a higher dimension in the universe. She'll come because it aligns with cosmic law.'

'What cosmic law?' Grace frowned, having trouble keeping up.

'Two of them, actually: "the higher dimensions always serve those below them", and "when we wish to serve the greater good and align with cosmic law, we will always prevail". She comes from a higher dimension, answering my invitation to serve our project for the benefit of humanity.'

'Okay. After the past year, I'm up for anything. What happens when we find her?'

'I'll ask her a few questions and request to share her vibration. That should entangle me with her future, and my future high-vibrational state then becomes a self-fulfilling prophecy,' Celeste explained.

Grace paused and considered Celeste's words. 'What about the learnings you would've gained along the way from other paths?'

'They'll still exist, of course. If I face those decisions with this new understanding of my destiny, then I may choose different paths at those crossroads. In short, I'll head towards my destiny like it's a homing beacon. I can't disrupt the free will of the other versions of me, though I can steer this particular awareness of Celeste towards my destination. Perhaps those decision points then no longer exist. There are no more forks in the road, so another universe isn't created.'

Grace shook her head slowly, then said, 'That's enough for now; I'm having trouble following all this. I just need your assurance that we aren't going to break anything. I don't want to carry that as a burden through life.'

Celeste laughed. 'We're only looking for one universe in a limitless number. The others won't even know we're there … at first, anyway.'

'I'm only slightly reassured, but I'm ready,' Grace replied. 'So tell me about your observer effect.'

'We're heading into the multiverse outside of time and space, so I offer three components to my search criteria. It has to be a version of me who finished the PhD, the highest state of happiness and an intention for service to humanity. That's it.'

Grace started with the usual protocols to expand Celeste's awareness beyond her current place in time and space. Celeste was ahead of her already. Instant access to Bob for many months now, stepping through a portal of light to embrace her light form and even the experience of visiting other lifetimes had now made her a natural traveller. From a long way away, she heard Grace's voice confirming her observer effect and asking for that version of her to come. She waited.

A presence emerged, slowly at first. In her mind's eye, a woman walked towards her, moving gracefully and confidently into her line of sight. Celeste stood, looking at this calm and confident version of herself, dressed in jeans and sandals with a loose-fitting top in a turquoise pattern. She was smiling peacefully. *I've been expecting you.*

At first, lost for something to say, Celeste eventually tried, 'Have you been waiting long?'

The other Celeste smiled. *All your life ... How about you call me Celeste-45; that will help you back in linear time. I'm about three years further along than you.*

'How come you're expecting me?' Celeste asked.

Because I once stood where you are and spoke to me, as you are doing now, came the reply.

That makes sense, Celeste thought. 'What can you tell me?'

I can tell you to keep going and trust that you're on the right path, Celeste-45 said. *Much will fall into place, and you're already making an enormous difference to the world. Very soon, this will expand even further. You've done well to connect us by following the leads Bob offered you.*

'Are you happy?' Celeste asked.

I am very happy, and my life is incredibly full with all I'm bringing to the world. I found someone to work alongside me too. I no longer tread a solo path and now know the deep love of another person.

'Can I ask who?'

It's best I show you. With that, Celeste-45 sent her the feeling of a male energy. It was familiar, yet unfamiliar, and Celeste knew she'd not felt that energy in her life until now. She couldn't make out the details of the person's features, just a sense of a blue energy around the torso, neck and shoulders. Not knowing what to do with the experience, she tucked it away for reflection later.

What other questions do you have? Celeste-45 asked.

'How do I solve the uncertainty problem? It's the last piece

I need.'

Celeste-45 smiled. *Bob has already given you some hints.*

'I know, but you know him. He's a little short on detail.'

I can tell you that it will come to you. You also need to look up an old friend or two to get some help. The only other thing is to focus on the illusion hint. That will help.

In the background, Grace, who would've heard the snippets of conversation Celeste shared, gently reminded Celeste of her original intention—to blend with the vibration of her other self.

Celeste-45 and Celeste moved together and combined their energy fields in an explosion of light and energy so profound that tears came to Celeste. She experienced a heart full of love and a soul full of purpose. It steadied her and brought to her a profound certainty that all would unfold in the most beautiful way. After what felt like a long time, she returned to what now seemed like the harsh environment of the physical realm. The echoes of her experience rippled gently out from her in all directions.

Grace held a supportive space for a moment while Celeste gathered her thoughts. 'Looks like it worked out okay, then?' Grace asked hopefully.

Celeste got out of the chair and hugged Grace with a full and open heart. 'Thank you, Grace. This is life-changing.' She strode out of the room, heading for the paper charts in the studio while the thoughts were still fresh.

Grace watched her go, knowing something big was coming.

CHAPTER 54

A few days later, Celeste was on the phone to the best quantum mathematician she knew.

'Are you sure about this, Celeste?' Riccardo asked.

'Humour me, Riccardo; there are a dozen bottles of your favourite wine in it for you. I seem to remember you enjoy whites,' she replied.

'The Heisenberg equation wasn't designed for this type of application. It measures uncertainty, not certainty. You're asking to reverse the whole concept.'

Celeste imagined Riccardo throwing his hands in the air. 'I know, but I need an equation that predicts a location. I want you to work backwards. Can you still use Planck's constant to create a level of certainty?'

'I'm not sure. I've been doing this for twenty years, and no-one has ever come close to asking for something like this. I need some time to think about it. Tell me your minimum calculation scenario.' Riccardo sounded flustered after this debate with Celeste.

'I need an equation that takes the last known position of a particle before it winks out of existence and then provides a new predicted position for its return. You can assume the disappearing and reappearing velocity are equal, and you can use Planck's constant if necessary,' Celeste said.

'That may be possible, though it'll have to be tested experimentally. It goes against the laws of physics as we know them. The whole uncertainty principle is based on non-predictability.'

She smiled. 'Yes, Riccardo, I know that.'

Three days later, she had the equation and asked the team to give it a test run. After a bit of quiet time around the table as calculations were made, Raz said, 'The equation checks out. It gives a location easily enough. Though without experimentation, we just don't know if anything will show up there.'

Grace nodded in agreement.

Skye said, 'This is why I never liked the maths component, and why I prefer space. I'd rather calculate the orbit of a large planet than the position of a troublesome particle that has disappeared.'

'You won't need to,' Celeste assured her. 'Raz, can you automate the equation in a small application? I need us to be able to cut and paste from a screen in another system, drop it into the app and then find the value of the new position.'

'Yes, I should be able to use universal code. I'll model it from the system we take it from. By the way, what system is that?' he asked.

'The operating system in CERN,' she replied.

Raz hesitated, a little surprised … 'Um, sure … Give me a day.'

CHAPTER 55

Celeste set up a Zoom call to Geneva. 'Guten Tag, Dieter, it has been some time since we spoke. Thank you for your emails.'

'It is good to see you, Celeste. How is life in the "down unter"?' He'd never quite mastered that phrase.

'Fine, thank you. How did you go with my proposal?'

Following Celeste-45's advice, Celeste had indeed looked up an old friend. Dieter was an experimental physicist at CERN. They'd worked together in her time there and, as a young, up-and-coming physicist, Dieter had been quite taken by her. A solid friendship had formed, and Celeste had helped him out of a few tough spots, so he was in her debt. She was now calling it in.

'There is a three-year wait for experimental time on the Large Hadron Collider, but I have a couple of compact linear colliders for small-scale experimentation. Your Project Shed is not part of our collaboration scheme. So technically I can't give you access, though there is always a way. I may finally have the possibility to repay your kindness from the past.'

'What've you come up with?' Celeste asked.

'We need to undertake maintenance on these smaller machines from time to time. Usually, this is done on a Sunday when the laboratory is empty. Following maintenance, we must use and test the machines, so we generate a stream of particles and let it run for an hour or more. During this time, we could observe the particles you want us to and run the prediction equation in parallel to this post-maintenance test.'

'I'm very grateful, Dieter. Did you find some volunteers to partake in the experiment?'

'My whole team of ten have volunteered. They are very excited about the flipping of uncertainty to certainty for subatomic particles. They will be suitable, as their mathematics is world class and their English is perfect. Perhaps more perfect even than the Australian version.' He grinned through the screen.

Ah. Swiss humour. Probably an ancient ancestor of dad jokes. 'Quite so!' Celeste agreed. 'I'll look forward to briefing them.' If Dieter said his team's mathematics was world class, then it would be so. They'd have the precision of a Swiss watch.

'This equation that you have constructed, does it have a name?' Dieter asked.

Celeste grinned. 'Good question. We're calling it the "interdimensional certainty principle".'

Dieter nodded. 'A wonderful name. So, before the briefing next week, you need the team to be one hundred per cent satisfied with the equation and also the program we use for calculation?'

'Correct, and we need each of them to undertake the experiment with our intention as stated in the email,' Celeste said.

'I have that here.' He reached for his notes and read, '"Particles that leave the third dimension reappear as predicted by the observer".'

'That's it precisely. That's the definition of the

interdimensional certainty principle.'

A week later, the briefing was in full swing via a video call with Dieter and his team of ten. 'We need you to be sure of your calculations at all times,' she told them. 'If you wish to do them manually before trusting the system, that's more than acceptable. When you observe the coordinates of the prediction, carry that certainty with you. Remember, you're observing these particles as they return from another dimension, so certainty is paramount.'

Late that Sunday evening, she sat in her office, eagerly anticipating the results. What was taking them so long?

Finally, her computer signalled a call coming through, and Dieter appeared on her screen. 'My apologies for being late, Celeste. We had to check and double check our observations. My team is in shock. We can't believe what we have just witnessed!'

She nodded expectantly. 'What did you find?'

'Until now, these particles that come back into observation have always arrived with complete randomness. It is unbelievable that we can now predict their arrival. We took one hundred observations, and they appeared at exactly the point predicted … every single time! We have also confirmed, through the subatomic mass, that they are the same particles that previously disappeared. The equation is one hundred per cent accurate. There will need to be further experiments, but the first test of the interdimensional certainty principle has confirmed this phenomenon.'

Celeste smiled. 'Dieter, thank you for what you've done here. Let me congratulate you and the team.'

'Wait … there is more to say! These particles slowed down to minimal velocity after they reappeared. It was as though they wanted to be measured, like they were helping us. This is unlike any phenomenon we have ever seen. My people are bewildered. I have just sent you all the data.'

'Perhaps I can help you understand why, Dieter. I'd like to

introduce you to something called cosmic law.'

CHAPTER 56

Celeste had come full circle and was sitting in front of her PhD review board for her last ever meeting.

Having seen her other lifetimes, experienced her existence as another form of being and made discoveries that traditional scientists never make, she sat there powerfully, in the full knowing of her multidimensional self.

Dr Bart, QB and Schrodinger beamed at her.

QB spoke first. 'This is an incredible result. Of course, we always knew you'd be successful.'

No, you didn't, though you did give me great incentive to prove you wrong. Outwardly, she just smiled.

Dr Bart had trouble keeping a straight face. Schrodinger looked like he was thinking about the memoir he was going to write in which he'd focus on his role in mentoring a young quantum physicist who'd changed the field forever.

Dr Bart spoke next. 'By the authority of the Board of Trustees of the University of New South Wales, and as recommended by the Faculty of the School of Physics, I have great pleasure in conferring upon you the degree of doctor of philosophy. A copy of your doctoral thesis, titled 'The Emerging Phenomenon of Quantum Metaphysics', will be held in the university library and made available to the public.'

The three of them applauded.

'Just so you know,' he continued, 'we have arranged a small private graduation ceremony for you before you make the Project Shed presentation in Burrows Hall in three months' time. That presentation is already booked out, and the hall holds over five hundred people! They're now proposing a livestream as well. They're calling your thesis the most important one since Everett's in 1957. And by the way, CERN are in uproar given what you did to them. You'd better walk us through that one, please, just so we're all on the same page. We do have an important relationship with them.'

Celeste nodded. 'Of course. But Dieter understands what happened to his team now. More importantly, he knows why I had to keep him in the dark. The elaborate equation designed was a prop. It simply calculated a random point in time and space. His people believe in mathematics because it's a discipline that's either right or wrong. Once they knew the maths was right and were certain that the particles would be there, they were. They found them at the predicted point every single time. The particles were called to that time and place by the observer effect of the technician looking for them.

'The big shock for Dieter's team,' she continued, 'was when the particles started to behave in a way that collaborated with the observer. They slowed down so they could be measured to prove the experiment was successful. This was what the observers truly wanted, without any doubt in their minds. They wanted to be successful.'

Dr Bart and QB nodded. Schrodinger squinted at her as if

he'd just returned from his daydream.

'The implications of the observer effect are well known,' Celeste went on, 'though what Dieter's team actually did was confirm that higher dimensions serve this dimension. As I've shared with you before, under cosmic law, the higher dimensions serve the lower dimensions when they ask for assistance, as long as the request is within the twin guiding principles of embracing free will and meeting a greater purpose. The environment created met those criteria. The final conclusion of this experiment is that the particles must have been in a higher dimension, otherwise they would not have slowed down to be measured after returning.'

'The last piece,' Dr Bart said.

Celeste smiled. 'Yes, so we now have a number of experimental techniques confirming that other dimensions exist and that we have access to them. This will be the subject of my presentation in three months' time. There is more to do beyond the thesis, though. The work of the Research Institute for Quantum Metaphysics is expanding, though that's a conversation for another time. Thank you all for your support over the past few years. Project Shed is officially complete now, and RIQM will now be assessing our next projects.'

Soon afterwards, she took her leave and travelled back to the mountains, ready to undertake yet another way for her to serve humanity.

She called the team together to again discuss the many worlds' interpretation. The waiting room area became their thinktank for the next few hours. With the completion of Project Shed, the participant journeys had tapered off, though some experimentation continued following Celeste's powerful meeting with her forty-five-year-old self.

Celeste started the discussion. 'Tell me how you're going with the future self scenarios.'

Raz spoke first. 'This has become one of the most powerful experiences, being able to tune into the preferred future and get that advice or support so badly needed. From what I've seen, it's working well.'

'Agreed,' Skye said. 'My cases are reporting a significant change in perspective and also ongoing contact with their other self. Once the link has been opened, that other aspect of them continues to be accessible afterwards.'

Both Grace and Abbey nodded in agreement.

'Okay, so now we've proven this makes a difference on an individual scale. How would we go about changing the world?'

No one replied. Though Celeste could hear the wheels turning inside their minds.

Eventually, Grace said, 'When we use the many worlds' interpretation to select a specific future that fits the intention of the person, I feel we're collapsing all lower vibrational paths, creating one positive future instead. We construct one specific destiny and everything heads towards that.'

Celeste nodded. 'Keep going.'

'Well, in a holographic universe where everything is connected, what we do at the small scale should translate to the larger scale. We don't need to take everyone on the planet into their best possible destiny, we simply need to create a vision of a world that carries the highest possible vibration, enrol people in this outcome and everyone's intention will take us towards that.'

'How would it work?' Celeste asked.

Grace continued, on a roll, 'I don't know if you've heard about the group meditation effect, but according to a well-known meditation group, many years ago when thousands of people in various cities in the USA meditated for peace, the crime rate supposedly went down for that period. Other factors may have been involved in causing that result, of course, but the logic is sound. Some meditation gurus say that the unified quantum field and consciousness are synonymous. If we place an intention into the field of humanity that is positive and is truly desired by the individuals, then the more they engage with it, the more certainty there is for that destiny.'

'Most people don't meditate,' Skye chimed in, 'but everyone loves a story. What if people talk about and share these visions of a positive future, and those stories create momentum to bring that destiny into being?'

Raz took a turn. 'Let's take people to their future selves and ask them to share with us a story that people most need to hear today. It'll be like time travel. We share the stories back here with others and gradually collapse all timelines into a better world.'

Celeste looked around at the team she'd become so proud of. 'So, basically, we leapfrog all the problems in the world today and bring the best future state of the world into our line of sight now. We can publish it as a collective vision of a new world. Put it out on social media and viralise it.' She felt the excitement building in the team. 'Looks like we have our next project.'

Celeste turned to Abbey. 'Abs, how many people have volunteered to be participants in future projects?'

'Just about everyone we've helped so far, over two and a half thousand,' came the reply.

Celeste smiled. 'Sounds like we have enough to create our own quantum consciousness effect. Skye, can you please design new protocols? Raz, we need a new database, along with supporting systems. Grace, can you design the project brief and do a new webpage? Abs, draft an invitation to our volunteer base. I'll brief the board on our new proposal and set a budget for the project. Let's do all we can by Friday afternoon. We'll share updates then.'

They scurried around for a few days and then, during the

Friday meeting, confirmed the project would be launched over the weekend. They'd take people into a future state of being with the intention of finding an inspiring story to share with the world back here.

Celeste had one last task to complete before launch—to visit the shed. As soon as Celeste sat in her chair, Bob hovered in his. *Hi, Bob, just checking in on this new project and wondered if you or the team have anything to offer?*

Scale will build quickly, he replied in her mind, *so you need to be prepared for that. It is time to spread the work being done further and place it in the hands of the network you have built.*

Celeste paused. *I'll give that some thought.* Her human mind was already humming.

Enrolment of others will be important in reaching the critical mass needed. As we have spoken of before, once the particle becomes the wave, it is unstoppable. What name will you select for this project?

Well ... we're designing a mass observer effect, or more accurately, a 'creator effect' for human consciousness into the collective intent for a positive shared future. We need a shorter name that speaks to that. I'm thinking Project DOD—designing our destiny.

Bob smiled. *It carries a beautiful intention, and in the emerging field of quantum metaphysics, it is also accurate.*

They were good to go.

CHAPTER 57

Expectation built around the presentation at the university. It was no longer just about her PhD. The Research Institute for Quantum Metaphysics, as the joint venture between the multinational corporation Collins Industries and UNSW, was causing a lot of discussion. When Bob had used the 'quantum metaphysics' term many months previously, it had seemed a good idea to bring that phrase into the general public's line of sight. Now she wasn't so sure. When she went public at the presentation, the term would sink or swim on her performance. Project DOD was at a critical stage as well, and the first round of data was due to be presented.

After working on it for days, one morning, Grace walked into Celeste's office and said, 'The data is ready for the first look. Do you want a pre-briefing?'

'We're all part of this, Grace. Ask the team to gather, and we'll have a look together.'

Grace had been reticent to speak about the emerging trends as she was eager to gauge their reactions when all together. Once the team was seated, she flashed some slides up on the wall.

'The first two hundred cases are now in for Project DOD, and interesting trends are emerging. I've had to design new ways of analysing data in time blocks because the trends have changed as time progressed. I divided the two hundred cases into five samples of forty cases each as they run in linear time. Sample one relates to the first forty cases; sample two, the next forty, and so on.

'Remember the protocols we're using: volunteers move outside time and space, and we ask their super observer to connect with information from the future that serves humanity. Usually, they connected through future versions of themselves who wanted to share a story. However, on some occasions, it was a different person, yet to be born. Like the future versions of our participants, they wished to share their story.'

The team's attention was riveted on the information presented on the slides.

'As always,' Grace said, 'we were greeted as though we were expected. These do appear to be future selves who are coming through. The time range is between five years and seventy-five years from now. This appears to be self-selected by the super observer, as we aren't giving them a specific time frame.

'We're seeing the same results in the random event generators and the heart coherence software as we did with Project Shed. The participant is no longer in the system being measured, though we still receive information through their voice, so this information can only be coming from another dimension. Looks like what we discovered in Shed is transportable to other projects.'

Raz asked, 'Why is it sometimes an older version of them and sometimes not?'

Grace paused, then spoke slowly and deliberately. 'My theory is that the participant is no longer alive. They've passed over and reincarnated into another body. Using standard protocols, we're able to access the next incarnation because the super observer is quantumly entangled with the next body in the same way. We never actually said it has to be this life that comes forward. We simply asked for a 'future version of themselves'. We may theorise that the super observer is either synonymous with the person's soul or, at the very least, has access to a level of quantum memory outside time and space.' She paused and waited for them for digest what she said.

'Holy Crap!' Skye said. 'So you're saying that in wanting to *design our destiny* for humanity, we've enrolled our participants' future incarnations in this project? … Umm, that's if you believe in reincarnation, of course.'

Grace smiled, having got the effect she wanted. 'Or another theory could be that we're mining the collective consciousness of humanity at a future date and hitting a random human subject. I have no idea why we would default to that particular person, though. The other thing to note is that all these people are younger. The further away from the present date we go across all samples, the younger the person at the other end is, as though they have to finish this current incarnation first. I would've thought that if we were randomly going into the collective, we'd have a mix of ages. This supports my first reincarnation theory. By the way, none of this has to do with the five samples in linear time yet; these are initial discoveries from the overall data.'

Celeste said, 'Why don't we ask the super about these incarnations when those younger ages come up?'

Grace nodded. 'I was going to recommend that. Skye, are we able to change the protocols?'

'Sure,' she replied. 'I'd recommend an open statement like, *Tell me of the connection between you and the participant.* Let's see what comes from that. I'll organise a couple of supporting directives too.'

Grace continued, 'Thank you; I'll let you know how that goes across the next sample of participants. But there's something even more important coming through in those linear sample groups. First, the background.

'At the end of each week, with the help of the social media company we engaged, we're publishing stories of the future. People who follow us have shared further, and we're slowly going viral. We published the first forty stories online, and they were all quite different. The participants shared reflections of a positive world across a wide variety of subjects. We were literally seeing "many worlds". People who visit our website or follow us on social media read and share them widely.'

'Excellent,' Celeste said.

Grace smiled. 'We then published the second batch of forty, and the different participants shared more similar stories, as though an overlap was emerging. For example, twelve separate participants reported the breakdown of the third-world and first-world structure into something that was more equal in terms of rich and poor. A type of social reset, if you like, or a more humane redistribution of wealth. These stories were even more popular.

'In the third group of forty stories, themes emerged about a shift in science. The further we went into the future, the more we saw a field of what they referred to as *metascience* emerging. One of the participants actually told us that they're a metascientist working on behalf of humanity. Details were few, though the year was reported as 2080. This was one of the people who came forward at a younger age, someone who wouldn't be alive today. After we shared those stories, the readership increased by four hundred per cent. Almost a million people now follow us, though we have no idea how many people have shared content with their own networks.'

'And the fourth group?' Celeste prompted.

'In the fourth group, the information started to overlap and align even further into key themes, and the number of our followers continued to grow. By the time we got to the fifth group, five themes about a future world had emerged. Almost all the stories touched on these in some way. The consistency in the participants' stories has become stronger the further we go. They're describing a far more common view of the world than the first group.'

'What are the five themes?' Skye asked.

'The first theme is a different type of leadership replacing the governments of today, one that advocates for all people equally and for the sustainability of the planet. The second is a series of world restoration projects, tens of thousands of them funded by the wealth previously held by a few people. The third theme is energetic medicine consisting of alternative-health modalities, ancient healing arts and the best of allopathic medicine. The fourth is the world of metascience, which blends physical and non-physical study together, and we hear about the "progressive application of consciousness". The last theme is one of new technologies. Many of the participants talked about free energy and the closure of the fossil fuel industry. They also talk about the retirement of all wireless technologies and the use of telepathy into the quantum field as a replacement for the internet.'

Celeste's eyes widened, as shocked as the others, though something deep inside resonated with the idea. 'Okay, Grace,' she said, 'I know you'll have a theory on why these themes are getting stronger. Let's hear it.'

Grace paused for effect. 'I believe we're collapsing future timelines that hold negative outcomes for humanity by directing our thoughts into positive outcomes in the here and now. The more we share our findings, the more people become enrolled, and the more strongly the characteristics of this new world emerge. We've initiated a time loop, building a positive future through these participants that's gaining momentum. Negative scenarios for humanity's future are ceasing to exist within the multiverse.'

Silence blanketed the room as they digested her words.

'Spell it out for us, Grace,' Celeste said eventually. She understood but wanted the others to hear it as well.

Grace's eyes lit with enthusiasm. 'We're literally *designing our destiny*. From this small sample, it looks like it's working. Humanity is being progressively placed on one path towards a greater future.'

'How do we get the scale, though?' Abbey asked.

Celeste turned to Grace. 'Tell them about the consciousness magnification effect.'

Grace smiled. 'The term "consciousness magnification effect" was coined by an international meditation group after some of their research appeared to show that we only need the square root of one per cent to kick start a change in consciousness. In our terms, it's saying that the observer effect multiplies when shared by others. Consciousness seems to have a magnification principle when shared in a common frequency of thought or intention. If we look at this more from our perspective as facilitators of quantum phenomena, we are infusing particles with a specific vibration and sending them out to collide with others. They are then absorbed into a growing wave, which moves holographically through the collective consciousness. This is the ripple effect of our work.'

Raz scribbled some numbers on a piece of paper.

Grace continued sharing her thoughts. 'This was the original concept behind the random number generator machines and the Schumann resonances where large, shared events in human history show a spike in the magnetic field of the Earth. It's the same principle as our smaller machines that we've used to confirm the absence of disruption when working with our participants.'

Raz looked up from his paper. 'I haven't evaluated the research you're referring to, but if those figures are correct, that's the square root of one per cent of eight billion people, which is'—he looked at his paper—'only 8,944.'

Grace nodded enthusiastically. 'And we're probably well past that already with our followers.'

Abbey and Skye's eyes sparkled with inspiration, but Raz frowned, apparently unconvinced. 'But even if it is true that we only need the square root of one per cent to kickstart a change in consciousness,' he said, 'there must be countless people out there thinking about the worst future possible. How do we counteract that?'

The team looked to Celeste for a response.

'I think we have enough momentum and supporting results to keep going, and enough people willing to keep working with us to have a positive effect, regardless of whether those figures can be validated or not,' Celeste said. 'It'll be up to the board to decide how big this becomes. Given what may be emerging, we can't stop; the future of humanity is at stake. I imagine that competing futures will drop away as we build more momentum. However, this is all theory; no one has ever done this before. We really are in unchartered waters regarding the experimentation of consciousness in the quantum field.'

The team remained quiet for the rest of the day. Though inspired by the initial results, they felt the burden of responsibility for the potential of Project DOD. Celeste sought counsel with Bob.

Bob, what's going on here? Are we really creating a new future for the world?

Something is unfolding that will change the future of humanity. You are about to discover that the universe responds to your collective intention. You proved it with the CERN team on the smallest scale, and now you are taking that into a larger scale. You have created a ripple that exists beyond time and space. You talk often of the super observer and the wisdom it holds, as it is not bound by time and space as we are in human form. Imagine the power of activating hundreds or even thousands of super observers—maybe even in their millions, eventually—towards a single high-vibrational destiny for your world. This is quantum metaphysics, the gift you are bringing to humanity.

What if we get it wrong? What if we slip up? What if something happens like it did to my father? It's all right for you all back on the other side, but I'm on the ground here, carrying the load. She'd never challenged him like this before, but fear made her speak up.

He replied with the 'Bob smile' that oozed patience. *There are safeguards in place. If you do anything outside cosmic law, it won't work. Your project is showing results because you are honouring the free will of the participants by asking them to tell any story that serves humanity. The super observers of the participants are working with you. Remember the parameters of free will and greater purpose. They permeate your endeavours. If you ever move outside these, the project will simply fade away. You are unable to break the universe, no matter how hard you try.*

Celeste sensed a Bob joke, but it was hard to tell.

There is more, he continued. *You are accessing higher dimensional states, asking them to give you information. It could be said that the future of humanity is held in a higher dimension, without war, greed, hate or fear. As a result, they reach out to help, and in doing so, they bring even more light to our present from the future. It creates a time loop for the greater good of all, a spiralling effect towards a more advanced state of being. Once humans learn to move outside of time, they can repair anything in their collective past and move towards higher states. All advanced civilisations in the universe have done this. Including the one you and I are from. As we have discussed before, this has been veiled from you while you are in human form. We cannot do it for you. Finally, know that we are always with you, Celeste; we have shown you this.*

Okay, I feel somewhat reassured. She relaxed a little.

Bob tilted his head in query. *There are other things on your mind? Remember, our support for you goes way beyond our projects in the third dimension.*

Yeah, I find the circumstances of my father's passing distressing. It doesn't sit well with me, and I wonder if I'm supposed to do something about it.

That is complicated, Bob agreed. *Remember your empath sensitivities for energy. Sit back and observe; don't absorb the situation. A path will open for you to pursue if you choose to. You wanted to learn about the energy of emotion in human form, and this meets that intention also. We discussed this together before you came to be Celeste.*

Suddenly, he was gone, leaving Celeste feeling a little unresolved.

CHAPTER 58

The next few weeks flew by, and finally the day of the presentation arrived.

Lillian from Gabe's office had called to say that transport had been arranged for the whole team. They speculated on what type of helicopter would be sent from Collins Industries and were somewhat relieved when a stretch limousine pulled into the driveway.

Celeste rehearsed with them as they travelled. They each fired possible questions at her that might come from the diverse audience made up of the university community and the public and private sectors. All in all, a crowd of almost six hundred were expected. This was the launch of the Research Institute for Quantum Metaphysics two years' work, and the careers of the whole team were on the line. The brands of both the university and Collins Industries hinged on what she said and how she came across. Celeste had to breathe deeply to stay in a cool, calm and collected state of being.

They arrived early and Celeste had time to brief the audio-visual team who would be supporting the event. Just to add to the pressure, the livestream was indeed going ahead.

She took a walk around campus to allow her energy to settle, and her phone pinged while passing the events building. It was Dr Bart:

I have a suggestion for the presentation. Stop by the catering area and I'll fill you in.

Celeste replied:

OK.

The catering area was part of the events building, and she knew it well. It seemed deserted when she arrived. No sign of Dr Bart, so she called his phone and heard it ringing in the distance.

Somewhat bemused by the cloak and dagger approach employed by her mentor, she followed the sound into a back room. *Must be a top-secret suggestion.*

Dr Bart's phone sat on a table in the back room, ringing. She approached it, starting to feel a little uneasy, and jumped as the door closed behind her. Hearing the door bolted from the outside, Celeste whirled around and pushed against it, but even with all her weight against it, the heavy metal door wouldn't budge.

She stood there, stunned, confusion taking hold as she began to understand her predicament. Her concern escalated as she realised this had nothing to do with Dr Bart. To make matters worse, a humming noise started in the background, and a burst of cold air came through a vent in the wall. To her horror, Celeste realised she was in a freezer room, and someone had turned the power on.

She looked at her watch: 6.30 pm. The presentation started in thirty minutes, and no-one knew where she was. Matters became even worse when she realised her phone couldn't get a signal with the door closed. She was trapped, out of contact and would probably freeze to death before anyone found her.

Celeste started to panic as her temperature began to drop. The sealed room contained mostly empty shelving used to store food for large events. A couple of canvas sheets sat on a shelf in the corner. She grabbed one, wrapped it around her shoulders and turned her mind to her predicament, knowing it was a matter of life or death.

After engaging her problem-solving skills and assessing all the facts, she realised she had no way out of this. She was physically constrained in a hostile environment with no escape. A wave of anger moved through her, followed by a deep sadness from another time. The old feelings of Zac fading away before his time came back into her knowing, and she almost surrendered to her fate.

A phrase entered her mind from elsewhere: *Determination is great, but stubbornness is even better when pointed in the right direction.* Something within her kicked in. *No, Zac, not again …*

It called for something more, and the last two years had taught her that so much more was available to her when she got out of her own way.

Her natural instincts were to keep moving and stay warm for as long as possible, but she had to transcend her human thoughts and move into something beyond them, so she sat on the concrete floor on another piece of canvas and tried to tune into Bob. Panic rose, but she breathed through it and found a better connection and a more relaxed state. Bob came into focus.

Well done, Celeste. I've been watching and waiting.

How do we get out of this one, Bob? I'm out of time and everything is at risk.

You know I can't interfere physically, Celeste, and you are the only one I make contact with.

So that's it, Bob, the end of this journey, just like it was for my father?

There is one thing we can do, though it must honour universal law. You and I are connected across time and space. You and others are connected here in this physical realm. We can use you as a bridge to get help, though it depends on the person we reach out to, and they need to be open to using their own free will to feel the connection at their end. Are you ready?

Celeste nodded and let go. In an explosion of light, Bob stepped into her and blended their consciousnesses. She felt the light tribe from her home dimension surrounding her, and then, as one mind, they thought of the one person who might understand. They reached out to Abbey.

Chapter 59

The team were getting worried. Celeste had disappeared.

Abbey, feeling worn and stressed, said to the others, 'There's no sign of her, and her phone is off. Something has happened. I just know it.' She turned to Dr Bart. 'Have you heard anything?'

'No,' he replied, concern being etched more deeply into his face by the minute. 'Though I did lose my phone this afternoon.'

It was 6.50 pm. Time had almost run out. Abbey decided to check the ladies' bathroom one more time.

Nature called when she arrived, and she sat for a moment, relieving herself, the concentration of her task lifting her away from her stress. Though for just a few seconds, it was enough. Abbey noticed a light coming under the door of her cubicle, as if a floodlight had been switched on in the main part of the bathroom. She stood, adjusted her attire and opened the door.

A man of sorts—more of a hologram than a physical being—stood in front of her. He looked about sixty and had long hair and a flowing beard. Abbey's eyes widened, and her jaw dropped open. She swore for the second time in living memory.

'Well, fuck me! You must be Interdimensional Bob!'

'I am, and Celeste has sent me to find you. She needs your help.'

'Well, lead the way, I-Bob, and stop loitering in the ladies' toilets.'

A picture appeared in Abbey's mind, and she ran, knowing exactly where to go.

CHAPTER 60

Celeste had almost given up hope. She was starting to fade—teeth chattering, fingers and toes growing numb. The sheet of canvas did little to alleviate her downward spiral, and she sank to the floor, preparing herself for the worst.

Did someone shake her shoulders, or was she dreaming? Celeste opened her eyes.

Abbey's face appeared in front of her. 'Lest … Lest … wake up,' her friend said urgently.

Energy surged into her body from Abbey's hands on her shoulders. It felt like the whole universe was downloading into her being. A tidal wave of energy jolted her into an awakened state.

Abbey pulled her to her feet. 'We are really late. Can you run?'

'If you help me, Abs.'

They joined hands and left the cool room, running towards the auditorium.

'I can't believe that worked,' Celeste said through still-chattering teeth.

'Yes, just met my first interdimensional being while I had my pants around my ankles,' Abbey quipped as they ran through the side door of the hall.

Celeste felt the restlessness in the crowd. It was 7.15 pm now, and people were wondering what was going on. The relief on Professor Robinson, Gabe and Dr Bart's faces was palpable. Raz, Grace and Skye rushed forward, clearly noticing Celeste's crumpled clothes and pale complexion. Grace smoothed her hair and brushed her down.

Celeste stood before all of them and declared, 'I'm okay, just give me a second and we're good to go.' She paused and closed her eyes for just a moment, centring herself and connecting with the part of her who chose to come here, to bring this work to the world and represent those from another place. It calmed her, and she stepped onto the stage and took her seat at the side, next to Professor Robinson.

She was ready.

Abbey, Skye, Raz, Grace and Dr Bart took their seats in the middle of the reserved seating, with Gabe and Amanda Collins, Jack Hadley and Paul O'Malley at one end, QB and Schrodinger at the other.

The lights faded, and a spotlight shone on the podium. Robinson stepped into view. 'On behalf of the University of New South Wales, Collins Industries and the Research Institute for Quantum Metaphysics, we wish you a warm welcome this evening. It was just two years ago that an idea was formed between business and academia to create a research institute with one brief: to undertake cutting-edge research into quantum physics, specifically designed to serve humanity. Tonight, we will share with you what has happened since.

'If you haven't heard of Dr Celeste Kelly, then you haven't been paying attention … well, to anything, really.' Some in the audience laughed. 'Celeste has a long history with UNSW and has been a part of some of our great scientific endeavours for the best part of two decades. She was the natural person to lead this new venture, and tonight you'll get a snapshot of what she and her team have been doing. Please, welcome Dr Celeste Kelly …'

The crowd erupted in applause, and Celeste felt the wave of energy and support from the huge crowd. She stood looking out at the people before her. This was the moment where she could share messages that would shift humanity further onto a timeline that served the people of this world. She stood there of her own free will for a greater purpose and with the full support of cosmic law behind her.

The big screen came to life, showing visuals to support her words.

'Thank you for your patience, and I apologise for the delay in proceedings. I was in another dimension and lost track of time.' A few chuckles rippled from the audience. The spotlight brought a welcome warmth to her body, and she moved into her flow.

'I stand before you tonight thanks to a handful of remarkable people, and the first thing I wish to do is recognise their contribution to our understanding of the quantum realm in which we exist. Albert Einstein told us that, "Time and space are modes in which we think and not conditions in which we live." After two years, our team has found a deeper meaning in these words. As quantum physicists, we've always theorised that time and space are malleable to our intention, and I'm here to tell you that is indeed so. We have created windows to the past, portals to the future, and the universe is within our reach. Einstein was as much a seer as he was a scientist. He left us clues to what the universe holds to be discovered when we were finally ready. Sometimes, I feel like I met him somewhere along the way. Who knows, maybe in a past life?'

Chuckles came from the audience, even though she

wasn't joking.

'When Hugh Everett published his paper in 1957, claiming that the wave function doesn't collapse but continues on, creating limitless different realities, he was told he was crazy. What right did he, as a PhD candidate, have to conceptualise something so revolutionary? In time, his ideas came to be known as the many worlds' interpretation, and too late in his life, he was hailed as a genius. These days, alternate realities, parallel universes and other dimensions are generally accepted, if not by all of science, then certainly by popular culture. As for me and my team, we've found them to be real, and we know that within them lies the future of humanity.

'Also, I wish to recognise Werner Heisenberg. By more clearly designing how uncertainty could be measured, he built a path to certainty. What appears to be strange behaviour in this reality simply seeks a multidimensional reframe. Particles are "slippery" as they prepare to leave this reality and enter another. Though they'll return when asked.' She paused for effect. 'More on this later.

'When Ed Witten brought us M-theory in 1995, amalgamating five different versions of string theory, he showed us the most remarkable concept. You add another dimension and the universe comes together. Witten moved us to ten, not nine, spatial dimensions. The maths tells us that they exist, so where are they? Maths is a black-and-white discipline; it is either right or wrong, and that has served us since ancient times. If the maths is right, then these dimensions must exist.

'So Einstein was challenging reality as we know it and telling us to think differently. Everett was telling us the multiverse exists. Witten mathematically proved the other dimensions, and Heisenberg confirmed that the building blocks of the universe itself behaved differently than they should ... and then we stumbled across the discovery that we actually influence the universe all the time.

'Science discovered the observer effect, and that was the turning point. While still many are yet to grasp this principle, the name doesn't do it justice. We don't just observe the universe, we shape it, and it responds to our every whim. Up until now, we haven't realised the incredible power this offers us, even within our own lives.

'So in Project Shed, we went looking for other dimensions. We wanted to access them, find out what was there and see how this could bring greater benefit to humanity. We found answers to those questions, and I'm here tonight to share them with you ...'

The crowd leaned forward in their chairs. The screen behind her that had shown the faces of all the scientists she'd mentioned went blank momentarily before running a number of pictures of the RIQM environment, the numerous participants and her team at work.

'This is how we did it ... It occurred to us that we, as individuals, are part of the universe and quantumly entangled with it, therefore we should naturally have access to the other dimensions. We used courageous volunteer participants as a bridge to these other dimensions. We asked for those volunteers to come ... and wow, did they come, in their hundreds, in fact. They were seeking something for themselves and, in their quests, offered a precious gift to all of us. All of them were brave people wanting to explore, to find answers that had eluded them through traditional means ... and they found those answers.'

She then explained in detail the set-up for Project Shed, the system they used for measuring participants' distress, the protocols they used and the results.

'Participants were able to tell us the source of the distress, how to resolve it or what they needed to do to recover. The participant was being guided by another version of themselves, one that could only be coming from another dimension. Our readings confirmed that the participant's awareness had left the system, joined their super observer, then returned with that wisdom. Another surprise to us was that the participant remembered the conversation once the experiment was over. There could only be one reason for this. The fact that we also could hear the voice proved that the phenomenon existed in multiple dimensions concurrently.

'Solutions that had evaded the participant, in some cases for decades, were offered in a journey taking roughly an hour. We went looking for other dimensions, hoping to explore the multiverse, and we not only did that but also ended up offering over two thousand participants a life-changing experience.

'People reported complete recovery from emotional issues such as anxiety, depression, grief, addictions and a whole range of various traumas. Some of our participants reported the complete healing of psychosomatic illnesses, and those with dedicated physical issues completely recovered or reported unprecedented improvement compared to their normal recovery plans.

'On average, they entered the system at a self-assessed personal scale of two point three, and an hour or so later self-scored at eight point eight, leveling off after a number of weeks at roughly eight point two. This was a little over three hundred and fifty per cent increase in their sense of wellbeing and has remained that way ever since. This occurred almost by accident. Or did it? Were we steered by a greater power towards a discovery that served humanity? Perhaps we will know that answer some day.

'Einstein said, "You can't solve a problem at the same level of thinking at which it was created." From our experience, he was right. I see that phrase as one of the clues to discovering aspects of the universe that have been hidden from us until now. This is why I refer to him as a seer as well as a scientist. Perhaps he was even more than that, an advocate for a greater power, here to serve humanity...

'I believe we found the other dimensions that Witten and others have theorised. The super observers of the participants helped them not just heal but also to explore. Participants were given insights into their family of birth, the purpose for their lifetime and how they can serve humanity. It was as though the super observers we met expected us and wanted to help. We suspected that these higher dimensions wanted us to succeed. The super observer was honouring the intention the participant had set—their deliberate intention, their own observer effect. In short, our request for help was being answered from another dimension. Or was it? How could we prove it?

'We took Einstein at his word and did something that no one would be expecting. With deepest respect and apologies to Heisenberg, we invented our own phenomenon called the interdimensional certainty principle, which stated that particles that leave the third dimension reappear as predicted by the observer. At times, when they hit certain velocities, particles disappear in the colliders. We believed they crossed some form of interdimensional bridge. So we put together an equation that would predict a random place in time and space and set up an experiment in one of the linear Hadron colliders in CERN.

'Now, this is where it gets interesting. For the experiment to work, we simply had to convince the team at CERN that their maths was infallible, and therefore they would find the particles that had disappeared returning in the predicted point in time and space. Well, they did just that. In one hundred predictions and subsequent observations, we had the perfect score of one hundred per cent success. Though the experiment still had one more factor to consider. When the particles returned from the other dimension, they immediately slowed down so they could be measured by mass, thus allowing us to prove that they were the same ones that left. They were helping ...' Celeste paused for effect.

'The equation we gave them had nothing behind it other than to convince the experimental team that they were good at mathematics. We were asking them to do something other than what they thought they were doing. It was their own observer effect that brought the particles back to the predicted point in time and space.

'So we had shown that the phenomenon we'd seen, where the super observer was helping the participant at the macro level, was confirmed also at the subatomic level. We had matched a result from the macro and micro levels of the universe. Any quantum physicist will tell you that the macro world and the subatomic world behave differently ... well, we proved the opposite. Dimensions higher than ours respond to the intentions that we set and want us to succeed, and we found that this holds true for the universe both large and small.'

She paused and surveyed the crowd. They were riveted and silent. 'Though for us, this wasn't enough.' The crowd laughed, and Celeste continued. 'We wanted to explore the multiverse and find something there to serve humanity. We started to explore at the individual level. We asked versions of future selves to share wisdom through our courageous volunteer participants. These conversations offered a true expression of our multidimensional selves. Future versions of our participants reached back across time and space to help supply the answers to the questions of today, though only in a way that served a greater purpose and honoured the free will of those participants. We had a sense of less positive timelines collapsing for those participants and setting them free to explore their greatest destinies. This is what life in the multiverse looks like when we live a life according to our quantum potential.'

Again, she paused and looked at her audience. No one moved a muscle. 'This signalled the end of Project Shed. We found other dimensions, just as Witten had envisaged in M-theory. We'd been accessing and leveraging Everett's multiverse to serve the people courageous enough to meet their other selves. We flipped Heisenberg's work towards certainty from the start he'd given us. But most importantly, we started to understand more of what the higher dimensions offer the lower ones in terms of loving service. We were no longer scientists; we'd left that behind. We moved from being quantum physicists to metaphysicists. However, we had one more thing to do …

'Our brief at the Research Institute for Quantum Metaphysics is to undertake cutting-edge research into quantum physics, specifically designed *to serve humanity*. You could say that all the people we'd helped along the way did serve humanity at the individual level, but we wondered what would be the big contribution we could make that would create a better world for the generations that follow us.

'So we dreamed big and came up with Project DOD, designing our destiny. We decided to take participants into an amazing future and ask them to tell us a story that would serve people in these times. This would bring hope and inspiration to a world with too many shadows and not enough light. We would take these stories and viralise them through our media strategies to bring a ripple of light into humanity and slowly dissolve any other futures that may carry a lower vibration, characterised by some form of cataclysm or collapse.'

Celeste summarised the results of Project DOD and then continued by saying, 'We had theories about how this could happen, though we found the very best way to find out was to ask the super observers themselves. I'll now play a video recording that typifies the responses we received. You'll hear our person off-camera ask the question of the super observer, speaking through the participant named Jonathan.'

The video clip started, and Grace's voice could be heard off-camera. 'Tell me of the connection between you and Jonathan ...'

'I am the incarnation following the person who sits with you now. There are many of us who have been here helping humanity across a range of lifetimes, taking various roles and serving in different ways. We leave one body and join another as part of the evolution for the people of this planet. I come to you today to bring hope to a troubled world, and I am grateful to have the chance to reach back across time to help in my life before this one. Know that you will be successful, and we look back on these times with great pride and joy.'

The clip ended, and Celeste noticed some scepticism on the faces of some in the audience. She continued. 'We, as a team, had to accept that we were face-to-face with the concept of reincarnation. As metaphysicists, this fits with our emerging view of the super observer reaching us from other dimensions and the multidimensional nature of the human form. Why, indeed, would we assume that various other separate expressions of our participants couldn't reach out across time and space to help each other? We'd been building a path towards this for two years, and it was right there before us. If particles can wink in and out of existence, then how could we not return to the physical realm for another lifetime in human form? We'd already proven that the large and small can, in fact, behave in the same way. This was simply another example.' Celeste paused for effect once more. 'We had set out to build a better future for humanity and found a working model of quantum consciousness that included reincarnation.'

Shocked into silence, no one in the auditorium spoke. But Celeste knew the information was bouncing around in their belief systems. Their expressions ranged from disdain and suspicion, through fascinated and deep consideration, all the way to delighted. It didn't matter to Celeste. It was up to them what they did with it. She noticed a handful rise from their seats and leave the auditorium. Presumably, this was too far from their comfort zones.

'Believe it or not,' she continued, 'this was just a side issue. Now, back to the one thousand participants in Project DOD … As I mentioned, by the end of the second group, five main themes at a high level kept coming up, and they became even stronger and more detailed in the next six hundred participants. These five themes may seem like science fiction to you, and I can assure you that's how they looked to us!

'We have hundreds of testimonies, recordings and transcripts that support what I'm about to tell you regarding the future of humanity. Tonight is the first time we've publicly shared the five themes of the future, and here they are, through the testimonies of eyewitnesses from that future. I've selected five videos that typify what we've been hearing. Our first theme is technology. This is Jakob, who calls himself a "technopath" in 2050.'

The video started on the big screen, and the project participant said, 'The world of technology is different now for two reasons. The first is that all technologies have been designed so they emit no radiation. Gradually, EMF radiation was minimised, and it was eradicated completely in 2045. We've found ways to rebirth technology with a connection to the vibrational energy field of people; that means everything is connected, and your own thought forms contribute to this field. An example of this is when you're working with a computer and send information through your thought forms. Those thoughts are picked up from the field and generate words on a screen. We no longer use a keyboard. It's like typing your thoughts through intention. There are no wires, no radio waves, no implants, just pure thought, read by the computer directly from the field.'

Celeste watched the audience. Every face was riveted to the screen.

'The second change has been the discovery of quantum networking,' the participant continued, 'as an extension of quantum computing. The old binary code was very traditional, but when we managed to have code in its superposition—meaning all possibilities—entangled with the thought forms of a user, technology was reborn. This same technique is used to establish a worldwide web of thought forms, where you can ask a question into the field, and the answer appears on your screen. It's as though the universe matches a question with an answer because they carry the same vibrational frequency.

'We drive technology with our thoughts rather than our fingers moving across a keyboard. We just bypassed one step and our name for it is technopathy—like telepathy for technology. We're now starting research that will finally retire the screens and have the answers to questions move into your awareness as soon as you think of your question.'

Again, there was silence. Celeste stood on the stage, feeling calm and powerful. 'Our second theme is about something called metascience. This video is of Chloe in the year 2058; she's an astrolist.'

The big screen came to life once more, and Chloe said,

'Many years ago, we replaced science with something that held a deeper integrity, passion and purpose. There had been widespread influences on research funding, and in many cases, the results of scientific studies had been driven towards particular goals for profit or prestige. Some fields of study had been minimised or ignored, even though powerful trends were emerging.

'We started over with metascience, a blending of the physical and non-physical areas of research and study, on an equal footing. We now study the progressive application of consciousness, as it echoes into the real world for the good of humanity.

'The paranormal and the normal, ancient medicinal arts and modern healing methods now exist side-by-side for exploration by enquiring minds. For example, the field of astroconsciousness contains the best of astrology, astronomy and astrophysics. We study the universe through ancient wisdom and modern science under the context of a quantum view of the possibilities.

'All levels of education teach the metasciences now. The World Unity Collective fund all research initiatives that contribute to the three principles of leadership. All explorations carry a purity of intent and a deep and profound energy to serve humanity. The people who lead the metasciences are inspirational and seen as heroes in our community with their breakthrough mindsets and the new ways of thinking they offer.'

The clip ended, and the audience remained silent. Celeste continued. 'This next theme discusses the new world leadership under the World Unity Collective and covers the three principles of leadership that Chloe mentioned. In this video, we hear from Gareth, a planetary advocate in 2078.'

Once again, the screen came to life, showing a man seated in a chair in a house in the Blue Mountains, but the voice that spoke through him came from somewhere else. 'When the old leadership approach was replaced by the World Unity Collective, the whole planet became different overnight. These leaders of world consciousness are selected for their integrity and ethics, a history of service to others and their humanitarian and sustainability experience. The three philosophies of world leadership embraced by these people are: We are all connected, and that which affects one, affects all; our reason for being is to raise our own and others' vibration; we are the custodians of the Earth, and her wellbeing is our legacy to future generations.

'In every country, there are two groups: the people ambassadors and the planetary advocates. These people make the new laws of society and work together for the common goal of having a positive living experience for every single person on this planet. These two groups work together beautifully and collaboratively. There are no politics or ideology that contravenes the three philosophies. We develop our leaders from an early age.'

The silence at the end of this clip was so deep that you really could've heard a pin drop in the hall. Celeste continued. 'The next theme is health. This clip comes from Asha, who says he's a wellness guide in 2052.'

The video showed a woman sitting back in a chair with her eyes closed. She said, 'The health of our people in all parts of the world has greatly improved. A focus on naturally grown organic foods, education about the natural immunity of our systems, enhanced by sunlight, fresh water and exercise, greatly improved the health of the average person. The pharmaceutical industry has been retired, apart from a few critical lifesaving medicines. Natural herbal remedies with no side effects have become the norm. We have combined the best of natural medicine with allopathic discoveries to bring about deep and lasting change in the physical health and wellbeing of our people.

'Physical health is maintained through new technologies that work with frequency and vibration. Mental health is enhanced through a knowledge of the different levels of mind and how a healthy subconscious is key to a vibrant and heathy life, through the mind-body connection. Spiritual health is encouraged, offering a transcendent approach that embraces the internal journey through meditation and self-exploration.

'It is well known and acknowledged that the future of humanity will be in the hands of our children. As a result, everything we do focusses on the nurture, safety and unconditional love for our children. We know humanity is evolving and that the new humans being born will be different from the generation before. We watch for this and support that evolution through vibrant health systems.'

The clip ended, and all eyes turned to Celeste. 'Our final theme is important, as it helps us understand how we arrived, through the world restoration projects, in the new world being described to us. In this video, we hear from Georg in 2038. He calls himself a project mentor.'

'The billionaires of the old world donated half their wealth to the restoration of our planet. They agreed to do so once the World Unity Collective swept to power across the planet. These restoration resources are benefitting areas of the world that most need it. They offer solutions that, previously, were almost unimaginable. The gap between the first and third worlds has all but disappeared. There are now over 50,000 projects underway around the globe, staffed by 750 million people so far. They have been inspired to serve in some capacity, which is why we refer to these project roles as 'callings', one step on the path in a life of purpose. People are inspired, as they have a level of fulfillment rarely found in the careers of the old world. They are lovingly supported at every level as they go about these life-changing projects.'

Celeste spoke once more: 'So there you have it, a snapshot of a future that seems to be emerging with more and more certainty. The more we share what we're hearing from participants in our projects, the stronger the five themes are becoming.

'Our theory is that we're gathering a collective intent towards this shared future. We've seen large-scale consciousness phenomena like the group meditation effect, the IONS Global Consciousness Project and even the Schumann resonance, which continues to be measured daily. If we continue to maintain this project's momentum towards a better future, then I believe that humanity has one destiny only, a bright and wonderful one, and it is our role at the Research Institute for Quantum Metaphysics to ensure that happens.

'My challenge to all of you is to hold this vision of the future I've described. My team and I hear these stories every day. For us, there is only one future for humanity, and we want you to join us in bringing that into being. In conclusion, I wish to share with you what we have learned about the universe.'

Celeste looked up to the video screen and read aloud the words written in dot points.

We have learned that:

The universe is based on free will, and this must always be offered the respect it deserves.

The universe seeks to evolve and remember its magnificence more fully, and the higher dimensions assist us when asked.

When you work with an intention to serve the

*greater good and have a purity of purpose, then the
universe ensures that you will prevail.*

*We are multidimensional beings, living in a
universe of limitless possibilities, and nothing is
beyond our reach.*

*When we as a species work with the full knowledge
of these cosmic laws, then humanity will flourish,
and we will take our place amongst the stars.*

Celeste turned back to the audience. 'I would like to finish on
a personal note … I'm a leader of this work and also a passionate
advocate. I was buried in grief for two years following the loss
of both my parents. It was my own super observer who showed
me that my pain was a choice and offered me a different road
to the one I was on. I took it. I have personally stepped into the
multiverse. It was my forty-five-year-old self who gave me the
idea for the experiment at CERN.

'I am blessed to have the most wonderful team: Abbey, Grace,
Raz and Skye … and none of what I've shared with you this
evening would've been possible without the incredible support
of that team, our university and Collins Industries, who continue
to be the champions for the Research Institute for Quantum
Metaphysics. Thank you all for coming tonight. I'm told we have
time for just a few questions.'

People with roving microphones moved through the audience.

The first question came from an older gentleman towards the
rear of the audience.

'Thank you, Dr Kelly, for a controversial presentation,' he
said. 'How do you account for the fact that you've apparently
been more successful in alleviating mental health issues than a

multi-billion-dollar medical industry?'

Bob's words about responding in a way that was 'powerful and personable' to people locked in the old ways of seeing things came back to her. She smiled and asked, 'Are you from the medical industry?'

'I'm a retired doctor and a member of the Australian Medical Association,' came the blunt reply.

'Thank you for being here tonight. I will offer you this. It's time for us to see all people in their magnificence. We have two thousand cases that cannot be ignored, people who have transcended the issues in their life by touching a greater part of themselves. We showed them how; they did the rest ... and it is mind blowing. I will readily share that information in any way that brings new mindsets and understanding to your profession.

'I've heard how the medical industry offers medication as the first choice, rather than explore the wisdom behind the condition. And I'm reliably informed that the mental health of our society has never been this bad and is getting worse. I don't have medical training, but I am a good scientist. All I've shared tonight has come from science and the willingness to explore new ways. I invite you and anyone else you know to join us on that quest. The real question is more for those within your profession: Are you willing to consider new ways to help the patients you see? ... Next question.'

The man sat, his face red, clearly in a state of non-belief. A woman on the other side of the audience stood up. One of the helpers handed her a microphone. 'Are you advocating for reincarnation?' she asked.

'My role as a scientist is to report what I find and offer theories supported by data. My team has done this, though I have to say that once you go looking, there is an enormous amount of credible research done in Western society on the subject. We have reviewed that, done our own research and come to the conclusion that it is either a real phenomenon or is information made available from the collective unconsciousness. If I had to hang my hat on a conclusion, I'd go with the mix of both, though personal memories held in the collective hold a stronger connection due to a closer degree of quantum entanglement. You can't see what I've seen in the last two years and remain a non-believer. Next question …'

'From what you've found, what is the future of science?' asked a younger person down the front, probably a current student.

Celeste smiled at her, remembering when she'd sat in this same auditorium twenty years earlier, asking those types of questions.

'We've already heard about the possibilities of metascience from our future selves. I like to think that we're entering the golden age being described—in fact, I hold a deep personal intention for that to be so. There are, however, ethical questions that need to be brought before every scientist on this planet and considered for every scientific endeavour, and it comes down to this: Are we serving humanity in what we are doing? Is this good for the Earth and the people of this unique planet? If those questions don't bring a positive response, then we have some very real and necessary soul searching to do. Have we been compromised by power, status or money? Have we lost our way? Are we embracing what science was originally founded to do? Remember, scientific exploration was originally conceived as a way to take humanity forward for the good of everyone. So my answer to the future of science hinges on what we ask ourselves in the present. I believe we'll start to ask those questions, just as I believe in the future that has been described to us.' Celeste nodded encouragement to the young woman, who took her seat once more.

The next question came from a young man on the other side of the auditorium. 'As you've stepped into the future, have you had any luck with horse-racing tips or lottery numbers?'

The crowd laughed, and Celeste smiled. 'The information we receive is for the greater good of the world and the individuals who take the journey. Self-interest doesn't get a look-in from what we've seen so far. I feel it would go against those rules of cosmic law that we're working with. It's a shame, though, as it'd be a great way to fund new projects.'

The crowd laughed.

'I have time for one last question,' Celeste said.

A man stood in the centre of the crowd and was handed the mike. Well-dressed and somewhere in his thirties, he had the confidence of a business person. Something about him aroused Celeste's suspicion, though she couldn't quite place the source of her unease. She was especially vigilant, given her chilling experience just prior to the presentation.

'How will you maintain the momentum of this work you've started?'

'We're planning that now. I'll be presenting to other faculties soon. Our institute will be starting an internship for psychology and medical students from the university next semester. We'll be using some of the new models we've created to educate the next generation of professionals. And to aid our expansion, we're looking for larger premises.

'At present, we're forming alliances with organisations such as the Institute of Noetic Sciences, the University of Virginia's Division of Perceptual Studies, the Michael Newton Institute, the Monroe Institute and a few more. I'll mainly be on the road presenting our findings. We need to spread the word, to the four corners of the world, of the true potential of who we are as human beings. It's time to bring a new future for humanity into our line of sight and move towards it,' Celeste replied, committing his face to memory.

From the corner of her eye, she caught the stage manager gesturing for her to wind up the evening.

'I'm being asked to close now,' she said. 'Thank you for being here tonight and for supporting the work of the Research Institute for Quantum Metaphysics. Together, we can create a better future for our world.' Celeste stood before the crowd, placed her hand on her heart and bowed her head slightly.

Nothing happened for a full two seconds as the audience sat in stunned silence from all they'd heard and seen. The sceptics remained seated, lost in thought, while many of them rose, and the sound of thunderous applause filled the hall. She looked down at her team. Abbey and Skye were hugging. Grace had tears rolling down her cheeks, and Raz stood on his chair, doing a victory dance.

A wave of people swept forward, and Celeste braced herself. The questions would go on for days, months, even years …

Out of the corner of her eye, she spotted Gabe Collins. Their eyes met, and he punched the air with a victory salute. *Looks like it went well,* Celeste thought as she disappeared into the throng.

Two hours passed before they could clear a path back to the limousine. Celeste felt a bit like a rock star with the team running interference.

A couple of grad students pushed through as she stooped to enter the vehicle. 'Dr Kelly!' one of them said. 'We just have to ask. We know DOD stands for designing our destiny, but what does SHED stand for? We think it might be Searching Heroically for Extra Dimensions.'

Celeste looked them in the eye and shrugged. 'I do like that, but it's far simpler. You just never know what you'll find in your shed.'

With that, they settled into the limo for the long ride back to the mountains. She and Abbey had quite a story to tell the others, and the warm environment in the safe company of her team was exactly what she needed.

CHAPTER 61

Back at the institute, they celebrated with a few bottles of champagne, just the five of them. It helped also to set aside the attempt on Celeste's life. She'd taken the time to brief Gabe and Jack later in the evening, and they retained Dr Bart's phone for further investigation.

The next morning, it was after nine before she finally rose from her bed in the studio. She'd given everyone the day off, and the team had certainly earned it. She showered, changed into jeans and a sweater, and then wandered into the house that had become an institute. The cappuccino machine in the big kitchen offered better coffee.

This was to be a day of relaxation. Celeste didn't want to focus on all that had transpired the night before. She walked past her office and noticed her mobile phone on the desk. The alerts showed countless text messages, and her email inbox was overflowing. She'd need to sift through them soon, but not now. Already she'd received invitations to present to other faculties at the university—at the schools of medical sciences, physics and biomedical engineering.

It could all wait.

After finishing her coffee, she braced for the cool air and stepped outside, more conscious of the security cameras than usual. The trees were a collage of amber and red, with leaves floating downwards in the autumn morning breeze.

Celeste wandered into the shed where so much had unfolded, and she sat once more in her chair. Bob didn't appear, so she let him be. There was no need for a conversation today.

After a while, the secret room behind the wall drew her. She pushed the rug out of the way, touched the catch in the panel and entered the room. A little wave of sadness came back as she remembered her father in human form—in contrast to knowing his energy as part of her light tribe. Today, she felt more like a daughter.

She decided, then and there of her own free will, that she would continue her father's work for one very important reason. It was the best way to flush out those who'd taken his life and robbed both her and her mother of his wonderful presence in their lives. She didn't doubt that the two attempts on her own life were somehow connected as well.

Deep inside her, that fire, already lit, was growing. Bob and her father had told her she was the backup plan, though that was no longer true. It was time for her to lead it now, and there would be others to help, including a forty-five-year-old version of her, who no doubt held some of the answers she needed.

She closed the room, left the shed and walked across the lawn, wondering how she'd start, how her life would now unfold and, most importantly, how she would expand RIQM into the design of free energy for the world.

A car came up the driveway. A man got out and walked towards her. He looked older, had lost weight, and his hair was a little more grey at the temples. But though different, he was instantly familiar from that time long ago. He stopped some metres away, unsure about advancing further. 'Hello, Celeste,' Carlo said. 'Please hear me out for just two minutes.'

She said nothing, but tears built behind her eyes.

'I've spent almost a year rebuilding my life. You showed me the illusion of who I was and opened my heart more than I could ever imagine. I've now reshaped my family in a way that has brought peace to all of us.' He paused.

Celeste noticed the deep-blue scarf around his neck and remembered the message from her forty-five-year-old self.

'So I'm free now … and I offer myself to you. If that's not possible, I'll leave right now, and you won't see me again. I leave it to you, though I want you to know that I love you in ways I'm still trying to understand …'

Suddenly, Celeste saw them in a changed landscape.

Behind Carlo stood the defender of the city who'd been killed by the Vikings and an RAF pilot who'd never come back from the Battle of Britain. Alongside him stood a Native American shot down in battle. Many more, such as explorers who'd never returned and soldiers who never survived the wars throughout history, gathered behind Carlo. Lifetime after lifetime, he'd always put duty ahead of love.

She finally understood. This time would be different. This time, he'd decided that love would be his choice, though it had to be hers also. This time, in a reversal of roles, it had been his turn for pain and hers for duty. Behind her, Celeste felt a crowd of women gather from across time and space, those who'd lost the love of their lives in other times, all waiting patiently for her decision.

She surrendered to her heart and ran to him, her crowd running with her. She threw herself into his arms, their actions mirrored in their matching pairs, reuniting their energies across time and space in the ways of the universe.

Something very deep and very old healed in an instant, and the universe rejoiced in the power of love.

CHAPTER 62

Two interdimensional beings stood on the veranda, watching a moment for which they'd been waiting over a thousand years.

'Looks like you were right,' Bob said.

'Always believe in love,' Wal replied. 'It holds the universe together. Sometimes, it just takes a while. It could go anywhere from here, though when one of yours works with one of mine, it seems to carry a greater chance of success. Let's wait and see what unfolds. By the way, I like the name you chose—Beyond Our Body; how very accurate!'

Bob smiled. 'We use that a great deal, as it touches our greater knowing. What about Wal? Where did that come from?'

'Simple …We Are Limitless. Same reason; it's a reminder.'

'So beyond our body we are limitless.' Bob chuckled. 'Or is it … we are limitless beyond our body?'

'Either will work, given time and space as they know it doesn't really exist.'

He smiled. 'No wonder we make a great team, Wal.'

'We do indeed, Bob.' She smiled in return.

They laughed together for a moment, then disappeared into the universe.

ACKNOWLEDGEMENTS

I am so very grateful for Melina, my beautiful partner and companion across various dimensions and metaphysical landscapes. She was by my side in this project from the moment the first chart hit the wall. Her advice, support and suggestions—even the one to write my first book of fiction—brings my energy into alignment and my creativity to the surface.

My author reading cohort of Brett Harrison, Cloudy Eldridge, Jennifer Cluff, Jane Jacobs, Bruce Meder and Barry Eaton all shone a light on different aspects of the early draft that I tentatively sent to fellow authors. The uplifting support offered in return warmed my heart.

Encouragement from your own children is like nothing else on Earth, and I'm grateful to my two beautiful daughters, Alex and Kate, for being the test cases for the next generation of readers.

Thank you, Val Hood, for opening a door to the other side that I didn't realise was there and putting me in touch with my quantum spirit helpers.

Thanks to Samantha O'Hare, who actually attended Blue Mountains' Grammar School, though not with Celeste and Abbey.

To the facilitators of consciousness all around the world that I have taught, worked with and journeyed alongside for almost two decades, thank you from the depths of my soul. This story echoes the work we bring in these times.

To the clients who showed me the way over the years, you have my deepest respect for your courage and the trust you placed in me. Without you, this book would not have been possible.

I did a great deal of research before approaching Tahlia Newland and the team at AIA Publishing. They offer a first novel writer an incredible mix of expertise, encouragement and coaching that drastically improves a heartfelt manuscript.

Good editors make improvements, great editors coach you to be a better author.

ABOUT THE AUTHOR

Peter Smith has been a consciousness explorer for over twenty years. He left a promising career as a banking executive to chase his dreams and follow the call of his soul.

He began by exploring some of his own past lives, then trained as a hypnotherapist and took clients on journeys that transcended time and space. Over time, he founded two hypnotherapy schools, the modality of hypnoenergetics and became president of the Michael Newton Institute for Life Between Lives from 2009 to 2019.

His journey led him to create the Institute for Quantum Consciousness and build a network of facilitators all around the world who take clients on journeys that show them their magnificence, transcend old therapeutic systems and blend science and spirituality. Pete is determined to blaze new trails for others to follow, and this book embraces many of the ideas and concepts he has researched, taught and offered to his clients during his metaphysical career.

Previous published works include *Hypnoenergetics – The Four*

Dimensions (Barker-Deane, 2011) and *Quantum Consciousness – Journey Through Other Realms* (Llewellyn Publishing, 2018). Pete has written over a dozen forewords for nonfiction books in the consciousness genre and is a sought-after speaker in his chosen field. He has published short stories and poems and written articles for *Nexus Magazine* and the *Journal of Humanistic Psychology*. *The Transcendence of Celeste Kelly* is his first novel.

Pete can someti—mes be found amusing the crowd at the Poetry Slam in his local town of Bellingen, Australia, close to where he lives with Melina and various forms of wildlife.

More about the author at www.quantumconsciousness.com. au and his life's work at www.instituteforquantumconsciousness. com.

Milton Keynes UK
Ingram Content Group UK Ltd.
UKHW010953080124
435661UK00001B/224